"Much more than a [...] fascinating textbook on how the FBI tracks and captures kidnappers. From high-speed surveillance tricks to high-tech laboratory sleuthing, it's all in this gripping minute-by-minute account. Only a longtime FBI insider like Art Nehrbass could have written a crime novel that rings so true."—Carl Hiaasen, author of *Tourist Season*

"Taut, tense fiction with all the chilling drama and stark detail of real life. Nobody knows the dark hearts of the lawless and the dedication of real live heroes better than Art Nehrbass, a helluva lawman, now one helluva writer."—Edna Buchanan, Pulitzer Prize-winning *Miami Herald* reporter and author of *Contents Under Pressure*

"Spare, taut . . . pure police procedural."
—*Library Journal*

ARTHUR F. NEHRBASS

DEAD EASY

AN ONYX BOOK

ONYX
Published by the Penguin Group
Penguin Books USA Inc., 375 Hudson Street,
New York, New York 10014, U.S.A.
Penguin Books Ltd, 27 Wrights Lane,
London W8 5TZ, England
Penguin Books Australia Ltd, Ringwood,
Victoria, Australia
Penguin Books Canada Ltd, 10 Alcorn Avenue,
Toronto, Ontario, Canada M4V 3B2
Penguin Books (N.Z.) Ltd, 182–190 Wairau Road,
Auckland 10, New Zealand

Penguin Books Ltd, Registered Offices:
Harmondsworth, Middlesex, England

Published by Onyx, an imprint of Dutton Signet, a division of
Penguin Books USA Inc. Previously published in a Dutton edition.

First Onyx Printing, October, 1993
10 9 8 7 6 5 4 3 2 1

 REGISTERED TRADEMARK—MARCA REGISTRADA

Printed in the United States of America

PUBLISHER'S NOTE
This is a work of fiction. Names, characters, places, and incidents
either are the product of the author's imagination or are used ficti-
tiously, and any resemblance to actual persons, living or dead, events,
or locales is entirely coincidental.

To Elaine,
for her unfailing confidence and encouragement.

To Harlean,
with whom I conspired.

DEAD
EASY

CHAPTER
1

Iacta alea est
(The die is cast.)
—JULIUS CAESAR, *De bello gallico*

Donald Stanley had always been a loser. He had never succeeded at anything.

He'd done some time for petty things. Nothing that he considered serious. Bad checks, shoplifting and car theft were things that "happened" when you were trying to score big.

He would agree that his plans had not always worked out, but would add that it was because the dice were loaded against him, and people he depended on always let him down. Many of his friends, those who he should have been able to depend on, went out of their way to screw him.

Today, though, he was going to make it big. He had it all worked out.

The alarm clock went off at 7:00, an unaccustomed way and time for Stanley to wake.

"Shit, it's still dark. It can't be time!"

Mona, lying next to him, came up like a shot. "Donnie, you're not really gonna do this?

You're not gonna grab that woman, are you? Ain't no way we'd get away with a kidnappin'."

"Get off my ass. I don't need your crap this early in the fuckin' morning. You'll do what I goddamn tell you. Now shut up and get your ass out of bed and get me some coffee."

Mona slid out of bed and put on a robe. "Damn, it's cold. Thought Miami was supposed to be warm in February." She looked at Donnie, lying back on his pillow, his hands behind his head, thinking. Mona was remembering the TV show two weeks before that started him off on this kidnapping scheme. "That damn TV show," she said. "I wish you'd never seen that crazy movie."

"I ain't gonna tell you again to shut up. Once more and your face'll be so bad it'll be a month before a john will even look at you."

Mona moved toward the small kitchen, thinking about Donnie, and smiled slightly. She could see Donnie, his two-hundred-pound, six-foot-one body stretched out on the bed; even after their nightly tussle, and his sleep, his black hair was still center-parted.

Mona's eyes scanned the house as she reached for the coffee pot. "This place sure is the sticks; Redlands, what a name. Ain't nobody within almost a mile. Damn house is fallin' down."

Stanley and Mona were staying in a small two-bedroom house in the Redlands, on the fringes of the Everglades, in the extreme southwestern part of Dade County. It was an old house, by Miami standards, built between 1915 and 1920. Besides the two bedrooms, it had a single bathroom, small kitchen, living room and a small dining area. It was sparsely furnished. The most noteworthy piece of furniture was the new television, recently stolen.

The house, and its surrounding land of twenty acres, had been bought by Donald Stanley's cousin, Richard, some years before as an investment. The house was lived in, off and on, by anyone needing a place to stay who was friendly with Richard Stanley. Richard had allowed him to live there, rent free, just to have someone there. He had been there about six months living off his thievery and Mona's occasional hooking.

Stanley, clad only in the pants to his one suit, shuffled barefoot into the kitchen. Looking at Mona, he said, "What you waitin' on? Move that lazy ass. We got work to do. We ain't got all fuckin' day to grab that bitch."

Stanley could see Mona's body under the housecoat. He approved of her skills, the ways she could use her body. But he was concerned with her continuing opposition to his plan.

Robert Stockton had awakened as usual at 6:30, in his comfortable home in affluent Cape Cutler. Jean got up with him and by 7:00 had just finished serving breakfast. Sitting opposite him, she looked across the table at the top of her husband's head peeking just above the newspaper he was reading while he ate.

"Rob, how about coming home early today, and we'll catch the matinee of that movie I told you about last night. Maybe we could even have dinner out."

A grunt was his answer. "What? I didn't hear you. I'm reading."

"Look at me, Rob. Forget the paper and listen. I'm trying to talk to you."

"And I'm trying to read the paper."

"You're impossible. You're getting worse every day. I can never seem to talk to you when you're home, and *that* isn't very often."

As he continued to read his paper, ignoring her, she flared up. "You're married to that damn business, Rob. You've got a wife and three children. Remember us? The kids have forgotten what you look like. You're either at work or hiding behind a newspaper or buried in account books in your den."

"Have you finished beating up on me? If so, maybe you'll pause long enough to consider where the hell this house comes from, where your car comes from, where every damn thing you have comes from. It comes from that damn business you seem to hate so much. You want me to quit? You want to go on welfare, food stamps, buy secondhand clothes? No, you don't. You want all this, so stay off my back."

"Rob, that's not fair," she said, backing down a bit. "I'm not against our business. All I asked was to talk over the breakfast table about going out to the movies."

"Okay, tell you what. Let's do dinner but no matinee. I can't get home before six. I've got meetings with some of my foremen this morning, a contractor in the afternoon, and then with some people I'm thinking of subbing some work to."

"Never mind, we'll try it another time."

"Now if that isn't just like a woman. Here I say yes, and then you say no." He quickly folded the paper in a loose mass, and tucked it under his arm. "This is senseless. I'm taking the paper to work so I can read it in peace." Rising from his half-eaten breakfast, without a good-bye, he left Jean sitting at the table with a stunned and hurt expression.

She sat for a minute, and then began blaming herself for the morning confrontation. The day was starting badly. She had always tried to send Rob off in a good frame of mind. It was her flare-up that had set him off.

She rose from the table and was clearing their plates when their three children stormed the kitchen. The entry of three happy, hungry, talkative youngsters turned her frown into a smile, and Jean was soon caught up in their excitement about their day off from school.

Steve, the seventeen-year-old, was clearly in charge. Ben, at twelve, followed his big brother's lead. Amy had just turned fourteen and discovered she was a young lady. She wasn't sure she liked the idea.

Steve began frying some eggs and turned to Ben. "You want me to toss some in for you, squirt?"

"Yeah, I'll take two, but I make my own toast. You burn it. Amy, you want toast?"

"No thanks. I'm just havin' cereal and juice."

Steve jumped on her. "You on a diet? Boyfriend don't like baby fat?"

Amy reddened. "I'm not fat and I don't have a boyfriend. I just don't want to eat too much before water skiing. You two'll never get up on the slalom if you eat all that."

Ben had to get his two cents in. "You do so

have a boyfriend. Jimmy Custer says he kissed you."

Amy screamed, "Ben, that's a lie! Jimmy never said that. It never happened."

Jean came to her daughter's rescue. "Okay, you three. Sit down and eat. What are the big plans for today? We should have a holiday every Monday to get you guys up early and wide awake. Strange that school never has this effect on you."

Ben and Steve ate hurriedly, talking between bites and as they chewed. Amy, in keeping with her new self-image, ate more slowly.

Steve led off. "We thought we'd drop the boat in at Black Point and run down to Caesar's Cut, do some skiin' on the way and then go out through the cut. The wind's down and we can probably run out a way to a reef and snorkel. If we're lucky we might find some lobster."

"Steve said he'd teach me some trick skiin'," Ben contributed.

"Steve, you be careful with Ben. Keep the boat speed down," Jean said, concerned. "If you do snorkle make sure your dive flag's up and stay near the boat. Today is a holiday, and that means lots of cowboys who don't know how to handle a boat will be out."

"Don't worry, Mom," Steve said wearily. He rose from the table and started gathering Cokes for the cooler as Amy made sandwiches. "Depending on weather, we should be home about four or five."

By 8:30 they had packed the cooler, the car, hitched up the trailer and were on their way.

Jean cleaned up the breakfast things and then settled down at the kitchen table with her last mug of coffee to enjoy her favorite time of the day. Robert was off to work, the children were gone, there were no demands on her. She was free for about the next hour. She savored the solitude and the pleasure of uninterrupted thoughts and daydreams. Mostly she dwelled on the Caribbean vacation she and Robert had been planning for the entire family. It would be so good to have everyone doing something together.

Her hands were pleasantly warmed by the coffee in the mug she was holding. She habitually wrapped both hands about her morning mugs of coffee for that reason. The kitchen was quiet, comfortable. The February morning sun promised a bright Miami day.

At thirty-six, Jean was an attractive woman, with gray eyes and light-brown hair which she wore in a mass of curls that accented a trim figure that drew appreciative glances. She noted the admiring looks, and in a moment of irritation had thought she'd like to see some of those looks from Rob. A new swimsuit for the vacation might help.

She was relaxed, content and in a world of contemplation. Her immediate future, that infinitesimal microsecond after "now," was not in her thoughts.

Donald Stanley and Mona drove up to 7220 S.W. 181st Street about fifteen minutes after they had seen the three children leave with the boat. Stanley reached for the brass dolphin knocker on the door and gave two sharp raps.

Jean came out of her reverie, and she reluctantly left her coffee and pleasant thoughts to go to the front door. She addressed the people at the door through the speaker. "Good morning, may I help you?" She observed the pair through the wide-angle viewer in the door: a tall, dark-haired man wearing glasses, dressed in a business suit, and a tall, thin blond woman.

"Is this the Stockton house?" Stanley replied. Jean answered in the affirmative, and Stanley continued: "My name is Anderson, this is my wife, Sue. We were passing Old Cutler Road and about 200th Street, and stopped to help some people who had just been in an accident. There were three young people involved who were trailering a boat, and they asked us to contact their mother to drive down and help them. They gave this address and the name Stockton."

Mona's presence, Stanley's appearance and demeanor coupled with the message—calculated to appeal to a mother—caused Jean to open the door and allow them in.

Stanley and Mona entered the foyer and glanced around, the smell of breakfast unmistakable. Immediately Mona engaged Jean in conversation. "Not to worry, Mrs. Stockton. The kids weren't hurt, just shook up and worried about what you were going to say."

As Jean concentrated on Mona, Stanley got behind Jean and had tape over her mouth and her hands pinned before she could react. Stanley forced her onto her stomach on the foyer rug.

Jean was totally surprised by the attack. It took several seconds for the assault on her to fully register. A wave of terror engulfed her; she had never experienced such consuming fear. It occupied her whole being; her normal defense mechanisms seemed frozen.

Her first conscious reaction was a feeling of certainty they intended to kill her. Her next emotion was panic that her children might unexpectedly return and be killed. Her body told her that her hands were being tied behind her back. She tried to speak or scream, she was never sure which. Only muted, unintelligible sounds came out. There was adhesive tape across her mouth. As the man rolled her over on her back, her wrists were crossed in the small of her back and she was aware of the discomfort as she lay on her hands. Jean looked to the side and saw Stanley, her eyes reflecting the terror of a small, helpless animal caught in a cruel trap.

The fright that shone in her eyes excited Stanley. She was helpless now, he owned her, totally dominated her. He had noticed when they entered that she was still in her nightgown and robe. The robe had been pulled open during the attack, and her front was now covered only by her nightgown. He dropped to his knees next to her and touched her stomach. Her eyes went wide with fright and he became even more excited. She had never experienced such a feeling of utter helplessness. She couldn't scream. Her hands were taped behind her back. A rush of black thoughts engulfed her. Did he mean to rape her? But what was the woman doing there? Her mind raced for an escape, but no solution was there.

As Jean's eyes reflected her fright Stanley smiled evilly, his excitement rising. "This is real. This broad is really frightened and I can do anything I damn well please with her. She's mine."

As she squirmed, trying to avoid his touch, his right hand moved to the pillow case in his jacket pocket. He intended to cover Jean's head with it so her exposure to them would be limited to the capture. The hand stopped at the pocket though. He was fascinated by the fright he saw. He couldn't cover it. This was too good. He savored his arousal.

His left hand moved to the hem of her nightgown and he pulled it up to her abdomen. Jean clamped her legs tight and tried to roll to her side, but Stanley clamped his hand on her thigh. Then, placing his left knee on her thigh, he began, with both hands, to explore her body.

Jean screamed but no sound penetrated the tape over her mouth. She kicked both legs with all her strength, throwing him off balance. He recovered in an instant and was soon astride her, one leg on each side of her hips. From this position he was able to slide back and immobilize her thrashing legs. His exploration of her now continued with only the minor inconvenience of her torso twisting to avoid his touch.

As she cringed under his heavy, groping hands, she saw the pure depravity in his eyes and grinning mouth. She saw him feasting on her nakedness and instinctively drew her legs tighter together. His hands were all over her, painfully pinching her nipples and squeezing her breasts, sliding down her stomach. As he forced his hand between her legs she thrashed violently, screamed her silent scream, but he was too strong. She saw the woman she presumed to be his wife watching with a blank look on her face.

Mona had been watching with mixed feelings.

They had participated in multipartner sex before, and she was somewhat intrigued by what Stanley was doing. At the same time though, she didn't like seeing Stanley so excited by this woman. She felt slightly threatened.

"Play later," she snapped. "We need to get outta here before somebody comes, and I don't mean you."

Stanley reluctantly paused. "All right. We take her to the house. This bitch is good. No shit from you. You want to play with us okay, but we get to the house, she's gonna play my games."

Mona agreed. "Do what you want at the house, but you screw around here, somebody's gonna catch us."

There was a pause in the movement of his hands on her. "Okay, let's go," he said. Then without a word, almost automatically, his left hand went between her thighs, and then his right, prying them apart as Jean struggled. He put his knees inside her thighs and his ankles over her legs to hold them down.

Mona thought he intended to keep on going but he just wanted to inflict one more humiliation on Jean; he was enjoying himself immensely. His fondling of Jean caused her to struggle, and the struggle stimulated his appetite for her.

"The children, oh God, the children," she thought. "Don't let them come home now." Silently she implored God not to let this happen to her, not to her, not to her. There was a sharp pain in her vagina, and she screamed again and again without sound, yanking away desperately, and then it stopped.

Stanley had noticed a small scar. Through his

excitement, which was rapidly overcoming Mona's advice, a great idea came to him. He stopped his exploration of Jean and with both hands fully exposed the scar on the inside of her right thigh. It was about three inches long and ran vertically from the very spot where the groin becomes leg down the center of her thigh. It appeared to be old. Its ridges were still somewhat distinct but it had flattened out to be just about level with the surrounding flesh. He ran his fingers back and forth over it, enjoying the irregular feel of it. He could feel Jean's whole body shiver every time he touched it.

He got up. "Calm down, I'm finished with you now. Listen. Listen! I want nothin' from you—you're safe. Your husband's gonna pay for your return and we don't want to hurt you. I need proof for him we got you. You got a small scar on the inside of your right leg, and I want to know where and when you got it. If you promise not to scream, I'll take off the tape. If you scream, I'll smash in your face. Do you understand?"

Jean moved her head up and down. Stanley ripped off the tape, and Jean gasped in pain. "Six or seven, fell off a bike." She swallowed and the tape was slapped over her mouth again.

Mona and Stanley rolled her up in the hall rug, a seven-by-seven square, blue, with a leaping white dolphin in the center. The rug had been a gift from a contractor on a job Robert had had.

Stanley hadn't considered how Jean would be removed from the house. This was one of the "details" that in his conception of planning took care of itself, and in this instance the rug was a perfect cover. If anyone saw them leave, they would see two people carrying a rolled-up carpet, assuming it was to be cleaned.

Before they left, Stanley nodded to Mona and said, "Use a tissue to take the note out of the envelope in your purse, and drop it on that table over there in the living room. Then use the tissue to set that candlestick on top of it so it don't blow away."

Mona, as always, did as she was told.

Jean, now tightly rolled up in the rug, felt herself being lifted. Both she and the rug were bent at the middle and she was sure she had been lifted onto his shoulder. She felt him move. She could see some light come through the top of the rug over her head. She had some trouble breathing, as the rug was right up against her nose. She imagined she could smell the family in the rug. Without bidding, a collage of faces of people who had stepped on the rug flashed before her. She took comfort in the familiarity of the rug. In the faint light in the roll she could make out the tail of the dolphin, out of focus, directly in front of her face. Dust filled her nostrils and she sneezed. This was greeted with a warning to be quiet and a hard punch into the rug, which absorbed the force of the blow. She was able to move her head down toward her chest and create a pocket, the top of her forehead taking the pressure of the rug.

As they walked out of the house, Mona turned and closed the door.

Jean sensed she was being carried a short distance and then she was dropped onto a hard surface, heard a slamming noise, and then there was only complete blackness.

She heard a car motor cranking and start, and

suddenly she realized she was in the trunk of a car; they were taking her someplace. Thoughts born of fear crowded her mind: "Where are they taking me? What will he do to me when he gets me there? Home, I won't be in my home."

This last realization frightened her more than the others. She would be in a strange place, their place; totally in their power. "God help me. Don't let this happen to me."

CHAPTER
2

He is torn from the tent in which he trusted,
and is brought to the king of terrors.
—Job 18:14

Stanley, at the wheel of his cousin's ten-
year-old Chevy Caprice, had never
been so satisfied with anything he had ever at-
tempted as he now was with this operation. He
had never absolutely and totally owned and dominated anyone. He felt Godlike. He had the power
of life and death. In the trunk of the car he was
driving was a woman who would live or die at
his whim. He could literally do anything he
wanted to her.

They were heading west on 184th Street. The
sun, in a deep blue and cloudless sky, was up
over the bay and reflected off his rear window
and side-view mirror. The area was middle-class
residential; the houses were all ranch-style with
stucco exteriors. Every house had palm trees and
some had coconut palms. The backyard pools
that were in use were heated. The air temperature would soon be in the middle seventies, but
seventy-degree water was too cold for Miamians

to use. Stanley crossed Route 1 and intended to continue west to Krome Avenue where he would turn south into the truck-farming area. He could then angle west again until he reached the house.

Stanley was full of himself. "Mona, we did it. We goddamn did it. I told you I could do it. Shit, Stockton don't even know his wife's gone. He's got no idea she's in the trunk of my car, that she belongs to Donald Stanley." He took great pleasure in that thought. Taking the woman away from another man made the whole thing much more exciting. "Mona, this score's goin' to be fuckin' dead easy."

Stanley retraced with Mona how this had all started: "Remember how we were watching that program on the new TV that I just got with the hot card?" he asked, turning to Mona. "As soon as I saw it I knew it was my score. That asshole on television, I saw right away the mistakes the guy made, and knew I could do a kidnap right. It would just take a little planning. The first thing we needed was somebody to grab, somebody who had money."

He smirked, remembering how he had gotten his cousin Richard to come by the house, and how he had gotten him talking about local people who had some bucks; Stockton was one. A couple of years before he had worked for Richard on several jobs and had been on a house where Stockton's company did the roofing and plumbing.

That's when Stanley decided to have a look at Stockton. After a few days of watching the Stockton house and family, Stanley decided on grabbing the wife. There had to be money—the house was evidence of that. He had reasoned, "The old man leaves in the morning and then the kids are off for school. The broad's alone after that for at least an hour or two before she ever leaves the house." Stanley had even figured out how to get to Stockton and set up the ransom so he'd be clean if the shit hit the fan.

Mona was quiet. She was watching Stanley's face. She had never seen him so up. She was uneasy, and in the back of her mind there was growing apprehension about Stanley's fascination with Jean. Mona would not have put the name "jealous" to it, but that was what it was beginning to feel like.

Mona began chewing on the middle knuckle of her right middle finger. "Donnie, what you going to do when we get to the house?"

"Now what the fuck you think I'm going to do? This broad's just screaming for a 'Donald Special' screw. Join in or not, I'm turning that broad inside out."

"Donnie, that's rape. They'll give you life."

"I can't believe I'm hearing this. First they got to catch me, which they won't. I told you, it's all figured out. Besides, what the hell you think they'd give us for this grab? Might as well take all the prizes. You only got to pay once."

"Donnie, I'm scared for you. If you want to screw her, go ahead. Then let's dump her somewhere and go away. When she's missed, the cops are going to be all over this town, and you and me's going to get caught sure as shit."

They were driving through hundreds of acres of tomatoes ready for migrant hands to pick for shipment north. Stanley, exasperated at Mona for spoiling his moment of triumph, reached over and grabbed her by the hair at the back of her head. The car wobbled a bit, but Stanley firmed his left hand's grip on the wheel. He pulled down and back with his right hand until Mona was looking straight up to the ceiling. The car's headliner had come loose and was inches from her face, flapping in the breeze that was coming through the open windows.

"Now you hear me, bitch. This is my score. You fuck it up and I'll open your belly and feed you your guts. From now on you do just what I tell you. No more talk, no more bullshit. I want somethin' from you I'll tell you. You understand me?"

"Sure, Donnie," she whimpered, wincing at the pain. "I didn't mean nuthin'. I just don't want you should get hurt, that's all. I'll do what you want. You know I always do."

Stanley gave a satisfied grunt and released his hold.

For the last few minutes they had been on a dirt road that bordered a palm-tree nursery. A left turn put them in their dirt drive and, after a hundred yards, at the soiled white house and brown barn and its couple of outbuildings scattered about. There was rusting construction equipment on the grounds and a general air of neglect. The sparse grass had not been mowed in over a month. There were some untrimmed fruit trees surrounded by the rotting fruit they had dropped.

Stanley stopped in front of the house. "Get the pad and pencil in the bag in the back." Mona leaned over the back of her seat and retrieved the bag while Stanley listened intently for any sounds from the trunk. He laughed out loud. Mona looked at him quizzically, but he ignored her. He was thinking, "I really scared the shit out of that broad when I told her she had better be quiet. She's another one that'll do what I tell her to."

For the first time he wondered about Jean's ability to breathe in the rolled-up rug in the trunk. "Well, there's nothin' I can do about that now. She'll have to take her chances. I hope to hell she lives; she'll be fun alive."

As Stanley began walking toward the house, Mona touched his arm. "Ain't you gonna get her out of the trunk?"

Stanley never paused. "After we finish the note for the call. She'll keep."

There was nothing Jean could do to help herself. Her tied wrists and the tightly rolled rug immobilized her. Jean was perspiring and shivering—one from the heat of the trunk and warmth of the rug, the other from fright. The car had not moved for a full two minutes, the motor had been switched off. Her thoughts dwelled on what would happen to her when he took her out of the trunk. She wanted out of the trunk. It was hot, dark and she couldn't move in the rug. But the specter of rape frightened her more than the confinement in the trunk. She knew that what he had almost done in her home he would certainly do now.

Inside, Stanley was seated at the kitchen table. He spent a long time composing his telephone message to Stockton, and Mona wrote and rewrote what he told her. He had decided that it would be better to write it all down and read it to Stockton so nothing would be forgotten or left out. This was important, and if things went the way he wanted he would not have to talk to Stockton again. The message had to be right—it was worth $250,000.

Stanley read over the finished note. "It looks good, but we need to put some more in about not going to the cops. That's the only problem we could have." Seeing Mona's look of alarm, he scowled. "I'm ready for that, though. If the cops show, I'll know and we'll just walk away."

Mona didn't seem relieved, and he went on. "Look. If we do this right and panic Stockton, he'll get the money, follow my instructions and by evening we'll be rich. That stroke with the scar was pure genius." Stanley remembered, very pleased with himself.

Reading the message again, he was at the point where he was telling Stockton to "draw out $250,000 in twenty-dollar bills," when he realized there was a hole in his plan.

He turned to Mona. "I need a signal that Stockton's got the money and is ready. Right here, after 'bills,' put in, 'When you have the money, park your pickup off the road at Old Cutler and 184th Street, and use the Datsun.' "

He stood up, all business, full of self-importance. "Okay, I got to make the call. I don't want her in the trunk while I'm drivin' around, so I'm gonna get her out and put her on the floor in the spare bedroom. Just let her be. Don't do nuthin'. Let her be wrapped in the rug till I get back."

Mona nodded and Stanley went out to the car and lifted Jean out of the trunk.

Jean saw light and detected the unmistakable smells of farm country as she felt herself being lifted. She sensed the time had come: He would unroll the rug and rape her. She recalled the evil, depraved leer as he had looked at her, and she shivered. He might go beyond rape. With the shiver she involuntarily wet herself.

As Stanley carried her she felt him stepping up some stairs and as he entered the house, she smelled the dampness, a feeling of mildew in the air.

He dropped her on the floor in the spare bedroom and looked down on the rolled-up rug, envisioning the woman inside. Despite what he had told Mona, he grabbed the end of the rug and, lifting it, propelled Jean out of the roll. His look became truly rapacious. Then he saw she had urinated over herself and the rug.

Jean saw the face she feared.

He reached down and grabbed her right breast, squeezing until she let out a stifled cry of pain. Then he smiled and turned to Mona. "Clean her up so when I get back I don't have to contend with her piss. Leave her hands taped. When she's clean, put her on the bed. Don't screw this up or I'll break your fuckin' neck. You understand?"

"Yeah, Donnie, I know what you want. I'll clean her, and she'll be here for you when you get back."

He sensed reluctance in her, and stopped for a moment.

"When I screw her you want in?"

"I don't know, Donnie. I don't think so, if it's all right with you."

"It was just an offer. But you're gonna watch. You're gonna see me do it the way it oughta be done. Maybe it'll teach you how to handle that ass of yours better."

Mona made no reply. Her head dropped under Stanley's rebuke.

Fifteen minutes from the house Stanley pulled into the almost empty parking lot of a line of small shops on Dixie Highway. There were about eight storefronts and several rows of parking spaces in front of each store. Stanley reread the message, now including the "ready" signal, and walked to a pay phone.

Stanley had been really hyper when he grabbed Jean. Now that he was actually about to talk to Stockton, he again began to pump adrenaline. He was excited, nervous and frightened, although he wouldn't admit it, even to himself. His hands were shaking and he was sweating.

He had eyeglasses with him that he didn't need and used only to give himself a mature, "professorial" look. He was so rattled that he put them on. He had trouble focusing his eyes and his mind was filled with dozens of conflicting thoughts and "what ifs." He willed his total concentration toward reading the message to Stockton just as quickly as he could, and then to get off the phone and get the hell away from this place. His quarter connected him to Stockton's office. A woman answered, "Stockton Company."

* * *

Mona eyed Jean nervously. Even in her di-
sheveled condition Mona could see she was a
beautiful woman. Without thinking, Mona bent
down and removed the tape from Jean's mouth.
After a moment's hesitation Jean responded with
a simple "Thank you."

"Ain't no point in your hollerin'. Nobody could
hear you; we're in the boonies. Donnie wants me
to clean you up. I'm gettin' a basin and some
towels."

Mona left her, and Jean looked about the small
sparse room. It had only a double bed and
dresser. There was a small door which could be
a closet. The walls were painted ivory with the
plaster chipped and peeling. The floor was bare
pine. The only light she saw was a lamp on the
dresser, which also held a mirror. There were two
wooden casement windows, without curtains but
with the shades pulled. It was bright enough outside that the light penetrated the shades.

Mona returned with a basin of water, soap, a
wash cloth and towel. As she approached, Jean
said, "I can do that. There's no need for you to
wash me. Just take the tape off my hands."

"No. Donnie said I was to do it and not to untie
you." Mona soaped the cloth and began to wash
Jean's stomach, legs and groin.

Jean did not resist this very personal washing,
instead seeing a ray of hope for her in Mona.
"What's your name?"

"Mona." The answer was by reflex.

"Mona what?"

"Mona Little," she replied, not thinking, for
now Jean had her name. "I know that's a funny
name. My last name really is Little. My mother

was a hooker, like me, and she thought Mona Little would be a good name for a hooker."

The terror Jean felt with Stanley was subsiding into a composed approach with Mona. She had never thought herself capable of such control. "Are you and Donnie married?"

"Married? Us? No. Never thought about marrying nobody."

"Why have you kidnapped me?"

"Donnie's gonna get two hundred fifty thousand from your old man."

Mona was drying Jean's stomach with the towel. Jean raised up her head as much as she could. Looking directly at Mona, she asked, "He intends to rape me too, doesn't he?"

"Yeah, but Donnie's good. You play along with him like I do, and you'll like it."

"I don't want him. I love my husband. I don't want him to rape me or have any sex with me."

Mona began to wash between Jean's legs. "Honey, it don't take nothin' away. My momma turned me onto old johns when I was ten or eleven, and I've been screwin' ever since. It ain't wore out yet."

Jean had never met anyone like this, and she was her only hope to escape. "Tell me about yourself and how you met Donnie."

"You want to know about me?"

"Yes, I do."

"Nobody ever asked about me before."

"I'm asking. Tell me about yourself."

Jean was studying Mona as she talked. She saw a tall woman about thirty, slim, almost skinny. Her blond hair had to come from her beautician, but it looked good with her blue eyes. She was not unattractive, but rather was a person without a striking feature, who would disappear in a crowd.

Mona had finished washing and was now drying Jean's legs and groin. She was thinking about Jean's interest in her. "Ain't nothin' to tell. I was a trick baby and was turned out when I was ten."

Jean's voice quavered, as she begged, "Mona, I want to go back to my family. My children need me and I love my husband very much. You don't want Donnie to hurt me. If you'd untie me and let me go I'd never tell. You could tell Donnie I got away while you were getting fresh water to wash me with. You and Donnie seem happy together. This scheme of Donnie's is going to get you both in trouble, and Donnie may go away for a long time."

Mona looked Jean square in the eye. "I really want to help you. I like you. You asked about me. And I am afraid for Donnie, but I got to do what he tells me. I'll try. I'll try to do something to help you, only if I can do it without hurtin' Donnie."

As Robert Stockton hung up the phone, he paused, wondering irritably how soon it would ring again. His cluttered desk was covered with the blueprints, tools and material samples that were also scattered about his office.

The morning had started badly, and the telephone had been a contributing, continuing annoyance. The argument with Jean over breakfast had set the tone for a lousy day. What upset him, and had really ruined the morning, was that Jean was right. He did work too much. He did neglect her and the kids. He had no good answer for her, and so his frustration at being in an indefensible position had caused an outburst of anger.

He wondered what would happen if he refused to answer the phone this morning. He knew that fully two-thirds of the problems that damn phone brought were really non-problems, just pure aggravation. If left to normal procedures they solved themselves.

"Goddamn it," he muttered as the phone rang and Kim, his secretary, picked it up. He knew she would refer it to him. He could not train her to screen calls. Then he thought maybe it was Jean and he could apologize for his morning tantrum.

CHAPTER 3

The best laid schemes o' mice and men
Gang aft a-gley.
—ROBERT BURNS, "To a Mouse"

He reached for the phone, summoned by the imperative of a buzzer. "Telephones," he thought, "we live for them. No matter what we're doing we stop and respond." And so he did.

Kim said, "There's a man who says his name's Peter, who needs to talk to you about a problem your wife's having."

Curious, Rob took the call. He did not recognize the voice, though, and as he listened he went cold.

"Mr. Stockton, you may call me Peter. I have your wife, Jean. She is a lovely lady. She is fine for now, but cannot come to the phone to speak with you."

Rob's mind worked, "He's reading a speech to me. What the hell is this he's reading?"

"I left a note for you in your living room that will direct you where to deliver a small amount of money that will cause us to release your wife. Leave your office at once. Do not delay, even a second. Speak to no one, not even Kim. Make no telephone calls. Proceed directly to your bank and draw out $250,000 in twenty-dollar bills."

Rob's mind raced. "This can't be happening. Who is this asshole? Is somebody screwing with me?" He broke in, "What is this shit? Who the hell are you? Where is Jean?"

Stanley was taken by surprise. In his planning no one had talked back. He looked up from his note, staring through the phone at Stockton. "Shut up, you're not supposed to talk. Listen. Just listen to this."

He knew he mustn't get into a conversation, this had to be quick. He looked back down for his place in the written message and began reading again, but several sentences after—*not* at the point at which he had been interrupted by Stockton.

"It is now ten. You will be at the bank by ten-fifteen at the latest, and will have the cash by three, at the latest. If you do not, Jean is dead. You are to tell no one, not even the banker, what the cash is for. We will know if you do. From the bank go home and at three p.m. follow instructions in the note left there. You will not, I repeat, will not, hear from us again. Do it right the first time or she is dead. By the way, the tiny scar on the inside of her right leg is hardly noticeable. She told us she fell off her bike when she was six. Don't even consider calling the police. They can't help you. If they show up we will kill her and we will just disappear. The police will never find us, but we will know if you contact them. If you want to see Jean alive, pay us now." With that, the phone disconnected.

The voice of Peter was gone, the phone was now a dead, useless instrument. It had Jean and was about to cut off her life. It sat there impersonal, cold. It had conveyed this horror, and now it ignored him. The power only flowed one way. He was helpless against it. He tore the phone off his desk and threw it against the wall. It fell to the floor and spat its dial tone at him.

"Jesus Christ, what the hell is this? She's gone. Lost. Where? How? What do I do?" The air went out of him, and he slumped back in his chair.

Kim heard the noise of the phone hitting the wall, and entered his office. "Robert! What—!" She stopped in mid-sentence at the sight of his death-gray face and the broken phone on the floor.

The sound of her voice and her coming into the room brought him out of his stupor. He pushed himself up, and without a word, ran by her and out the office to his pickup.

Kim, expressing utter confusion, followed him in his flight. "Where are you going? What's wrong? Will you be back? Your appointments!"

The Ford pickup truck was unlocked and he was behind the wheel in seconds. Putting the key in the ignition took two tries. He careened out the driveway, oblivious to traffic. Rob was replaying the telephone call in his mind, trying to remember everything he had heard, trying to digest and understand what Peter had said.

Try as he might, though, his thoughts kept returning to the way he had parted from Jean that morning. "That lousy morning paper was more important to me than Jean. I didn't even say good-bye or kiss her."

There were hundreds of thoughts and images running through his head, but foremost was Jean. His thoughts revolved around what had happened to her. Was she alive? What had they done to her? Had they—he swallowed hard—raped her? Would they release her? Should he go to the police?

With a start, he remembered he had not fastened his seat belt. His mind, overloaded, had reverted to a problem it could deal with. He fastened his seat belt with one hand. The familiar, somehow satisfying, snap of the buckle brought him out of his uncontrolled mental wandering. He began to pay attention to traffic as he went over the call slowly.

He was convinced of its authenticity. Then suddenly a thought struck him. "I've been so rattled I never tried to call Jean. She's at home, she's got to be. This is some kind of trick, and I almost fell for it." But he was not convinced by his own argument. The scar, that damned scar. He saw a public phone and swerved right to the accompaniment of a protesting car horn.

The pickup pulled into a slot directly in front of the phone and Rob slipped his seat belt and was out of the truck in one movement, his hand already locating a quarter in his pants pocket. The quarter was in the slot and the number punched up almost instantly. He let the phone ring ten times, hung up and tried the number again.

The sour taste of vomit rose up in his throat as the phone in his home rang with no one to answer it. He knew. Jean was gone. He thought about calling neighbors or friends, but Jean had not mentioned going out. He knew the call was real.

Jean had been kidnapped. *Kidnapped* was a word seen in newspapers, an event that could not possibly be connected to him and his family. "No," he thought, "this is not possible. There has to be another explanation." Reality overcame his groping for escape. There was no point in trying to rationalize out of it. The call was real.

He considered the call as he walked back to the pickup, belted himself in and started the motor. As he pulled out into traffic, now in control of himself and the truck, he concluded that the call was professional, well thought out. "Hell, the guy had read it! They were obviously well prepared. The thing had to have been planned." The acid taste of fright again rose in his throat. He swallowed it down.

"I don't have a choice," he thought. "I've got to do what they want, and I've got to do it quickly. What's happening to Jean at this very moment? What are they doing to her? With her? 'A scar on the inside of her right leg.' " A very light scar and very high up, almost into her crotch. "The bastards!"

Waves of rage came over him and unconsciously he accelerated the pickup until he was roaring past other cars and weaving in and out of lanes. Horns and screeching brakes cut into his trancelike state. He remembered his assault on the office phone. The futility of his anger came through.

"I need to keep cool if I'm going to help Jean. I need to handle this right. I just need to get $250,000, and Jean will be free."

The bank, Barnett Bank, was just off to the left. Rob pulled into the driveway and turned to the right, toward the bank door and away from the drive-in teller lanes. He was sure that the vice president he always dealt with would advance him the cash without a problem. He had drawn several times that; his credit was excellent; his company was worth perhaps six to eight times that figure. But, Rob thought, "Jerry'll ask questions I'd better be prepared to answer without divulging the real reason for my need for cash."

Ordinarily he presented some documentation for the bank to transfer money to his company account, and Kim would prepare checks for him to sign. He did almost no cash business. He believed there might be close to $200,000 in the company account right now, since he was about to pay some material bills. There was also the payroll account. He regretted not looking at the checkbooks before he left the office. He felt there might be enough money there, but he was still searching for a plausible explanation for asking for $250,000 in cash—in twenties. "If there's no other way, I'll tell Jerry about the kidnapping," Rob thought.

Even thinking the word, *kidnapping*, set him to speculating. He willed his mind to stay on track and to tune out the speculations and wandering of his imagination. He knew that if he did not control this he would crack up. He was Jean's only hope.

As he got out of the truck a plausible story for his need for cash came to him. "Jerry might doubt the story, but I'm going to use it. I'll tell him that an eccentric in west Dade has some prime land he's willing to sell but'll accept only cash. There are still some old throwbacks in Florida who sound just like that. That's the best story I can think of. It'll have to do."

As he approached the glass door of the bank he became aware of his surroundings. He had been so intent on the task before him that he had not really seen the bank or the area around it; now he did. The parking lot was empty. But the parking lot was never empty! He put his hand to the door. The door was locked! The bank was closed. The word roared through his mind—*Closed!* How could a bank be closed on Monday at—he looked at his watch—10:17 in the morning? He saw the sign in the door: CLOSED FOR PRESIDENT'S DAY. It was not a holiday for him, and he had forgotten. He had forgotten!

Suddenly it came to him: Peter had forgotten too! What if Peter did not remember? He had no way of reaching Peter. There was no way to tell Peter the banks were closed. There was no way to tell Peter that he couldn't get the money today. Peter might, probably would, think that he was not going to pay. "They'll kill Jean. They'll kill Jean!" He sat heavily on the bank step, defeated. He was beaten.

He had been there almost ten minutes when a bank customer about to use the automated teller machine saw the bent figure holding his head in his hands. The customer hesitated a moment and then asked, "Can I help you? Are you all right?"

The voice brought Rob out of his mental shutdown and triggered his thought process. He realized he could not just give up. There had to be a way to contact Peter and find Jean. "I'm not going to find it sitting on bank steps," he thought. "The police. I should have gone to the police right away." He recalled that Peter had warned him not to go to the police, that "they" would know if he did. Now he felt he had no choice. The police were his only hope. They had to find Jean.

Without a response to the stranger's inquiry, he rose and got into the pickup and drove back to the phone he had used to call the house and called 911. Within a few minutes he would regret this call, but he had no frame of reference to guide him in his response to the problem thrust upon him. He had never been exposed to any situation even approximating this one.

A quiet female voice greeted him and asked whether this was an emergency. Without responding, Stockton shakily replied, "This is Robert Stockton. My wife, Jean, was kidnapped from our home by a man calling himself Peter. I'm on my way home now. I need you to find her."

The calm voice asked him for his address, then for a description of his wife, her full name and what had happened. While Rob was supplying this information, the 911 operator was dispatching two uniform units to the house.

It was less than a ten-minute drive to his home, but it seemed an hour. His imagination was again on fire. Questions crowded in on him. "How had Jean been taken? Had there been a fight? Was she hurt? Was she dead? What had they done to her? The scar—had she been raped? What were they doing to her now? What would happen when no money was delivered? Would they discover I called the police? Would that call, by me, kill her?"

When he arrived at his street and turned in he knew Jean was dead. There, parked in front of his home, were two "green and whites"—marked police cars—with spinning emergency lights. Now the whole world knew he had called the police.

The neighbors, Jinny from across the street and Phil and Helen from next door, together with four or five others he recognized but whose names did not register, were answering questions posed by the two uniformed officers. He heard some of the questions, and from the responses, he gathered the officers were inquiring about strange cars or strangers in the area and when Jean had last been seen. None of those responding to the officers indicated they had noticed anything out of the ordinary that morning, nor had they seen Jean.

Jinny was saying, "Yesterday there was a tall, thin man, maybe thirty-five, six-foot-two or three, very slender, black, who stopped about three houses down and let out four young black boys who then went door to door selling some laundry detergent. One came to my door and said the proceeds from the sale were to be used for drug rehabilitation. I don't remember the name of the product. I didn't buy any."

A neighbor whose name Rob couldn't recall said, "I saw them too. The car was a late-model, blue Lincoln two-door."

Rob walked up to the officers, and the conversation stopped. The neighbors moved aside to give him access to the police. The silence and movement were unmistakable, and one officer addressed him, "Mr. Stockton?"

Rob's reply was a very curt "Yes."

"I'm Kincaid, this is Officer Rodriguez. We were dispatched to follow up on your telephone complaint."

The neighbors were obviously uncomfortable around Rob, not knowing how to treat the police presence and Jean's apparent disappearance. They gave whispered expressions of concern and drifted back to their homes.

Every muscle in Rob's face was clearly defined, his eyes narrowed. He was exercising every ounce of self-control he had, but there was no mistaking the rage just below the surface. "In the call I received, I was warned not to call the police or my wife would be killed. Please, at least turn off your emergency lights."

The two officers were obviously chagrined. Kincaid apologized, "Sorry, Mr. Stockton, no-body told us." Both moved to their cars and turned off the lights.

Rodriguez approached Rob and said, "Maybe we better check your house."

Rob nodded and moved toward the house, followed by the two officers. They stopped at the front door, and Kincaid said, "We're sure there's no problem inside, but just to be safe, would you mind if Rodriguez and me went in alone? We'll do a quick check and come right back out and then we can all go in, okay?" Rob agreed and Kincaid reached for the door knob as Rob proffered his keys. The door swung open, unlocked.

Once again Rob felt the grip of fear. His face drained of color and he steadied himself on a wall. He feared he was about to be sick on the spot. He took a breath and the feeling began to lessen. After a few minutes the officers returned, Rob noted, holstering their guns.

Rodriguez said, "Come on in, the house is empty. Tell us exactly what's happened, and then take a look around to see if anything's missing."

Rob stepped into his house and was enveloped in the familiarity, the welcome, of his home. He could smell the breakfast his children had eaten. He sensed Jean, but she was not there. The welcome he had first felt on entering quickly gave way to a sense of evil, a vestige of those who had taken Jean.

Out of habit, he collapsed in his white reclining chair in the family room, waving the two officers to chairs. Kincaid took Jean's matching recliner and Rodriguez perched on the edge of the green and gold sofa. Rodriguez had a notebook and pencil, and Stockton began to talk.

"Between nine-thirty and ten this morning I got a phone call. The guy said his name was Peter. He said he had my wife, Jean. He described a light scar she has on the inside of her thigh, up almost to her groin. He told me she said she got it when she was six. He said I was to go to the bank and get $250,000 in twenties, and that if I called the police or told anyone they would know, and would kill her."

Rodriguez asked, "Does your wife have a car?"

"She has a red Datsun, and there's a white Chevrolet Blazer that we all use."

Kincaid said, "The red Datsun's in the garage, but there's no Blazer around. Where are your kids today?"

"They're in school." He stopped, and his mind began to catch up. "No, today's a holiday. The banks are closed too. I went to the bank to get the money and they were closed. I can't get the money. They don't know the banks are closed. They'll think I'm not going to pay."

Trying to calm him, Kincaid asked, "Could your wife be shopping or visiting someone? Do you know what she and the kids had planned for today? Is there anybody you could call that might know where she is?"

He put his head in his hands and thought, "Jean. What was Jean going to do today?" He felt guilt again as he realized that he was not attuned to family activities unless they affected him. He should be; this is what Jean had been telling him over breakfast, and even then he had not asked what they would be doing today. He damned himself for the unfeeling way he had behaved at breakfast. He returned to Kincaid's question, making a conscious effort to control his thoughts. "Was there a boat in the yard?"

Rodriguez answered, "No."

"Then the kids are out skiing and snorkeling. The wind is down and they wait for days like this in winter. I—I don't know of any plans my wife had."

"How about a walk through the house to see if anything is missing or disturbed?" suggested Rodriguez.

As they moved throughout the rooms, Kincaid asked, "What was your wife wearing when you left for work?"

Rob paused, his distress evident as he answered, "A blue nylon night dress and gray housecoat."

"Would you know if any specific items of your wife's clothes are gone?"

"No. I'm sure I couldn't spot a particular missing piece of clothing." He held himself in as long as he could and then screamed at them, "Missing clothing! Jesus Christ, my wife is missing! The goddamned house is empty! Who cares about missing fucking clothing!"

The officers, taken aback, were about to answer when they saw his expression change, as he realized that something was indeed missing: He hadn't noticed the large rug on the foyer floor when he came in. It was of no real value, a rug someone had given him, but Jean had decided it would look good in the foyer.

He hurried back to confirm his recollection. "The foyer rug is gone. It's about six or seven feet square, blue, I think, with a white fish—no, a white dolphin on it." As he was telling the officers about the missing rug he suddenly remembered, "I have left a note for you in your living room." "Damn," he thought. "What else have I forgotten?"

With a gasp he turned from the two officers, who stood there bewildered. Racing into the living room he looked wildly about. There it was. A folded piece of white paper. A pewter candlestick held it down on a lamp table. Rob snatched it up, tumbling the candlestick to the floor. He unfolded it and saw it was a photocopy of a piece of paper upon which pieces of what appeared to be newsprint had been attached: *if you good and not call police and have money and follow orders you will have her tonight put 250000 in brown Publix bag go to 3rd public phone at Winn Dixie Perrine you will find message under shelf wait 5 follow orders go now no stop or call we watching Put this in money bag*

The officers read the note over Rob's shoulder, having followed him into the living room and observed the discovery of the note. Rodriguez looked at Kincaid, who nodded and said, "Mr. Stockton, we need to contact detectives to follow up on this."

Rob reread the note in his hands. He was devastated. "If I haven't lost Jean with the phone call that brought the 'gangbuster' cops," he thought, "I'm certain to lose her now. It's ten-forty-five, I've got no money, police cars are in front of my house, and I'm supposed to be on my way with the money to the Winn Dixie supermarket. There's no way, no way I can save her. They're waiting for me now and I've got no money. How can I tell them? How can I make them understand?" Rob slumped into a chair. He had no answers.

Kincaid picked up the Stocktons' kitchen telephone and punched in a number. He was soon connected to someone in a group called GIU, which Rob later learned was a "General Investigations Unit." These were detectives assigned to district stations to do—just what the name implied—general, as opposed to specialized, investigations. Kincaid was soon explaining to a detective named García what had happened to this point.

Kincaid finally hung up and told Rob, "OCB— the Organized Crime Bureau of the department—investigates kidnappings where there has been a ransom demand. GIU is contacting them and they'll call us. OCB has detectives that know these kind of cases. They'll be calling in a few minutes."

Rob absorbed all of this in utter disbelief. Time was passing and a bunch of initials, GIU, OCB, without names or faces, was supposed to help. The cops obviously had no idea what to do. And here they were, parked out front for the whole world to see. Rob's facial muscles again began to harden, and his eyes closed, as anger grew within him.

"How could they not know?" he thought. "The whole goddamned neighborhood knew!"

Just then the phone rang. The Peter call flashed into his consciousness. Perhaps they realized it was a holiday. They were calling to make other arrangements. He snatched up the phone.

What he heard was, "Is this 7220 Southwest 181st Street?"

Rob answered, "Yes."

The voice identified itself: "This is Debbie Swift from Channel Eight. We heard over the police radio that someone has been kidnapped from your address. Can you give us any particulars, or let us talk to the police?"

Stockton was struck dumb. Now the whole world really knew the police were in on the kidnapping. It would be on the six o'clock news. Rob just could not cope, and he completely shut down. He sat in the chair with the phone in his hand hanging down by his side. His expression was blank. There was no more anger there. He just looked blank.

Rodriguez, observing Rob, saw he had some sort of problem. "Mr. Stockton, can I help?" Getting no response, he took the phone and asked, "Who is this?"

The reporter from Channel Eight repeated her request for information on the possible kidnapping.

"This is Officer Rodriguez. We've only been here a few minutes and don't know what we got. It could be just a missing person. If anything develops I'll have somebody get in touch with you."

The reporter replied, "From what we've been told there's been a kidnapping and a ransom demand for a woman at that address. I need some information now. We want to send a broadcast van to the address."

As soon as he hung up, Rodriguez recontacted García and informed him of the Channel Eight inquiry and suggested he immediately pass it on to OCB. García agreed.

Rob heard the exchange but gave no response. He had given up. He remained in his chair. He was convinced there was nothing he could do and that Jean was lost.

CHAPTER 4

Hope lies to mortals,
And most believe her.
—A. E. HOUSMAN, *More Poems*

Al Lawrence, Special Agent in Charge of the Miami FBI office, was taking advantage of the holiday by catching up on long-promised repairs to a leaky kitchen faucet. The ringing phone was answered by his wife, Helen.

"Al, it's the office—Randy Jefferson."

"Okay. I'll be right there."

Al wiped his hands on a paper towel and picked up the kitchen extension. "Hello, Randy. Busy day?"

"Not until now. When you transferred in, you decided to personally supervise kidnappings for ransom. The boss can always change his mind, you know. I've got one that is starting out bad, and it's a holiday. There's a Detective Hernandez from Metro OCB on hold. He's reporting a kidnapping. I'll take the information, or we can do a conference call if you want to talk to him."

"I appreciate your offer to let me off my hook. Set up the conference call." Al settled into a desk chair at the small built-in kitchen desk between the pantry and oven that Helen used for the business of running their home. He pulled a yellow legal pad from a plastic divider attached to the wall, and a pen from the cup that held other assorted writing implements.

"Okay, boss, Hernandez is connected in."

"Hello, this is Al Lawrence."

"Octavio Hernandez, Metro, OCB. Sorry to bother you guys on a holiday, but I just got a call from GIU that I figured you ought to know about right away. A Robert Stockton called 911 and reported that his wife had been kidnapped from their home and that he was on his way there. The dispatcher was new, put it out on the air and sent two units to respond. They were marked. They searched the house, found no trace of her. The husband said he got a phone call demanding $250,000 ransom and the uniform unit reports a ransom note in the house. We're sorry about the uniform response, but shit happens. Do you guys want it, or should we handle?"

Foremost in Al's thoughts was the federal kidnapping statute that gave him the authority to investigate the case. The statute did not take effect until the victim had been gone for twenty-four hours. The law, passed after the kidnapping of the Lindbergh baby, presumed that if a kidnap victim was not returned within twenty-four hours, he or she had been transported interstate, the case thereby falling under federal jurisdiction.

Al was weighing the problem. If it later developed that she was not transported interstate, which was likely, the FBI would have no jurisdiction and the case would revert to the state. As it was, the state now had jurisdiction and the authority to investigate and prosecute.

It was unlikely that the victim, in this situation, would be returned within the twenty-four-hour period. But waiting twenty-four hours meant the FBI would inherit all the decisions made by the police, and to avoid taking over a case in which another agency had made the initial, critical decisions and commitments, Al saw only one realistic choice: come in now, even if it was without statutory authority.

One other thought crossed his mind: His assistant Milt would raise hell about not adhering to the law and the rule book.

His answer to Hernandez and Jefferson was short and to the point. "We'll take it. But since prosecution is probably going to be in state court, I'd appreciate some OCB people working with us."

Al, in making his request for local assistance, knew that this would give him a measure of control over other members of the police force who might stumble into this sensitive situation. In addition, Metro's OCB had excellent informants and other sources that could be of value.

Al added, "Pull out the uniform units and arrange for Stockton to call me at the FBI office in twenty minutes. It goes without saying we ought not to use police radios."

Hernandez, in concluding the conversation, informed Al of the Channel Eight inquiry and the possibility of a TV news crew on the scene.

"You guys got any more good news for me?

Randy, pull the kidnap plan and begin making your calls. I'm on my way."

Al swiveled in his chair and, rising, looked through the open kitchen windows at Helen on the patio watering some of her orchids, which had just come into bloom. Al smiled at the sight of his visiting four-year-old granddaughter, Ann, "helping" and being lovingly encouraged by Helen. This was another day in her life he would miss.

He called to Helen, "Sorry, I have to go in."

Helen's disappointment showed on her face. It was plain that she once again saw Al's work robbing them of a holiday together. Helen was counting the days until Al retired, giving them the opportunity to enjoy each other and spend some time with the boys and the grandchildren.

She brought Ann behind the fence that separated the pool from the rest of the patio, gave her something to keep her busy, and then joined Al in the bedroom.

Al was stripping off his T-shirt and shorts. "It looks like we've got a 'for real' kidnapping. Ransom note, missing wife, phone call, the complete package. By the way, you can use the sink. I just have to put the cover on the faucet base."

Resigned to the lost holiday, Helen started laying out the clothes he would need.

Al knew Helen was hurt and disappointed. "Sorry about this. I know you were planning a barbecue this afternoon, but there's no choice. I have to go." Al's apology was offered as much to lessen his own guilty feelings about leaving as to explain to Helen.

"I know," she said, smiling wanly. "But I'd be

less than honest if I didn't tell you I won't miss this sort of thing a bit when you finally retire."

As he passed his belt through the trouser loops he reached to the top of his dresser and threaded a holster on the belt. After fastening the belt he attached a leather cartridge carrier, holding a 6-round speed loader, and inserted a Smith & Wesson Combat Magnum in the holster. Many of the younger agents carried automatics; Al had tried one for a while in New York City, but he came back to the reliability of the revolver; he was just too used to that constant companion.

Al left the bedroom and headed for the garage that adjoined the house. Pausing at the door he took Helen in his arms and kissed her, holding her tightly for a moment. As he released her he said, "Expect me when you see me."

In the twenty-three years they had been in the FBI Helen could not begin to count the times she had heard that phrase.

After he hung up with Al, Jefferson reached for the lower file drawer of his desk and drew out a large manila envelope. On the face of the envelope was typed KIDNAP PLAN MIAMI OFFICE. The envelope contained a number of memoranda detailing instructions to various office elements in the event of a kidnapping. Jefferson selected a memorandum captioned "Personnel Assignment." This document listed not only the duties of office personnel in the event of a kidnapping, it also set forth the order or priority of notification to each person. Jefferson passed this to the special agent on duty with him, and he gathered up the clerical personnel in the office. They were placing calls within a minute of the conclusion of the Hernandez call.

As Al headed for the office he called the Assistant Special Agent in Charge on the scrambled car radio. "Two from One."

"One, go."

"Milt, start thinking about recommendations for inside men. What's your ETA?"

"About ten minutes."

"10-4."

Milt Jennings, having been promoted to Assistant Special Agent in Charge of Miami the year before, was only thirty-six and had come up fast. This was his first office as ASAC. Milt's advancement, in Al's opinion, had been too rapid: he was a good administrator but lacked experience and consequently took refuge in the "book." Al saw him as a "by-the-book" bureaucrat who was short on imagination, conviction and the ability to make tough decisions.

Milt had received a telephone call, as part of the kidnap plan, and had been briefed on the case, but as he drove to the office he was troubled. This kidnapping had gotten off to a bad start. The uniformed police response could well compromise the entire investigation. Why, after the police screwed it up, Al would jump in was beyond him. The FBI didn't even have authority to be in, and if the shit hit the fan on this, Al could be in trouble. "I need to call the Bureau early on," he thought, "and let the kidnap desk know that I was not consulted on this decision."

* * *

While Rob was unaware of the growing FBI preparations, time was rebuilding some of his composure. Without much foreboding he answered when the phone rang and talked to Hernandez.

"I've talked to the FBI," Hernandez told him, "and they're going to take over. I talked to the boss, Al Lawrence. You're to call him at 973-6000 in twenty minutes; he's on his way into the office now. Try to relax, it's going to be okay, the guy knows what he's doin'. The officers are going to leave now, but they'll be close by. You lock up and make the call, okay?" Rob, in something of a daze, agreed and at Hernandez's request handed the phone to one of the officers. Hernandez gave them their instructions, and they left.

Rob had never felt so alone. The house was more than empty. It was as though all the air, the life that makes a house a home, had been sucked out and what remained was a shell, filled with regrets and remorse and the horror of what had happened here.

He endured for twenty minutes and then reached out for the telephone to call the FBI number. He knew that this was all for nothing. The die had been cast when he found the bank closed. Jean was dead, or soon would be.

Milt was already in Al's office when he arrived. They were joined shortly by Xavier Restrepo, a supervisor. It was an open, spacious room, with Al's large, mahogany, standard government desk at one end. Behind it was a credenza with some books, and over the credenza a large FBI seal was affixed to the wall. The credenza was flanked by the United States and Florida flags held upright by floor stands.

Al's priority, upon arrival at the office, was damage control: Channel Eight. He quickly located the number and called. He identified himself and asked for Ralph Winslow, the assignment editor.

"Hello, this is Winslow."

"Ralph, this is Al Lawrence, FBI."

Al knew they were just doing their job, but he resented the imposition. He enjoyed a good relationship with the media, tried to be accessible, answered questions when he could and never lied to them.

"We've got a sensitive case working. Your reporter picked up a piece this morning, but right now it's pretty much a non-story. It could be a good one later on. Since we have a life in jeopardy, you know I can't talk about it, and I'm sure you'd rather not hear about it and take responsibility for that life. A release of what little you have could well cause a death. You know I'll release information as soon as I can."

Ralph was impressed by the fact that Al had called him without pressure and volunteered some information. "Thanks for the call, Al. Of course we don't want to screw something up. It's good you called. I was just about to send someone out on it. We'll sit on it for a while. I'll call you to check on progress and make sure we get to go with it as soon as possible."

Al wondered who else might have the bare information of a possible kidnapping, and just go with the story.

The phone rang within a minute of the media

call and Al turned in his chair and hit the button that activated the speaker. "Yes?"

The telephone operator said, "Mr. Lawrence, Robert Stockton is on the line." Al thanked her and Rob was plugged in.

"Mr. Stockton, this is Al Lawrence, I'm in charge of the Miami FBI office. I've been told briefly about your wife's abduction. You are on a speaker phone and Milt Jennings, the assistant in charge of the office, is here together with Xavier Restrepo, a supervisor. Please tell us exactly, as best you can recall, and in as much detail as possible, what has happened. We need you to give us this detail in order to assess the situation and suggest some possible responses, and hopefully, some solutions."

Rob, exhausted from the strain of the day, launched into a discordant monologue of fact, hurt and accusation. He began, "Someone calling himself Peter called me at work to tell me he had kidnapped my wife, Jean, and to get $250,000 from the bank in twenties and to deliver it to him. But the banks are closed today. I didn't realize that until I got to the bank. I don't have $250,000, but if the banks were open I could get it. Because the banks were closed I called the cops to find Jean, and they fucked it up. They came in marked cars with the lights flashing and parked in front of the house. The guy said he'd kill her if I called the cops. Then the fucking TV news called me at the house asking about the kidnapping. It'll be on the goddamned evening news. I found a note in the house telling me to go to a Winn Dixie in Perrine and to deliver the money there. I haven't done a fucking thing right in this goddamned mess, and Jean is probably dead by now. Now you guys get handed to me by the cops and you're going to hand it to somebody else. When the hell is somebody going to do something about finding Jean?" He stopped, exhausted, out of breath and beaten.

Al, sensing the fatigue and helplessness, tried to inject both calm and confidence in his voice. "Did this Peter give you a time or instructions as to when to go to the Winn Dixie and what to do when you got there?"

"No. Wait, yes, I remember now. I think he said, after I got the money from the bank. I think he said by three. The note in the house told me what to do."

Al glanced at his watch and read 11:43. "Do you have the note you found in your house?" Rob read through the note, and at Al's request, read it to them a second time.

"Put the note down and don't handle it anymore," Al instructed. "Stay in your house. Call your office. Tell them you will be home for the rest of the day. Make an excuse that someone is ill, but that if Peter calls again they should tell him to call you at home. Sit down and write out a complete physical description of Jean: height, weight, coloring, scars, the whole bit. Give us the name, address and telephone number of her doctor and dentist, also advise us of any occasion where she may have been fingerprinted. Find a good photograph of her and the negative, if possible. Do you understand what we are asking you to do?"

"Yes."

Al glanced at the legal pad in front of him on

which he had made some notes. "Within an hour a white panel Dodge van with signs reading 'Pleasure Floor Conditioning' will pull into your driveway. The driver will come to your door and identify himself. Open your garage door and the van will pull in. Also, we need your permission for the telephone company to trace all calls to your home and office."

"Yes, of course." Rob began to feel a sense of relief. Something was happening. Wheels were beginning to turn.

Al again glanced at his pad and then continued, "If Peter should call before we arrive, assure him that you will pay, that you want Jean back. Tell him about the banks being closed, but that you are going about getting some money from friends. Tell him you'll have some money tonight, and the rest when the banks open tomorrow. Impress upon him that you want to stay in touch with him. Ask him to call later and you'll tell him how much cash you've been able to get together today and to call to make arrangements for tomorrow's delivery of the whole amount. It is most important that we not lose contact with Peter. Do you understand?"

"Yes, I understand."

"Good, now repeat back to me what you are to collect for us, the manner of our arrival and how you are to handle Peter. I want to be sure we haven't forgotten anything."

Rob summarized what he had been told, and Al was satisfied he understood.

Milt was not satisfied. He considered Al to be impetuous, and felt they should have more information before sending the van. The SAC should not be questioning and giving instructions. The whole chain of command got disrupted when managers did this.

Al turned to Milt and Xavier. "Do you have any questions for Mr. Stockton, or any comment on what we have so far?"

Milt hesitated, not sure he wanted to participate in this interview, but then asked, "Was there anything familiar in Peter's voice? Do you suspect anyone in this?"

"No."

Milt added, "If you have children, where are they now?"

"We have three. They went out in the boat this morning. I don't know when they'll be back."

Milt continued, "You might give some thought as to how you're going to handle this with them, and whether you want them to remain in the house while this is working, or whether they should stay with friends or relatives."

"Okay, yes, I will."

"Mr. Stockton, this is Xavier. We'll ask you to accommodate two agents in your home until this is concluded. We'll explain this when we see you shortly." Stockton assented and the conversation was ended.

The office kidnap plan was being rapidly implemented. A select group of experienced support personnel were arriving at the office and setting up a major-case control desk. Their job, with analyst and computer assistance, would be to track all information that was developed, and to insure that all leads emanating from the investigation were assigned, covered and reported. It would be the job of the agents and supervisors to recognize what needed to be done in the case and to compose the leads.

The first clerk in had secured a prepackaged kit, made up months ago, from the storage room; it contained all the materials necessary to get the operation underway.

As soon as the "technical" agents arrived at the office they contacted the telephone company and began to arrange to trap and trace all incoming calls to Stockton's home. The special kidnap kit came off the shelf, and the techs began a check-out procedure to make sure it all worked.

As the agents arrived they each pulled memos from their desks detailing what role they were assigned in a kidnapping, reviewed them and secured the necessary equipment. One of the mundane but top priorities was gassing up all the cars now before there was a need for them.

Stanley was elated. As he drove back to the house, the fright of the telephone contact with Stockton was replaced with self-admiration for how well he had carried it off. He had about four hours to kill before the three o'clock contact. He knew precisely how he was going to fill up that time.

Stanley had his coat and tie off and was unbuttoning his shirt as he entered the kitchen. Seated at the table, drinking a Coke, was Mona, who had changed into a sheer blouse and a mini skirt that rode high on her thighs. As usual, she was not wearing any hose or underwear.

Stanley hardly noticed her. "Is she in the bedroom, cleaned up?"

Mona rose from the table and approached

Stanley, her body full against his. "Forget that stupid broad. I know what you like. She doesn't know anything. We can do it all."

"I told you before, I'm fucking her. You can join. If not, you watch." Stanley was out of his shirt, but stopped quickly. He would undress with Jean watching. She would see what was coming. It would build fright in her.

He slipped back into his shirt, and with one arm moved Mona out of the way and headed for the bedroom.

She watched Stanley enter the bedroom, and at the same instant heard Jean scream. Stanley was undressing. Jean, using her heels, had pushed herself up against the headboard. Her back rested there and her knees were drawn up tight to her chest. She presented a compact, tight figure.

"Mona, get your ass in here. Stand over there so you can look at the bed and see us in the mirror too."

Jean found her voice as Stanley dropped his pants to the floor and removed his briefs. She begged, "Please, don't do this! I have a husband and children I love very much. Please don't do this to me! Mona loves you, she wants you. I don't want you! Mona will do what you want. I'm no good for you. Please, leave me alone! Please! Please!"

Stanley stood nude before Jean. Her pleading was just what he wanted. He had never achieved an erection so quickly.

He was on her in an instant. Jean did not notice the lengths of rope he picked up from the bedroom floor, and she was surprised when her hands were freed and then quickly rebound individually. He sat astride her as he tied each hand to a bed post. One arm was pinned to the bed by his leg so he had two hands free to control the other one. She felt his penis on her chest and shuddered, closing her eyes. He was so strong that her struggling did not even slow his tying her. He slid down her body, controlling her thrashing legs. He managed to place a loop around each ankle and then over the foot board so her legs and arms were virtually immobilized.

Jean fought and screamed and cursed and cried. For uncounted, seemingly endless minutes, she struggled against the degradation, the pain, and the anguish. Finally, exhausted, she could no longer fight. For the next half hour she could only protest his attacks with feeble groans and screams of pain.

When it was over, Mona came up out of the corner she had squeezed herself into. She was shaken by the things she had seen Stanley do. She followed him into the kitchen, while Jean lay on the bed, her eyes closed, not moving.

Stanley got a beer from the refrigerator and Mona took a Coke. They sat drinking, in silence, Stanley still nude.

Mona broke the silence. "What we gonna do with her now?"

Although he had bragged continuously about how well he had planned everything, he hadn't thought about what to do with her once he had her. The big question he had not faced was whether she should stay alive. Especially now that she had seen him and Mona. And she had really seen him!

For a moment he regretted his exposure when he was playing with her. He began to consider what would happen if she were dead and he got caught. He decided that alive, for now anyway, was better than dead. Dead could mean "Old Sparky." He shook his head. No, he wasn't going to be caught. But he needed insurance.

Soon he would be moving for the money, the big one, the payoff. While dead broads don't point fingers, it would be better insurance right now to hide her until after Stockton paid off. That probably would be the best time to kill her, and maybe Mona too. He needed a place to hide her, just for the day. It'd be too risky to leave her in the house, alone.

There were a couple of hours before his next move with Stockton. The best place to hide her would also be one where he could have some more fun with her, before he killed her.

Stanley rose from the table. "We're gonna stash her. Get my clothes out of the bedroom and put 'em away. I'm changin' and then we're leavin'. Make me a sandwich."

Mona hurried to do as she was told. Stanley was soon in dungarees, cowboy boots and a Key West "Conch Republic" T-shirt.

He entered Jean's bedroom. Hearing his boots on the wooden floor, Jean opened her eyes, saw him, and screamed. "Please, no more. Please, don't hurt me again."

"Shut up, we're leavin'." Stanley grabbed her wrists and a piece of rope, and once again secured them behind her back. Jean was too exhausted to attempt even token resistance. He again taped her mouth, carried her out to the car and dumped her in the trunk. He returned to the bedroom and gathered up the rug. Dumping it on top of her, he said, "I hear a fuckin' sound outta you I'll really rip you open."

Stanley and Mona headed east to Krome and then north and west, into the Everglades, looking for a dirt road to nowhere, a place to stash Jean.

It was almost 2:00 before he found a dirt road that suited him. He had tried several, but they all ended in places he did not feel were secure enough. He was looking for a hammock, a growth of hardwood thick enough to conceal her and the fun he would have with her after he got the money. A place that would be dry. The road he was on now looked good. There was water on both sides, but up ahead was a hammock, and if the road curved that way it would be just what he was looking for. And so it did. Stanley pulled a little off the road and opened the trunk.

He easily lifted her out and carried her about forty feet to a small open spot among the trees and dropped her on the uneven ground. Mona carried the rug and dropped it beside her.

Jean was not fully conscious. Stanley's attack, the closeness of the trunk, and her physical exhaustion had taken their toll. She hardly felt the cuts and scrapes from the stones, twigs and roots. He had ripped the center of her gown in the bedroom. Her housecoat was torn also but still on her shoulders.

Stanley studied her. She was well put together. He knew every millimeter of her. She could be fun again; he hadn't finished with her. She was his. All his. He owned her. He could do anything he wanted. He began to want her now. But an unusual voice spoke in Stanley's mind: "Take your time with her *after* you get the money." He had taken so long to find the right place that time was starting to get short.

"After" was logical, but Stanley had problems grasping any "after." He never put off pleasure or gratification. Pleasure was a now thing, not a future thing. When he wanted, he wanted now, not later.

Jean was regaining her equilibrium and awareness. Quickly he looped an end of the rope around each wrist and tied it off. The free end of each was tied to the base of a tree, so her arms were outstretched, like a cross. He tied an end of rope around each ankle, pulled her legs wide apart and fastened the free rope ends to trees. Jean was tied spread eagle with her back on the weeds and earth.

Stanley looked down on her and thought, "She's open." He liked that idea, her being "open." He thought of her being open to him. And then he thought of her being open to all sorts of things the hammock might produce, or he might produce. Before Jean died he would have his fill. It would be fun to again show Mona how much he could enjoy someone else.

He motioned Mona toward the car and they drove away leaving Jean, nude except for the remains of night dress and housecoat crumpled under her back.

Jean was now fully aware of her surroundings. She had been enough awake to feebly resist when he tied her ankles. She had looked up into that face that carried threats of horror as he stared fixedly at her. She saw him finally make a sign to the woman, and they walked away. She heard a car start, and the motor fade in the distance.

Her reaction was one of relief that he was gone. She saw a canopy of oaks over her, and glancing to each side, saw she was in a small glade. She felt a slight touch on her face, then on an arm, a leg, her stomach. She realized they were bugs, mosquitoes probably. She twitched and rippled muscles and flesh trying to shoo them off. It was then she began to understand her plight. She was tied spread eagle in the woods, defenseless against any animal or bug that fancied her. As the horror mounted in her and the ants began to crawl up her left leg and over her face toward her left nostril, she silently screamed in terror.

CHAPTER 5

The first step is the hardest.
—MARIE DE VICHY-CHAMROND,
"Letter to d'Alembert"

The tech-work van was driven by Walt Freeman, the principal technical agent. Crowded in the back among the electronics equipment were Al and Milt, together with the two agents who had been selected as the inside men.

Milt had selected two other agents, but Al had disapproved and designated the two now in the van. Milt still chafed at this.

The selection of the two inside men was perhaps the most critical of the operational decisions that would be made. The success or failure of the investigation might well depend on the caliber of men selected for that unpleasant and stressful assignment. The inside men would be surreptitiously placed in the house and would have to stay there, without relief, throughout the entire investigation.

Their job would be to guide Stockton in future negotiations with the kidnappers, and provide assessments and suggestions to guide the investigation. They would be prepared to impersonate him, or impersonate a friend, and deal directly with the kidnappers. They would, among other things, be inside protection for the family, giving them what comfort and information they could, and, most importantly, they would record incoming contacts from the kidnappers and signal their receipt to the techs and agents who would be on surveillance.

Grover Carlson and Henry Adamski were both trained, experienced hostage negotiators. Carlson had also been SWAT trained, but at forty-eight had dropped out of that grueling regimen, leaving that part of FBI work to younger men. Adamski was nearly twenty years younger, and was fluent in Spanish, good insurance in case this kidnapping was narcotics-related. This was a growing problem in south Florida as the cocaine cartel exported its Colombian criminal habits as well as its dope.

Besides electronic gear and people, the van carried a 12-gauge shotgun and a silenced 9mm machine gun, both cased so as not to frighten the family. There had been no time to gather personal gear. Toilet articles and change of clothes for the inside men would be brought in later.

Al was no stranger to kidnappings. This was his third office as SAC, and he had been an Assistant Special Agent in Charge in two other offices. In his twenty-three years in the Bureau he had supervised five major kidnappings for ransom and had not lost a victim. He was an attorney, but had never practiced. His education fit perfectly in his job.

While the van was moving toward Cape Cutler, an agent from the FBI Homestead Resident Agency, who was near the Winn Dixie in Perrine, had been contacted on his scrambled car radio. The gist of the kidnap note was relayed, and he was told to chart and inspect the phone booths there, but to do it without being observed.

Phil Bentley was fifty-three, the Senior Resident Agent in Homestead, an area comprised principally of a large Air Force base and huge truck farms that fed much of the country.

Phil bridled some at the instructions he had just received. "The usual crap from Miami: How am I supposed to inspect public phones without being observed? I'm fresh out of invisible dust." When he got the message he was about fifteen minutes away from the Winn Dixie, covering a lead at the Ochoa Nursery farm.

Phil opened the trunk of his Bureau car and changed into the clothes he carried there: jeans, work boots and an old shirt. The change was carried, not for surveillance use, but for work. He needed these for his real "field" work, to save his suits. He told Jorge Ochoa he needed an hour of his time and one of his old pickups. He bent a few Bureau rules as Ochoa followed Phil's Bureau car to a parking lot about four lots away from the Winn Dixie. They parked next to each other, and Ochoa got in the Bureau car while Phil drove off in the pickup.

Phil parked the truck in an open spot just north of the Winn Dixie, and walked south spotting the three phones set up against the blank wall of the supermarket. The "third phone" could be either of the end phones, but was more likely the end phone counting from his left to right. He approached that phone but did not enter its two-sided enclosure. He noted the number and went into what he believed would be the first phone enclosure. Someone was on the center phone. He dropped a quarter in the coin slot and punched up the number of the third phone. At the beginning of the first ring he touched down his cradle, disconnecting the call.

"Well," Phil thought, "for a change a public phone is carrying its correct number." Phil stayed in the enclosure for a minute, carrying on an imaginary conversation. He jotted down the numbers of phone three and phone one. He squared himself to the phone enclosure, covering as much of the instrument as possible, and felt under the phone shelf: nothing but the usual chewing gum.

He hung up the hand piece and walked away about fifteen feet, stopped as though remembering something, and turned back and entered telephone three. He dropped his quarter and punched up the number of telephone number one, and again disconnected at the beginning of the first ring. Another correct pay phone number.

The phone enclosure had the usual two sides that encompassed the phone and extended down past a small shelf under the phone and to the bottom of two hinged phone-book holders that swung up to about shelf level where they could be opened and used. The two shredded phone books hung limp and wet under the shelf.

Phil again squared his body to the small enclosure, cradled the phone shoulder to ear and reached down, grasping one of the phone books and raising it almost to shelf level. With his other hand he opened the book and then slid that hand under the shelf. He could feel a folded piece of paper held to the underside of the shelf by what felt like cellophane tape. Making an on-scene judgment, he detached the tape from the shelf and withdrew tape and paper. With some difficulty, using only one hand, he opened the paper sufficiently to see that it was a photocopy of cut-up newspaper words. He made another quick decision and put the paper in his shirt pocket, dropped the phone book, and after a few seconds walked away and back to the pickup.

He drove back to the Bureau car. He and Ochoa again switched vehicles and Ochoa waited, at Phil's request. Phil carefully opened the folded paper and placed it in a clear plastic envelope designed to hold documents. The tape remained attached to the paper. The document was a clever way of passing a message: no handwriting or typewriting that could be identified, probably no fingerprints, and few hairs or fibers on the Xerox. It was probably the best one could do to avoid leaving identifiable evidence behind.

The note read, *put this with dollars go to Tony Roma's Place For Ribs Kendall under outside bench follow orders*. Phil got the office on the scrambled radio and related what had happened.

The occupants of the white van en route to the Stockton house also copied the transmission.

"Just what we expected," Al observed. "He's going to run a trail of notes to a drop point."

"He's smart," Henry added. "Even though he's using what are probably 'sterile' notes, he's having them put with the money so that when he clears the drop he gets all his notes back."

Phil queried the office: "I've got the message. Should I put it back?"

Al asked Walt for the mike. "This is One, read your transmission, Phil, good job. Keep the note, don't return it."

"10-4, boss."

Headquarters advised the telephone company of the numbers of the pay phones at Winn Dixie, which the phone company had been trying to identify in the event a trap and trace were needed. They, in turn, advised that a trap and trace was up on the phones in Stockton's home and office.

Phil sent Ochoa on his way with his thanks.

Al had anticipated a moving payoff, and this note confirmed it. "I should have insured that SPIT was alerted. They're part of the kidnap plan but need to be in on all developments as they occur."

"Al, we're just moving too fast on this," Milt said. "We should slow down and make sure that we've complied with all Bureau directives, as well as our own plan."

Milt got nothing but a withering glance as Al keyed the mike. "Station, One."

"One, go."

"I did not specifically insure that the Special Investigative Team is kept fully informed and that they are ready to move. Have Xavier make sure that this is done."

"10-4."

In their off-site office, SPIT picked up the transmission and began rechecking their gear; they talked to Xavier in order to come up to speed on the developments in the case.

SPIT had been a tough battle with Bureau Headquarters, but approval had given Miami three five-man teams of full-time surveillance people. Al thought how effective these people had been. He was fond of claiming that these guys and gals could follow you into your bathroom without being made.

Along with the street-surveillance group came four pilots and two high-wing Cessna aircraft, slow-flying, quiet surveillance machines. They were unshakable eyes in the sky. Coupling these assets with radio-tracking devices that could be attached to vehicles under surveillance, night-vision equipment, special body-pack radios, infra-red strobe markers and other specialty gear made for a powerful investigative tool.

Al was concerned about this slight oversight of not specifically alerting SPIT. "Milt, can you think of anything else we forgot?"

"Not right off. You have to expect to miss things when you try to do it yourself. I think we should have assigned these jobs, like this one of talking to Stockton, to agents and then we could have carefully checked to make sure that nothing was missed and that the agents had done a thorough job."

Al, an edge of impatience in his voice, said, "Milt, the manager in you is showing. You've succumbed to the Headquarters concept of an SAC being a manager. The FBI doesn't need green-eyeshaded managers counting paper clips in its Field Offices. For Christ's sake, Milt, try being a leader." Milt stiffened at this rebuke, and his resolve to inform Headquarters of the cavalier handling of this case was finalized.

Al was sure he had forgotten something else. "Of course. The Winn Dixie. Just because we found a note at the phones does not mean that Peter would not also use the phone." Stockton, Al recalled, had been told to wait at the phone for "five." Al keyed the mike: "This is One. Also advise Xavier to insure the phone company has trap and trace on the three phones at Winn Dixie when the payoff commences."

The van turned right off Old Cutler Road and threaded its way through Cape Cutler to Stockton's street. As they turned onto it, the people in the back could not see out, but they knew the locale. The homes were all on generous half-acre lots, each with at least a two-car garage and domed, screen-enclosed pool and patio. Prices were in the $300,000 to $400,000 range. The neighborhood could be characterized as consisting of substantial homes, but certainly not the pricey homes of some exclusive areas of Dade County.

The Stocktons' house did not back up to a canal. It was center block and had a house on either side, one to the rear and across the street.

As they approached the drive, Al leaned forward so that he could get a partial view through the windshield. He noted the house across the street from Stockton's. The van entered the driveway and Al saw the house. It was the usual ranch, L-shaped, except the legs of the L were equally long. The bedrooms would be in one leg, and the living area in the other. The pool and covered patio were fitted into the angle and filled it. Off a circular drive that went up to the main entrance was a branch that continued up to a two-car garage. The house was stucco and painted light blue with dark blue trim.

The van stopped in the driveway, and Walt got out and walked up to the front door.

After the call to Al, Rob had gone to his office that had been set up in one of the bedrooms. He sat at his desk and busied himself putting together the requested information. He located a recent photo of Jean and found the negative. The vital statistics came easily from memory. The work was important; the busy part more so. When the work was done, Rob's imagination took over. Unoccupied, his thoughts roamed.

Self-accusation predominated. He relived the breakfast exchange again and again. "Jean was reaching out to me. She wanted to communicate, to be more a part of me, and I pushed her away. I wasn't always like this."

They had married seventeen years before, when she was nineteen and newly pregnant. Theirs was a high-school romance, after meeting on a blind date.

He thought how shy she had been, and still was in many ways. They had been natural together. After that first date neither of them had ever dated anybody else. In his senior year they were definitely an "item," talked about in the yearbook, and everybody knew they'd be married.

They hadn't planned the first time they had made love, but they both knew it was going to happen. It was his old Ford. Somehow making love in the old car was one of the most exciting times of their lives. They were always careful, except for one evening.

Rob paused in his thoughts. He was not sure he could bear these vignettes of Jean. He recalled a specific evening. He was in his second year at the community college, attending nights and working days as a carpenter. Their time together was mostly weekends. On this particular evening two of Rob's classes were canceled, and he decided to drive over to her home on the hopes she would be there. He intended to surprise her and her parents with a short visit, but found Jean home alone. Her parents had gone to visit a cousin across town.

Jean had decided to stay home to take a long hot "soaky" bath, and finish preparing some job applications. She was fresh out of the tub when Rob arrived. He recalled her that evening, fresh and beautiful. That was the night that they made Steve and pushed up the wedding date.

He quit school and worked extra jobs, but the two of them did fine. Jean was always there. When he ran into problems he didn't think he could handle, it was her confidence in him that got him through. There wasn't a major decision in the business or in their lives that Jean didn't share. "Now she's gone," he thought, as his head fell into his cupped hands, "and I didn't even say good-bye this morning."

Guilt gave way to nightmarish thoughts of what was happening to Jean. As the minutes passed the thoughts became more horrible, and hope, if he had ever had any, disappeared. The doorbell brought him back to the present and he hurried to answer it. It offered an escape from his thoughts.

He looked through the wide-angle viewer in the door and saw the van and Walt, who was square to the door and holding a folding pocket case against his chest. The case was made up of two joined cards: the top contained printing and large blue letters FBI, the bottom card had printing and a photograph. Rob opened the door.

"Mr. Stockton? I'm Walt Freeman." As he said this he offered Stockton a closer look at his FBI credentials. "Would you open the garage door please? We'll pull in."

"Okay." Rob closed the door and walked to the garage area and activated the electric door opener.

Walt went back to the van, and as the garage opened, pulled in. Rob closed the door behind the van. They had finally arrived.

Passengers and equipment came out. Al saw the garage was occupied by a red Datsun, a small workbench, garden tools, and a ride-on lawn mower. After quick introductions he hurried into the house, anxious to begin. Grover and Henry carried their cased weapons, and each had a briefcase with paper, pens, lists of radio-call signs, county and state maps, evidence containers, fingerprint kits and other items they had quickly snatched up.

Once they were all in the kitchen, Al led off. "Let's start with the note. Where is it and where did you find it?"

"You told me to put it down. It's on my desk. I found it on the table in the living room held down by a candlestick."

"Grover, secure the note please and later dust the table and candlestick for latents."

The note was placed in a clear plastic envelope, which was taped closed.

"Mr. Stockton, we're going to get to know each other very well indeed. My name is Al. May I call you Robert or Bob?"

"Most people call me Rob."

"Thank you, Rob. We need written consents to intercept and record telephone calls to your home and business. We also need signed consents to intercept and record any calls to which you are a party, and any conversations to which you are a party."

Seeing Rob's puzzlement, Al explained further. "Peter might call the house, and the call must be recorded for evidence, as well as to insure that any instructions are understood. Recording of your conversation might also be necessary if you meet with the kidnappers in person."

Rob, dismayed by what he considered bureaucratic nonsense, responded testily. "Yes, yes, I consent. Show me where to sign and let's get to finding Jean." As he was signing, Al also gave him a consent for the telephone company to trap all incoming calls and trace them to the phone from which they originated.

With this out of the way, Walt, who had brought in his electronics gear, began to hard-wire a recorder into the phone system and to rig it with two sets of earphones. The installed equipment would allow any call to be answered normally, recorded, and simultaneously listened to by the two inside men. When Walt finished his intercept installation, he next turned to setting up a hundred-watt, scrambled, "suitcase" two-way radio that could communicate with FBI cars and the office. His immediate problem was installing an outside antenna for maximum efficiency. After checking around, he resolved this with a gutter mount on the patio overhang, which could not be viewed from the street. Walt then began to lay out and test his body bugs.

While he was busy with his tech stuff, Al contemplated how he would handle Stockton. To describe what was to come as "delicate" was an understatement. In the midst of an emotionally charged situation, direction, leadership and control had to be established.

Al studied his man. What he saw physically was a white male, thirty-eight, five-eleven, one hundred eighty-five pounds, short graying brown hair, getting a little thick around the middle, no facial hair, no glasses, deeply tanned from outdoor work. His eyes and brow had squint marks from many hours in the sun. He was obviously physically strong. On balance he was what a woman might term reasonably handsome. What Al really needed was to be able to describe the man inside.

Al's mental assessment flowed. "We know he's excitable, and apparently does not handle stress well. Therefore he likes to have things decided. From our conversation on the phone, he's into guilt, which will slow him down, distract him from what we have to do. We need to lift some of that guilt. Because of the bad response by the uniform units and because of the warning by Peter, he doesn't trust police, and that means us too. He has pretty much decided to do everything that Peter wants. He's terrified and mesmerized by Peter. The Bureau decrees that I must respect the family's wishes on dealing with the kidnapper. I can advise, but they decide."

Al felt that the advice he would be giving in this case would have to be couched in terms that allowed little choice. They could not just follow Peter's instructions slavishly. If his assessment of Stockton was accurate Stockton might ultimately be incapable of dealing with Peter, in which case, contrary to the "rules," Al, not Stockton, would have to make the fateful decisions.

C H A P T E R
6

Soothsayers make a better living in the
world than truthsayers.
—GEORG CHRISTOPH LICHTENBERG,
Aphorisms

Al's first priority was to have Rob detail everything he could tell them
about what had transpired that day, and indeed
many days before, that could even remotely be
connected with the kidnapping.

Rob immediately protested: "What's the purpose of this? How is this finding Jean? Why aren't
you out looking? Can't we prepare some money
for him? We're just wasting time!"

Al allowed him to run down. "We need to have
as complete a base of intelligence as possible
from which to operate. Right now you are the
main source for that intelligence."

Milt put a tape recorder on the kitchen table,
and the interview began. For a moment Rob's
attention was captured by a half-empty mug of
cold coffee. He knew Jean had left it there. That
mug was, at that moment, his only link to Jean.
He shook himself to hear what Al was saying.

"Please begin by recounting your conversation

with Peter, the time of day, accents, text, anything out of the ordinary."

Rob related the conversation in nearly the same terms as he had previously. Al was struck by Rob's emphasis on two points: the scar on the inside of her thigh and the warning not to call the police.

Questioning brought out some small details, but nothing of import. Rob thought the voice was not Floridian, not even southern, but he could not be more specific. He was certain only that it was male. He could offer no suggestion as to who might be responsible for the kidnapping. He had no enemies that he even remotely felt could be capable of this. After twenty minutes Al was satisfied that for the present, Rob's emotionally charged state of mind had given what it could. They had enough to begin. Al knew that as Stockton came to know Henry and Grover, he would gain confidence in them and calm down, at which more information could then be remembered and extracted.

Now it was time for hardball. Al looked at Milt with a knowing glance that was picked up by Henry and Grover. The two agents excused themselves to check on the progress of the technical installations.

This was the tough part of a kidnap case. Al was now about to become a bad guy, unsympathetic to Rob's horrible problem.

Al knew the role he was about to play was essential. He had done it many times before, but he still didn't like it. Sometimes kidnappings only masqueraded as kidnappings. There were pissed-off husbands who killed wives who had made their lives miserable but who, for one reason or another, they could not divorce. Other husbands wanted insurance, others had been cheated on. The list was endless. But many of these husbands, to mask the disappearance of their wife, had alleged a kidnapping.

Al asked in considerable detail about the relationship between Jean and Rob, inquired about mutual friends and organizations they belonged to; this would all be information for future leads, depending on what developed.

Al explored their marriage. "Rob, I have to know if you or Jean are into any affairs. Any girlfriends, boyfriends?"

"For Christ's sake, no! Jean and I are very much in love. Neither of us is fooling around."

Al also asked an uncomfortable Stockton about his financial affairs, including where Jean stood in this picture. Rob squirmed and objected to the closeness of some of the questioning. He became irate at one point.

"Am I under arrest? Aren't you supposed to advise me of my rights? What if Jean owns fifty percent of the company? Our wills are identical, we each take all from the other. That's what husbands and wives are supposed to do. What the fuck has this to do with her being kidnapped? Get off my fucking case and find Peter."

Then Al dropped the bomb. "Will you take a lie detector test concerning what you have told us this afternoon? If there is a problem or an embarrassment, now is the time to clear it up. I have to warn you that if you have given us false information, you face prosecution for fraud against the government, a violation of Title 18 U.S. Code Section 1001."

There was no easy way to do this. While Al personally believed him, he had been lied to by experts and occasionally fooled. Rob had to be tested.

Rob exploded. "You fucking son of a bitch! Get out! I don't need you and your radios. For all I know Jean's dead or being raped, and you sit here and smart-ass me about lying. You don't believe me! Well, I got news for you. I don't give a fuck whether you believe me! You, you're supposed to be helping; I haven't seen any help from anybody so far. Just get out and leave me alone!" Rob exhausted himself, and his head dropped onto his arms on the table.

Al let him rest for a moment, then placed a hand lightly, compassionately on his arm. Stockton had spent his anger. He swallowed his pride and agreed to a polygraph. Al realized he was tired and beaten; there really was no more fight left in him. His agreement to a polygraph was really all they were looking for. One would be arranged in the next day or two if the demands of the case permitted. His agreement under these conditions was an indicator of truthfulness.

Milt had maintained a neutral posture, following the exchange by eye movement. He had shifted uneasily in his seat when Stockton's head had dropped on his arms, but he took no active role.

The next question, Al felt, was sure to skyrocket him out of control. He did not really know Stockton, but this was Dade County and it had to be asked. It had been answered unexpectedly in the affirmative once or twice before, changing the entire character of the case. "Can you think of any motive, besides money, for kidnapping or harming your wife?"

"No."

"Do you, your wife, relatives or friends use or deal drugs?" The standard south Florida question.

"No." Rob had not gone ballistic.

"You will be polygraphed on these questions too, and again I caution you concerning possible fraud prosecution if you are not truthful." Rob, tired and whipped, made no response.

This part over, Al began his standard speech: "Mr. Stockton, Rob, the FBI has had considerable experience in kidnapping cases. Since 1933 I can think of only one case that has not been solved. I have personally supervised five kidnapping-for-ransom cases, and fortunately in all five the victim was rescued and the kidnappers arrested. Don't take this to mean that there are no problems here and that Jean will be home for dinner. While we can predict that certain things will happen in this case, and based on experience we will react in certain ways to what transpires, every case has its own peculiarities. Hopefully we will not be unprepared, but adjustments and decisions will have to be made. We will consult with you on major directions and we may ask for your permission or direction on occasion. There will be many more areas, operational areas, where I will make the decisions.

"Now, let's get clear on one thing. Our primary concern is and always will be the safe return of Jean. We will do nothing to jeopardize her well-being. Our whole investigation and involvement in this case is centered on her safe return. If we arrest Peter but fail Jean, we have failed in this case. When we ask you for a decision, we may not always be able to abide by it, but it will carry great weight with us. The ultimate responsibility for this investigation rests with me, and I can not delegate or dilute that responsibility. Whatever happens, I will always be responsible in my own mind, and without question, in the view of FBI Headquarters. So, as of now you have no responsibility for Jean's well-being. It is mine."

Al had given this speech before, and while he genuinely meant every word of it, he gave it for a purpose, and he could see it being accomplished as the expression on Rob's face lightened. Until this moment Rob had appeared drained, almost empty; now you could see him filling up. Someone was taking part of the responsibility for Jean. Part of the load left him and seemed to fly across to Al.

"One of the things you must decide for us is whether or not you want to pay off in real money, or whether you want us to dummy a package. If you decide to pay off in real money, may we follow the pick-up person and, if it appears advisable, arrest that person? If we pay off with a dummy package we will arrest if it looks like our fisur—sorry, Rob, FBI language—physical surveillance may be lost. Rest assured, whatever your decisions, we will pursue the kidnapper to prosecution. There is no possibility of a ransom payoff and our dropping the case."

Rob's gaze rested on the half-empty coffee mug on the kitchen table.

"I assure you that any arrest we make before Jean is safely returned will be for the primary purpose of forcing our hostage to divulge Jean's whereabouts. While we want to prosecute this man, we would, if absolutely necessary, trade him for your wife. It is possible that such an arrestee may have little or no information. In my experience, this is never the case. The person appearing to pick up the drop of money is always a principal. With only one exception, kidnapping conspiracies, in my experience, are made up of one to three people. In that exception, there were seven, but all knew everything that was happening."

Rob responded, "I have no money; the banks are closed. But I do want to give him the money."

"We cannot supply money for you, but I can offer suggestions. You could follow what is apparently going to be a string of contact points, and when and if you confront him or communicate directly with him, tell him this is a holiday and that the banks are closed. This may give us two shots at locating Jean. The first will be when you confront him with no money, which obviously is not your fault but caused by his poor planning. The second, presuming he understands and agrees to what you have presented, will be when you come at him tomorrow with all the money he has asked for. We may be able to turn the closed bank into an advantage if we can communicate with him and make him understand you want to cooperate, but that his timing was off."

Al backed his chair away from the kitchen table and laid his pen down on the yellow legal pad in front of him. Milt turned in his seat to more squarely face Al. Stockton was not aware of this move, but Al saw it as an indication of Milt's assessing his performance.

"This brings us to another area which we have, until now, assumed you would approve. I want your permission for Grover and Henry to live here in the house with you until this is resolved. We will get some clothes and toilet articles to them later.

"They are both well trained and experienced in hostage negotiation, and I suggest very strongly that you be guided by them in your dealings with Peter. Our best advice to you, based on experience in other cases, is that you introduce one of them to Peter as a brother, cousin, friend, lawyer or whatever might fly, on the basis of being too distraught to think or understand and that you are concerned you will mess up because of your condition. By doing this we will have an advantage in negotiation with Peter. They are not as emotionally involved as you, and they have broad and varied experience to interpret and remember what transpires. Your emotional involvement puts you at a distinct disadvantage. You should consider this suggestion very carefully; it has worked to our advantage many times."

Rob was overwhelmed, buried in information. He got up from the kitchen table and walked once around the kitchen. "I can get five thousand dollars from petty cash at the business and from funds in the house. If I can meet him today I want to give him that as a show of good faith."

"Rob, we can put a tiny electronic tracker in

the money which may lead us to where Jean is. We can also mark the money for later identification." While Al made the offer in good faith he did not expect Stockton to accept it. He was trading on the premise that people, after refusing a number of suggestions or offers, will be inclined to look more favorably on those they would have declined had they been offered them in the beginning.

"No. I prefer to lose it rather than lose a chance of getting Jean back. A clean, no-strings delivery will show Peter I want to pay. I have to convince him that when the banks open he'll get the whole amount."

"Okay, Rob, I don't disagree with that in principal. We won't mark the money, but we will run it through a camera. That way we'll have the serial numbers and there will be no indication to anyone of any tampering."

Rob nodded, and Al went on to the next tricky area. "We have no idea who this Peter is, Rob. He could be dangerous. You should wear a 'body bug,' a very small transmitter. You should try to meet and talk with Peter personally. The broadcast conversation will be monitored and recorded. The monitoring will allow us to know if you are in danger, and the recording will tell us a great deal about our man."

"Al, what if he searches me and finds it?"

"Let us demonstrate how we'll conceal it. I think you'll agree that he won't find it."

Al hesitated. Rob's strain showed clearly in his face. His hand was massaging his forehead. There were decisions yet to be made, and Al reluctantly continued. "You need to consider the advantage of an arrest if Peter shows. If he shows, we've got him. We're in a very strong position to convince him to tell us where Jean is. His arrest may produce information that will do that. If we let him go and don't arrest him, there's no guarantee he'll ever show again. He could get cold feet and walk away or be hit by a car. The future is 'if.' The present is certain."

"No! No arrest. I want to follow his instructions. I'm afraid if I don't I'll lose Jean."

Al countered, "Then we need to surveil the meeting and surveil him away from the meeting."

"He might see you."

"You have my assurance that the surveillance will be most discreet. There will be absolutely no chance that it will be detected."

Rob made no response, and Al took that for acquiescence. Milt jotted a note.

Al continued, "Rob, there's one more security arrangement we need to make, and I feel very strongly about this one. I want either Henry or Grover concealed in your car. We'll put him in the trunk with a radio and shotgun. The back seat will be modified so that he can come from the trunk into the car interior instantly."

"All right, if you think it necessary."

"Grover and Henry will brief you on how to act and what to say if you are able to contact Peter.

"Now let's talk about day two. The real payoff."

"I can't. I can't think anymore. I'm tired. Could we do that after we see what happens today?"

"Sure. We'll take it one step at a time."

Al was satisfied. It was a plan he could live

with. He would have preferred more latitude and, if operationally essential, he would take it. The discreet surveillance and no arrest might be judgment calls, but all things considered, it could work. The variable in the whole plan was Peter.

There were two telephone lines connected to the Stocktons' house. The main phone had been hardwired to a recorder. The other phone was for use by the Stockton children. Fifteen minutes before, the telephone company computer had changed its number and arranged for a busy signal on the old number. Walt was a busy man. The second phone with the new number would be an open line to the command post at the FBI office, a command post that Xavier was setting up while Al and Milt were with Rob.

From the first phone Rob called Kim at the office. "Kim, I've got a real serious family problem I'll fill you in on later. Right now I want you to call my foremen and tell them I'll be gone for two days and out of contact. You can say you don't know where, but you think it might be Washington. They'll just have to do the best they can. I want you to close the office after you talk to them and then take tomorrow off. Don't come in at all. Tell the foremen the office will be closed.

"One other thing, I'll need the money in petty cash. Put it all in an envelope. Someone will pick it up before you leave."

"Who?"

"I don't know yet. Just give it to a man who asks for the petty cash. I can't explain now."

"Rob, what's wrong? You've got me scared. Are you all right?"

"Kim, I really appreciate your concern and I'll

tell you everything later, but I just can't go into it now. Don't worry about me, though, I'm all right."

"Okay. I'll do as you ask. If I can help I'll be at home."

When Kim had finished and closed up the office, the telephone company arranged a call-forward setup for the office phone to a special phone in the FBI office. It would be answered and recorded by a Kim impersonator. Al confirmed that the trap and trace were now up on the office phone as well as the home phone.

As this was being done, Rob filled in Henry and Grover about his neighbors, and particularly the people across the street. Jinny and Joe Fleming had been neighbors for five years. They and the Stocktons were friendly but not close. Rob placed a call to them on the line that had previously been the children's. He explained to Jinny, "We've got a real serious problem. The FBI is with me, and they tell me you could be of great help. In a few minutes two FBI agents will be at your door. Please, Jinny, listen to what they have to say. I hope that you and Joe will agree to help me and Jean."

Within five minutes Jinny's doorbell rang and a man and woman were on the threshold displaying their FBI credentials, and Jinny let them in. Agent Sue Sullivan began, "What we are about to tell you must be kept in the strictest confidence; Jean's life might depend on it."

Jinny replied, "The police were here earlier, and it appeared from their questions that Jean was missing and might have been kidnapped."

Sue confirmed the fact that it did indeed appear that a kidnapping had taken place.

Jinny was impressed. "Just like a TV thriller," she thought.

Sue now put the reason for their visit to Jinny. "May we have your permission to stay in one of the rooms in the front of your house? We need to be in a position to observe everyone coming or going or passing the Stocktons'."

Jinny agreed. Sam, the other agent, asked Jinny if they could pull into the garage. She consented to that as well and opened the door. Sam went out and pulled the FBI car into the spot usually used by Joe.

Both agents began unloading gear from the Bureau car. Their job was to record the tag number and description of every car and its occupants that drove by the Stockton house. They were to obtain as many photographs as possible of each car as it drove by. They were also to photograph and record the description of anyone walking by the house.

As Al was preparing to leave the Stockton house via the van, he took Milt aside while Stockton was in another room. "We know the second meet site. We have to assume Peter does not know we already have his first note. If he does, it's all over and we need to be doing something else."

Milt was noncommittal, either by gesture or response.

Al continued, "Why not follow what trail there is right now, before we even put Stockton in position? If there are other notes we will be way ahead of Peter, and perhaps be better able to anticipate his moves. If the notes break to phone calls, we would still have more information than we do now.

"We could dry-clean the area with half a dozen agents, even create a diversion, while one makes a quick pass and retrieves the message. The risk is small, and I think acceptable, balancing the advantage of always being several steps ahead of Peter and his possible surveillance of Stockton and the area Stockton is in.

"The question is, do we tell Stockton and then just do it? Not tell Stockton and do it, or seek Stockton's concurrence?"

Milt did not hesitate. "There is absolutely no way I could be a party to this plan without the approval of the family. We must tell Stockton we're thinking about picking up the notes and get his permission."

"The 'manager' again. Why not just do it?"

Milt countered, "What if Peter detects us doing it, breaks off contact, and kills Jean? Stockton might sue us. Headquarters would have our heads."

"Milt, I don't see any successful suit, but at your insistence, I'll talk to Stockton."

Rob was horrified at the idea and gave a resounding "No!"

Al did not fault him. It was just too big a responsibility for him to assume. In retrospect, Al felt he should have just done it and not consulted Milt. Al reluctantly admitted to himself that he was prompted to consult Milt by an unaccustomed sense of self-preservation. He was beginning to feel Milt's opposition more keenly, and had come to the conclusion that, if the case went badly, Milt would probably save himself at Al's expense.

Al saw that Rob was intimidated by the omnipotence with which he had clothed Peter. Rob had never been exposed to anything approaching the deadly serious game he now found himself in. It was not worth a confrontation with Rob this early, so Al decided to pass and follow the trail as it unfolded. But he would leave Milt in the office.

Milt, Al and Walt left the Stockton house in the van.

Stanley maneuvered the Chevy into the passing lane, and glanced at his watch. "We'll be there with a little time to spare. Mona baby, this is it. The sun shines on us today."

Stanley was smiling and as happy as Mona had ever seen him. Mona was not smiling. Chewing on the middle knuckle of her right middle finger, she was thinking of Jean, and what Stanley had done to her. Thoughts were exploding in her head like a string of firecrackers. "What's Donnie really gonna do with her? When he gets the money will he tell where to find her? She's seen us both good. Donnie really worked her over. The cops'll go crazy tryin' to find us. Donnie's gotta know that."

She finally found enough courage to put one of these questions to him. "Donnie, when her old man pays off, how we gonna get her back to him?"

"Don't you worry about that, baby. Donnie'll take care of that. Probably better for us if she don't go back." His private thoughts, however, were more specific. He was thinking: "Yeah, she stays there in her tomb. She's good as buried, and there's room for one more in that tomb." Stanley, uncharacteristically, reached over with his right arm, put it around Mona's shoulders, and drew her close to him.

Mona smiled at the unusual touch, and put her head on his shoulder. In the next moment though she involuntarily shuddered at the thought that came to her. "If he leaves her there she's dead. I got to figure some way to get her back, but I can't hurt Donnie. If I get her back, she'll identify him for sure."

Donnie felt the shudder pass through her body. "You okay?"

"Yeah, just got a chill, I guess."

"When we see that truck of his at 184th and Old Cutler the good times'll roll and you won't get no more chills. You really hooked up with a winner this time."

CHAPTER
7

Learn to labor and to wait.
—LONGFELLOW, "A Psalm of Life"

It was 2:40 and Al was getting impatient. Milt, Xavier and he were in the radio room of the FBI offices. Sally, the unflappable radio operator, and two assistants were at the radio console and wall displays.

"Milt do you have direct communication with Stockton's house and with the telephone company established?" Al asked.

"Yes. The phone company will know before the Stockton phone even rings that there is an incoming. If it's a Peter call, the house will tell us and we'll broadcast the origin of the call. We should know the address of the originating call before Stockton even answers the phone."

"To save time, Milt, broadcast each address even if we don't know it's a kidnap call, and then follow up with advice as to whether it's hot or not."

Al turned to Sally. "How about a roll call? The units should all be pretty much in position by now." He watched as Sally began. As each unit number was called and then responded, a light came on opposite that agent's number. Anyone observing the board could see all the units in service.

Al was pleased. "Even with the holiday and short notice we didn't do badly. We've got sixty agents out there." He glanced over at the large wall map of Dade County with a plastic overlay on it and grids marked off with a letter of the alphabet assigned to each grid.

With the county divided into twelve sections they would have five agents per section. That was not great coverage for the size of the county, but they could adjust grid dispersion if they detected any trend, and even at this point they would be able to get a car to a phone in two to five minutes in their target areas. If they concentrated near shopping centers they might gain an edge. That's where pay phones were, and lots of people placed kidnappers at ease. Broward and Monroe counties to the north and south had not been set up for coverage. Monroe County consisted of the Keys, and, by their narrow geographical configuration, a place for an extortionist to avoid; he would trap himself in the Keys. Broward was a possibility because it was merely a land extension of Dade County. But since the two notes had designated south Dade locations, the heavy concentration was south and thinned as it went into north Dade and became nonexistent at the county line.

"Milt, two more items," Al continued. "Get a teletype off to Bureau Headquarters and surrounding offices, outlining what we've got. Also,

I think we ought not to go at three. Let's figure on three-thirty. Being on time is a police habit. Bad guys are always late. Another consideration is that delay might cause an anxious Peter to make a call to find out why. We need to play some psychological games with him. Let's try to condition him early on to problems, screw ups and some opposition from Stockton. Peter must be made to realize that not everything will go his way. If we can do this early, a later problem will be less likely to scare him off.

"Okay, Milt, it's yours. Xavier, let's load up my car and join the troops."

Milt hesitated. "Al, can we have a word in private?"

"Sure." Al moved out of the radio room and into the empty squad area.

"I'm sure you're aware that I disagree with the direction this investigation is taking."

Al's sarcasm showed. "That thought had occurred to me."

"I feel strongly about this and intend to incorporate my dissent in the teletype to the Bureau."

"No, Milt, that teletype is from me. From my office. You may, of course, communicate with Headquarters in any other fashion. If you like, I'll sign your communication attesting to these objections. I would hope that you know me well enough to understand that I do not ask others to suffer under my decisions.

"Will you send my teletype, or should I do that?"

"No, I'll send it and prepare a memo for our signatures expressing my dissent."

Al turned from Milt without further comment and moved to the preparation for the payoff.

Angry at his abrupt dismissal, Milt secured a copy of Jefferson's memo of the contact by Hernandez and the decision by Al. A case had been opened and assigned on the memo and a file number issued. Milt dictated, and sent, the following teletype:

To: Director, FBI [7-new]   IMMEDIATE
     SAC, Atlanta, Mobile, Jacksonville,
       Tampa

Fr: SAC, Miami [7-508]

Unsub, aka Peter; JEAN STOCKTON-VICTIM
Kidnapping

At approximately ten a.m. this date, ROBERT STOCKTON, a building contractor, received telcon from Unsub identifying himself as Peter who claimed to have abducted victim, wife of ROBERT STOCKTON, and demanded two hundred fifty thousand dollar ransom in twenty dollar bills to be paid three p.m. instant. STOCKTON directed to secure money from bank, Unsub apparently unaware of holiday. Note found in STOCKTON home, from which victim taken, directing STOCKTON to payoff location. Police initially contacted and responded STOCKTON home with marked units. F.B.I. assumed jurisdiction, police assisting. First drop scene covertly cleared and note directing STOCKTON to second Dade county location found. STOCKTON cooperative will attempt to make five thousand dollar "good faith" payoff tonight promising remainder tomorrow. Victim described: wfm, dob 1/12/55, Miami, SSN 056-23-6428, 65 inches, 125 lbs., light brown hair, curly short, gray eyes, two inch scar inside right thigh, three moles center of back at spine. Full coverage implemented, SAC on scene. Bureau will be kept advised. End.

Al had asked Xavier to drive his car and share on-scene direction with him. Lieutenant James Young and Sergeant Ray Abernathy of Metro's OCB would be in the command post to assist with any local police problems that might arise, and to be in a position to smooth an eventual turnover of the investigation should no federal jurisdiction develop.

Al began a check of equipment. "Xavier, do you have the hand-held radios?"

"They're already in the car. One for Stockton's body bug, and one for the SPIT channel so we can stay on the operational channel with the car radio."

"Okay. Let's get the shotgun out of the trunk and put it in the back seat with our vests. There're four gas masks in the trunk and gas shells for the shotgun. We can leave those there."

Al had full confidence in Xavier Restrepo. He had one of the Foreign Counter Intelligence desks. He was thirty-two, Cuban-born, and had been in the Bureau nine years. He was a top-flight hostage negotiator. Xavier had been "confirmed" in Al's eyes a year earlier when a U.S. airliner had been hijacked to Cuba by an American. The Cubans were having problems talking the hijacker out, and Al, in conversation with the Cuban commander on the scene, via Xavier's language skills, expressed concern that they might start shooting. The Cubans agreed to let Al come to Havana airport with one other agent. When asked if he would go into Cuba, Xavier never hesitated in his answer: "Let's go." His display of *cojones* made him, as far as Al was concerned.

Xavier was a questioner; he observed and studied. He was careful, not brash, highly intelligent and had a keen understanding of human nature. He could also act when called upon, swiftly and decisively. Al made him a part of all the major decisions in the office. He was on the "board of directors." He was, above all, a man to have near when you might have to go to the wall.

They were as ready as they could be under the circumstances and, as both strapped themselves in, Xavier started the car and drove out of the FBI garage. Al would be where the action centered, and so Xavier headed to the Perrine Shopping Center, where the Winn Dixie Supermarket was located.

As they drove, Al ruminated over how he should proceed next. Kidnappings were intriguing studies. In each case the subject had the same problem: How could the kidnapper obtain the cash payoff without exposing himself to possible arrest? He had to devise a way to grab the money with minimum risk. He usually set up a series of contacts, communication points where the person being directed by the subject to make the payoff is given verbal, usually telephone, instructions as to where to go next or what to do with the money. In lieu of verbal instructions the person could be directed to a series of notes concealed by the subject prior to the payoff.

This was much like a treasure hunt, but with the payoff person being moved by the subject from place to place. The purpose was obvious: to move the money about like a shell game, with the subject trying to detect police surveillance, and finally, maneuvering the money into a position where he could take it with relative safety.

The biggest hurdles for Al to overcome were to prevent detection of the surveillance and—that over which Al had the least control—the subject getting up enough nerve to grab the money.

Al had arranged for Larry Hunt, the agent who was designated as the "money man" in kidnap cases, to put Stockton's $5,000 together. Larry had photocopied the bills, dusted them with invisible fluorescent powder, and then wrapped them in a shopping bag.

Al had not consulted Stockton on the fluorescent powder, nor had he mentioned it to Milt. Again, the risks were minimal and the potential return great. Anyone touching the money would pick up the powder and leave it on anything he touched, including the door to his house. The powder fluoresced under ultraviolet light.

While Al and Xavier were heading for the drop point, Larry drove to the Stockton house, and as he approached he radioed the house, "Eleven-oh-one, open sesame." The garage door opened and he pulled in.

Grover opened the kitchen door to the garage for him and Larry whispered, "It's salted—UV powder." Grover nodded and brought Larry into the living room to Stockton, and introduced him.

"Mr. Stockton, I've counted the money and wrapped it in this bag. Please count it to make sure it's all there."

"That's fine. Let me have the bag and I'll take it from here."

Rob had written a note that was folded around the money bag, all of which went into a final, larger bag. The note read, *Peter, the banks are closed today. This is a holiday. I want my wife and*

will pay. This is all the cash I could raise. I can
get the whole amount tomorrow. Call me at home,
239-2624. I will not be in the office. Tell me what
you want me to do.

With that done, Grover held out the body bug.
"As you can see, Rob, it's only the size of a cig-
arette package but thinner. It transmits a half-
watt signal continuously for six hours. I'll show
you how to change batteries, just in case this
thing runs longer than anybody expects it to."

"Where will you put it so he won't see it?"

"If you werc going into a situation where somebody was going to physically search you, we'd
probably put it in your crotch or give you one
built into a telephone pager that you'd wear on
your belt, just like you would a regular pager.
We want to hear conversation and both ends of
any phone call, so this one will be used a little
differently. Take off your shirt and drop your
pants, we'll rig it, and I'll show you how to
use it."

Rob complied and Grover, using adhesive tape,
placed the transmitter at Stockton's belt line in
the small of his back.

"Wearing jeans, with a wide belt, the transmitter is entirely covered by the belt. Even without the belt it would not be visually detected.
Does it feel all right?"

"Yeah. With the belt fastened, no one will be
able to feel it."

"Okay. Now this is a combination antenna and
mike cord I'm going to tape to you. The mike is
about half the size of a pencil eraser, and I want
it below your left ear, since you're right-handed.

We also need a loop of spare cord on your left shoulder."

"Now what?"

"This is a receiver."

"No. I don't want any more gadgets. I really don't want this transmitter."

"This receiver is even smaller than the transmitter. You'll only be able to hear me on it. It transmits via an induction coil that fits inside your ear. There is no wire to your ear. This little flat coil is inside the right side of your collar and attaches to the receiver by this slender wire. We can put the receiver under your belt."

Since Rob still seemed wary, Grover continued. "It may be necessary to warn you of danger or give you some essential information. There's no way anyone can see this. If it looks like you're going to meet Peter in person and you're uncomfortable about having this in your ear, just take it out and throw it away."

"On the basis that I can throw it away if I want, I'll try it. No more!"

"Okay, no more. This really is all we wanted to give you. Now, I need to bring the mike cord from the transmitter out a ways from your collar and pass this small safety pin around it and then pin it to the inside of your shirt collar. You can feel the mike inside your collar. It can't slip farther down because the pin is too small for it to pass through. You can pull it up with your right hand and place it by your ear canal. Do that."

"That's easy enough. Now what?"

"Hold it with a finger. Take this telephone in your left hand and put the ear piece to your ear so the mike is between the phone and your ear.

Now we'll be able to hear everything said on the phone as it happens. Put the mike back under your collar and we can hear any face-to-face conversation as it happens. The conversation we hear will also be recorded."

Henry handed Rob a ballpoint pen and spiral note pad. "Even though we're recording, it's important you take notes of any conversation with Peter."

"Could we skip that?" Rob said, starting to look weary. "I would think the recording is enough. You're giving me too many things to do. I'm going to forget something important."

"Taking notes accomplishes several things. You should tell the subject you're taking notes to be sure you don't misunderstand, and since you are indeed taking notes, it will have the ring of truth. This will serve as a reason to tell the party to 'slow down so I can get it all down right,' thereby keeping him on the phone and giving us a better chance to spot him. It will also serve to reinforce your understanding of what is being told you. You can read part back to the subject, so he can hear what he says. Sometimes people don't hear what they say, and impart false or imperfect information."

A reason not stated to Rob was that radios sometimes fail and his notes might be all there was to rely on for direction.

The most important instructions that Stockton received were on how to handle Peter.

"Interrupt the speaker with questions," Henry told him. "The idea is to get him off any script he might try to read. You must try to discover areas that are vague or identify problems in what you are told to do. The purpose is to present problems to the subject to keep him, as much as possible, in a decision-making mode. You should ask to speak to Jean to assure yourself that she is all right. You must repeat back to him what he says so he fully understands the instructions himself. We can not overemphasize the importance of this repeat-back concept."

Rob was given an example of what the agents wanted:

Peter: "Get in your car and drive to the X restaurant on 36th Street and 24th Avenue."

Stockton: "I'm to drive to X restaurant at 36th Street and 24th Avenue."

"Of prime importance," Henry said, "is that you impress upon Peter that you want to cooperate. Repeat several times, that if somehow something is missed and you lose contact with each other or you don't arrive the way he expected, that he call you or somehow contact you to insure that no matter what happens you will be able to continue your efforts to get Jean back safely." Loss of contact with a kidnapper was a disastrous development and in this case could well spell doom for Jean. Peter was their only link to Jean.

Grover added, "You will, of course, tell Peter about the bank being closed and the $5,000 you have."

"You guys have given me such a jumbled and long list that I'm not sure I can handle it all." He began to wish he had allowed an agent to impersonate him. Someone else would be responsible for Jean.

Finally Rob was informed that Al had decided to go at 3:30.

"Now what the hell is that supposed to accomplish?" he yelled. "All it's going to do is screw up the whole thing. Peter said three. He'll think I'm not trying to comply. He may never show. No! I go at three. To hell with this."

Grover tried to explain Al's reasoning but had no success. Finally Henry said, "The boss said three-thirty. It's his call. He told you he'd make some calls; this is one. It's no longer open for discussion."

Rob was irritated, but accepted it.

At 3:30 he got in Jean's red Datsun. Grover, with a stockless pistol-grip shotgun and two hand-held radios, squeezed uncomfortably into the trunk. His bullet-proof Kevlar vest added to his discomfort. The car had been altered so that he could easily come through the backrest of the back seat just by pushing against it. He could also release the trunk lock from inside so the lid would spring open. One of the two radios he carried was on SPIT frequency, since they would always be the closest resource. The other radio was on the body bug Rob was now wearing. He could receive from Rob's transmitter and also talk to him.

A radio voice brought everyone to attention, "Package rolling." It had begun. It was 3:30. Rob was heading toward the Winn Dixie for the first drop.

CHAPTER 8

Remorse sleeps during a prosperous period but wakes up in adversity.
—ROUSSEAU, *Confessions*

Stanley, with a green light at 184th and Old Cutler, rolled through the intersection looking for Stockton's pickup. There was no one in sight, just some old guy selling fruit out of boxes. He went to 168th Street and turned around in the 7-Eleven parking lot and came back. He looked at his watch—3:10.

Mona craned her neck, looking about the intersection. "Donnie, I don't see no pickup."

Stanley, exasperated, replied, "You don't see no pickup because there ain't no fuckin' pickup there. I got eyes too. He probably got a problem getting all the bucks together. Let's get a Coke."

Concerned, Stanley drove to the Publix supermarket at Franjo Road. Mona went in and got two cans of Coke and some potato chips. They sat for a few minutes eating and then Stanley, impatient, pulled out of the shopping-center parking lot and headed north on Old Cutler.

They passed 184th Street for the third time.

There was no truck. Stanley looked at his watch—3:35. He was perplexed; he hadn't anticipated this happening. He wondered what, if anything, he should do. "Why hasn't Stockton placed the ready signal?"

Mona was biting the middle knuckle of the middle finger of her right hand.

Rob had barely left home when a car, boat and trailer pulled into the yard. Henry had moved the portable hundred-watt briefcase radio, which was now on the surveillance channel, into the living room. From there he could see the approach to the house. He remained well back so he could not be seen.

The children opened the garage door and were coming through to the kitchen. Henry opened the kitchen door and walked out to meet them. Their surprise was evident. He introduced himself. "Hi, I'm Henry Adamski, with the FBI." He displayed his credentials as he spoke. "I need you to come inside now, please."

Henry felt this approach was the safest he could make. He not only remained concealed in the garage in the event Peter was somehow surveilling the house but he also felt the children would not feel as threatened if the approach were outside the house proper. Henry knew he had to be as unthreatening as possible.

Surprised, the children looked at each other.

Amy was the first to speak. "What's wrong?"

"Your father had to leave to help with a problem involving your mother; she needs the help of all three of you right now, and your father asked me to explain it to you. I can't do it here. I have some special equipment in the house that I need to be with in order to help her. We need your help in this. You may look at my identification again if you like, and you can go across the street and talk to Jinny, who is also helping."

The children seemed dubious and then Amy said, "Okay," and they followed Henry into the kitchen.

Henry began his explanation. "There is no good way to say this except straight out and honest. Your mother was kidnapped this morning and is being held for ransom. As far as we all can tell she is all right. Your father had a communication from the kidnappers, and he is out right now with other FBI people working to get her back home."

Henry said it all in a fast burst to get it all out quickly. He noted the gasps and tears forming in their eyes, and unspoken questions. "Your father is going to need your help, and so will I. Let me show you what we've brought in your home, and what you'll be seeing and hearing. Then I'll try to answer your questions before I put you to work."

The children did not move. Amy's hands went to her face and she burst into uncontrollable sobs, calling for her mother. Ben, trying to hold back tears, was also crying. Steve's eyes were filled with tears as he bit his lower lip. His voice broke in midsentence: "When will . . . our father be back?"

"There's no way of knowing. You all have to be brave and control yourselves if you're going to help."

Amy ran to her room.

Henry moved into the living room and the boys

followed. He showed them his equipment and explained what they might be hearing over the radio. He also walked them through the telephone coverage, explaining that the kidnapper could attempt to contact the home via telephone, and that only he or their father should answer the telephone. The boys found that their telephone had been preempted and they could not use it.

After absorbing what they could of the situation and Amy rejoined them, still crying, they asked a few questions about their mother. Seeing that they were confused and unsure, Henry asked each of them to get a pad of paper and some pencils and to begin writing the name, address and telephone number of everyone they knew, and their relationship to that person. The task had a dual objective: The information was essential to a thorough investigation, and should Jean not be located that night, Rob would soon be doing the same thing. It was most likely that the kidnapper had a relationship to the Stocktons, or to someone known to the Stocktons, and had chosen them based on his knowledge of them. Identifying that someone would help unravel the kidnapping. Beyond that, Henry knew work is medicine when someone feels himself powerless against the forces arrayed against him; the work gives a sense of direction.

Finally, Henry asked if they would like to stay with relatives or friends, and was very pleased when the question drew a resounding *"No!"* from all of them. They very strongly expressed their intention to stay home and help find their mother. And so they went to work writing, pausing whenever the radio spoke, listening for some hopeful message.

SPIT had completed their survey of the Winn Dixie area, and some were at the second drop, Tony Roma's. SPIT was not supposed to make arrests, but this afternoon they would be the agents closest to the action, and if things turned to shit, as they sometimes did, they would probably catch it, so they were all tooled up. Each car had a shotgun on the floor of the back seat, covered by a newspaper or blanket, and each agent was carrying his sidearm, which was not usual for SPIT.

Radio communication was essential to the success of a case such as this and so chatter was strictly forbidden. Much of the conversation would be by transmitter button clicks. Voice transmission, when necessary, would be short and to the point.

Al's car was about two blocks from the Winn Dixie, parked behind an auto parts store. He was monitoring the body bug. He heard Rob leave his car and could envision him walking to the phone bank and to the third phone.

Rob had been carefully prepped on this drop, since the FBI already had cleared it. In his pocket was a Xerox of the Xerox Phil had located under the phone shelf earlier; it was folded and had tape attached, just like the original note. Rob simulated finding the message. He stood in the enclosed area for a minute, groped about and Al heard, "I'm pretending to look for it, now I got it, I'm looking at it, I put it in my pocket."

Al, smiling with pleasure, looked at Xavier. "He's good, starting off like a pro."

"That's because he was trained by pros. They don't come any better than Grover and Henry. You picked the right pair for this job."

Al, still smiling, but not with pleasure this time, said, "They weren't the first choice."

"I know, but they were *your* first choice."

After waiting for the required five minutes, Rob broadcast, "Heading back to the car, now." Heeding Grover's admonition to go slow, he started the car and headed for the second drop on Kendall Drive. Preceding him, already in place, were elements of SPIT. Other SPIT personnel boxed him as he moved to Kendall Drive. The five cars assigned to the sector containing the Winn Dixie were on the outer perimeter, and as Rob approached the new drop point, and the new sector, they dropped off and returned to their sector.

The FBI knew that Peter could "hit" Rob's car at any time. Peter would assume that the Stockton car was carrying the $250,000, and Rob could get hurt. Full coverage of him was essential as he moved or stopped. Every traffic light was viewed as a hazard.

Unknown to Rob, his ignition system had been wired with a kill switch, one of Al's tactical decisions—one that Milt would not have approved of.

The headquarters radio had the ability to emit a coded radio signal—the same kind of signal that sets off a paging device—that would activate a tiny receiver under Stockton's car hood that would cut the coil on the engine, stopping the car wherever it was. It would seem and sound like engine failure. It would prevent Peter from seizing Rob. If the seizure of the car were only for the money, they would follow and not use the kill switch.

Grover, of course, would have to be protected. If Peter were to go for the trunk, everyone would move in—and if Peter were lucky he would just be arrested.

In addition, a concealed transponder, or homing device, had been placed on the car to make it simple to find, even if the surveillance lost it, which was almost impossible. The transponder, usually referred to as a "tracker," emitted a continuous radio signal which was received by direction-finding equipment that pinpointed the location of the transponder, and thus the car to which it was attached.

Even before Stockton arrived, the license-plate numbers of all cars in the Winn Dixie area had been recorded. Now, as SPIT moved through traffic, hand-held tape recorders were recording additional license-plate numbers and car descriptions of any vehicle that attracted SPIT attention. All these would eventually go into the computer. Any repeat became a suspect who would receive direct surveillance for the rest of that evening by some of the sector agents, and follow-up investigation.

Rob arrived at Tony Roma's and announced the fact to his body bug. He found a place to park and exited the car, again advising the bug what he was doing. He saw a wooden bench off to one side of the main entrance to the restaurant. It was apparently intended to accommodate patrons waiting to enter, or for those waiting for cars to be brought up. Rob now began to have doubts about his adamant rejection of Al's suggestion that they be allowed to "roll up" all the drop notes before he started on this trail. He did not know where this one might be, and had no idea what its contents would direct him to do. It was an uncomfortable, disconcerting feeling. Jean's fate might hang on the unknown contents of this note and his ability to satisfactorily comply. He was on his own here, alone.

As Rob approached the bench he saw that a man and woman were seated on it, talking, apparently waiting to be called into the restaurant. Rob thought this peculiar since it was much too late for lunch, and too early for dinner. As he approached the bench, the two occupants rose and walked toward the parking area still in conversation. Rob looked about, and saw only a car entering and two exiting the general area, which was also a shopping center. He saw no one that he felt was observing him.

He stood for a moment in front of the bench, just eyeing it. From his right side he saw a car enter the restaurant parking area and pull into an open parking spot about forty feet from him. He sat on the bench. The male who had just parked got out of his car, a blue Toyota, about three years old. He wore jeans, white tennis shoes and a gray T-shirt. He walked into the restaurant.

After he had passed, Stockton, sitting in the middle of the bench, slowly, furtively, began to run his hand under the edge of the seat. "Gum! More gum!" he muttered furiously. Then his hand touched a taped piece of folded paper. He removed it, held it in his hand and looked about. He saw no one in particular, just movement of people. He paused, and then opened the piece of paper and began to read: *good we close together you near end center phone at 7-11 old Cutler 168 street*—this too was a Xeroxed reproduction of cut-up newspaper words and letters. It ended: *put this in money bag*

Rob walked back to the Datsun and got in. Starting the engine, he paused long enough to read the note into his body bug. The SPIT team that had surveillance responsibility on the outer edge of the drop immediately started closing in on the new site. The close-in SPIT crew from the Tony Roma drop would take the outer edge. The two units would continue this leap-frog arrangement as the trail progressed.

Rob followed the directions in the note and drove out of the Tony Roma lot toward the new drop site at a moderate pace, giving SPIT plenty of time to set up before he got there.

Grover, who had been listening to the SPIT surveillance, spoke through the receiver in Stockton's ear. "You're doing great. The surveillance is with us and they're picking up good info. Just relax and stay with it. Might have to hire you as an agent when we're done."

Stockton grinned. He was pleased. He needed the encouragement.

Al rubbed his chin, wondering, as he expressed his impatience to Xavier. "How many message drops has he set up?"

Xavier was moving quickly through traffic to be in place before Stockton approached the new site. "Al, I suspect he's going to run a trail of notes, watching and waiting until he feels secure, and then we'll get a telephone contact."

"You're right, of course, just my normal abnormal impatience."

An agent assigned to the sector encompassing the 7-Eleven was less than two miles away when the office radio retransmitted the note's contents. Less than five minutes after Rob had read the new instructions the numbers of the three pay phones, including the center phone, were recorded and transmitted. Anyone observing the agent securing the numbers would have seen a thirtyish, casually dressed woman who probably forgot to tell her husband something when she left home on an errand.

A trap and trace was up in minutes. So far the telephone company computer was doing the work. The numbers were all computer accessible, and the trap and trace could be programmed by computer against the numbers. If some numbers came up that were not computer accessible, then old-fashioned wire tracing in the frame room, which was time-consuming, would be required.

During the twenty-five-minute drive to the 7-Eleven, Rob found himself praying it would be a contact from Peter by phone. He rehearsed in his mind what he had been instructed to do. As he approached 77th Avenue and 152nd Street, he announced his position. SPIT was with him, still recording license plates and descriptions of cars that appeared to show any interest in Rob or stayed close to him too long.

After what seemed an interminable time, Rob sighted the 7-Eleven. He announced over his bug, "I'm comin' up on the 7-Eleven now, see a parking slot north end, turning into lot now, pulling into slot just south of the flower store." He heard

Grover's voice on his receiver, "You're doing great; go slow, don't rush it. You got lots of help all around you."

At 4:00 Stanley again drove by the intersection of Old Cutler Road and 184th Street. Stockton's truck was still not there. Now, at about four-thirty, Stanley drove by another time with the same result. "Now what do we do?" he wondered out loud.

"Donnie, I told you it was gonna be trouble. It ain't gonna work. He ain't gonna deal. We gotta let his wife go before we're in more trouble. Donnie, she'll die out there."

Mona received a backhand slap and retreated to the passenger door, biting her knuckle.

"Shut the fuck up. I got enough problems without listenin' to you. He'll deal. He's got to deal. Somethin's just delayin' him, that's all."

Leaving the car, Rob walked toward the phone bank. One phone was in use, and he overheard a boy of about seventeen trying to convince someone, hopefully a girl, that tonight was the night. As Stockton stood by the phones he noticed a number of people in the 7-Eleven. As he waited, several others arrived and departed. At last the boy hung up with a curt comment. Tonight was apparently not the night he thought it would be. In spite of his worry Rob smiled.

While he was waiting, SPIT was trying to ascertain if anyone was attempting to watch Rob; the task was to discover a countersurveillance.

Audrey, a one-year SPIT veteran with six years of agent service, called Grover on the radio. "Pal,

Aud." Pal was the designator for Grover, and Audrey used her nickname as a designator.

Grover responded with two quick depressions of his transmit button which were received as two clicks, and indicated an affirmative.

Audrey then transmitted, "Tell package look for note, no pay phone observation of site."

Her advice was based on the collective experience of the agents in extortion-type cases. They knew that subjects, almost without exception, use pay phones for communication. They also knew that, whenever possible, the subject uses a pay phone from which he can observe the recipient of the call at the other pay phone. The observation allows him to know when to call the victim. Observation also gives him the opportunity to watch the recipient's reaction, and perhaps to "make" a police surveillance. Audrey concluded that the absence of telephone contact, coupled with the lack of an observation pay phone, equalled a message drop.

Grover transmitted to Rob's receiver: "Check phone for notes." Rob walked into the enclosure, seeing nothing, he ran his hand under the shelf beneath the phone until he finally felt a piece of folded paper stuck there with cellophane tape. He lifted the tape and paper and walked back to the car. Once in the car he opened the paper and read aloud for the benefit of his bug: *put me in bag Big Daddy's 152 Street park close to Dixie at 7 clock look final instructions Midway Mall entrance west phone*

Rob added, "The note's a copy like the others."

Al, receiving the bug transmission, noted to Xavier, "He's smart. He wants Stockton in an open, very viewable area for over an hour! Hell, more than that. It's about four-fifty now. He'll be at the liquor store parking lot by five and it's only about twenty minutes to the Midway Mall, so Stockton will be exposed to the heavy traffic of Route 1, Dixie Highway, and 152nd Street for about ninety minutes. Seven p.m. will put the drop during darkness, which is typical. At least Peter is predictable there. Damn, I just realized: If this thing goes beyond nine, I hope Stockton remembers how to change batteries on the bug."

Xavier responded, "If he has a battery problem we can have a SPIT guy meet him in a toilet enclosure and do it for him. Slight risk, but Peter has to expect there might be a nervous pee."

Once again the new location was on the air within moments of retrieving the note. Within eight minutes one of the agents on sector surveillance was on the phone to headquarters. "Milt, Jerry. Got the numbers at Midway, west phone, 265-3121, others 265-3211, 265-3752."

The agent had made a pass under the west phone and phone counter and reported by radio to Al. "One, Jerry. Made pass under west phone and shelf. No note. Telephone contact possible. Target phone can be observed from pay phones in front of three stores."

Al relayed this to Grover.

Within minutes the telephone company had the trap and trace up.

Xavier was concerned. "I don't like this exposed stationary position. Peter could easily do an almost undetectable drive-by, or he could be in a fixed surveillance—observing without moving or being observed. He could be a store man-

ager, employee, customer, anything. He brings
Stockton here, sets up on him for an hour, sees
nothing, then he gets in a car, drives up to Stockton, parks next to him, shoots him and grabs the
money. By the time Grover or anyone could help,
Stockton might be dead."

Xavier was reading his boss's mind, because
Al was about to pull SPIT back, exposing Stockton to an even greater degree.

Al replied, "SPIT stationary or moving could
be made if Peter has a fixed fisur and is recording
what he sees."

Al picked up the mike, depressed the transmit
button and transmitted to the sector cars around
the new drop, "Sector Charlie." Two clicks followed. "Select optimum parking slot, stationary
fisur preferred."

His answer was two clicks.

As Rob was turning left on 152nd Street, the
sector leader transmitted, "One, Charlie." The
answer from Al was two clicks. "Package, park
north side Big Daddy, by lounge, not facing
lounge but slots north facing Route 1, as far from
lounge as possible. Copy?"

Al responded with two clicks and raised Grover
on SPIT frequency. "Pal, One. Park facing highway, north side Big Daddy, northernmost Big
Daddy slot. Copy?"

Grover acknowledged and transmitted the
message to Rob, who was then about five blocks
from the site.

Al queried SPIT and the sector: "SPIT Alpha,
Charlie, from One, any good fixed fisur location?"
Abe replied, "10-4. Large parking area, good ve-
hicle cover to north; to east stores, good foot

cover. West of highway all open, little cover. South side and north side of 1-5-2, half block east good cover for car to record 1-5-2 traffic. East side highway observation, south 1-5-2, in shopping center lot."

Al responded, "SPIT, select stationary points Abe suggests; Abe, all your units are rovers close in, try not to create patterns. This is long wait, Peter will try to make us. If any vehicle pulls next to package, immediately put unit next to him. Be alert for heist."

The SPIT supervisor assigned spots to his people, and the sector supervisor, on a separate frequency, set up drive-bys. Not everyone was in position when Rob pulled into the slot, but his stationary, close-in coverage was there.

Grover, in the trunk, was saying a silent prayer of thanks that it was not summer. He was hot now and summer would have been impossible. This would be a long ninety minutes in an airless trunk.

Stanley was in turmoil. Four times he had decided to abandon the scheme, and each time had changed his mind. "What's with this bastard? Why the fuck isn't the truck out there? He's got to pay off; he can't let his old lady rot."

Mona responded, "Donnie, let's forget this. Let's go home. Call somebody and tell them where she is. Somethin's wrong."

Stanley shouted, "Shut the fuck up, I'm thinkin'." What he was thinking, among other things, was that he didn't like the way Mona was talking. "I ain't walkin' away from two hundred

fifty big ones. There's gotta be a reason for this.
I just have to figure out what."

Jean was fully awake. Every nerve and body
sense was alert and sensitized. She moved muscles, twisted her torso, moved legs and arms as
much as she could, snorted through her nose,
twitched her face to shoo flies, gnats, ants, mosquitoes and all the other crawling or flying things
that were infesting her body. She was rapidly
exhausting herself. Her mind raced, unable to
cope with the enormity of her utter helplessness.
She was losing. The ants ignored her movements.
The flies, gnats and mosquitoes either ignored
her or, after being chased, settled in new areas
to feast on fresh meat. She was aware of small
animal bodies coming out of the surrounding
brush and moving closer as darkness increased.
Fear had been with her ever since her abduction.
Horror and panic were her companions. Now
came the ultimate, the feeling that she had been
abandoned by God and by all; and her will to
survive began to slacken.

CHAPTER 9

Great deeds are usually wrought at great risks.
—Herodotus, *The Histories*, VII

Rob was parked facing Route 1, Dixie Highway. The north-south artery, four lanes to a side, was almost one continuous shopping center from Miami to Homestead. Cars flowed past his windshield in a constant stream.

"Somewhere out there is Jean . . . and Peter," Rob said to Grover via the bug, oblivious to the fact that all within half a mile could hear him. "Grover, I'm not sure I can handle this. My mind keeps seeing pictures of Jean and the guy who's got her. He's got to have done something to her. How else would he know about that scar on her upper leg? Grover, I'm losing it. Sitting with nothing to do, I can't handle it."

"Rob, I can't resolve your concerns. I wish I could. You've got to concentrate all your energy on just getting her back. There's nothing you can do about where Jean is right now or what has happened. You can do something about what is going to happen in the next second or minute or hour, and that is where we belong."

"You're right," Rob said quickly. "I'll be okay." But he wasn't. It made sense. It was logical. He bought it. But he still saw Jean and Peter and was tortured by what he saw.

The agents around the Datsun had by now filled cassette tapes and notebooks with license plates and descriptions. It would be a busy night for the computer operators. A few targets had been identified and were getting close attention because they had come by too often or showed what appeared to the surveilling agents to be an interest in Stockton.

Stanley made a decision. "Shit, that's too god-damned much to screw with. I got to find out what happened and if it's still alive." He cranked his engine, slipped into gear and moved into the night.

Everybody was alert, on edge. Just the waiting heightened the tension. Waiting for the unknown, the unexpected. Where was Peter? From which direction would he come?

Al had been mulling over this question some more. "You know Peter has to believe there is $250,000 in Stockton's car. As you said, he could pull up next to Stockton, have the money in seconds, perhaps shoot him, and be out on U.S. 1, all in a minute. If we can't get to the car before he leaves, we need to have blockers in place ahead of him to stop him."

Xavier contacted headquarters. "Station, One."

"One, go."

"Bring in eight sector cars, not Midway sector, position at drives north package to enter highway as blockers if Unsub picks up and moves."

Headquarters made the necessary contacts, and within ten minutes cars began to position themselves so they could quickly pull onto the highway. In crowded traffic, the stop would be a box. The cars would pull out onto the highway before Peter reached their position, or they would get cars ahead of Peter. Three or four cars ahead of him would prevent forward movement while a car on each side prevented movement left or right. With a car behind, Peter was boxed, and any danger to other traffic minimized.

The danger was if Peter responded with gunfire. If all agents returned fire they could by their very positions bring each other under friendly fire. For this reason fire control would be worked out among the cars as they prepared to make the stop.

Al was reasonably satisfied that they had done all that could be done. It was now a waiting game. "I think I've spent half my Bureau career waiting for something to happen, and most of that in a car."

Xavier had taken up a stationary position about a block north of Stockton, parked among a large number of cars in a shopping center parking area. They could reach Stockton through the lot without going onto the highway.

At 6:10 a SPIT unit broke the silence of the radio. "Green GM style car north Big Daddy, heading for package. Pulling in passenger side, I'm moving, backup."

Al responded, "One, backup."

As he approached the green car, Charlie Rogers, the SPIT agent, saw the headlights and tail lights go off, a sign of parking. The driver and passenger in the green car exited talking and walked toward the cocktail lounge.

Al was almost at the rear of all three cars as the green car people cleared the area. Charlie announced on the radio, "Cool," and Xavier continued back to their parking slot. Charlie walked into the lounge to get a better look at the two. He located a pay phone, called headquarters and while looking at the pair dictated their description. He took the opportunity to visit the men's room, a rare treat during a surveillance, and moved back to his position prior to the green car move.

There were several more "alarms" involving cars parking close to Stockton, before it was time to leave. But no one attributed any significance to any of them, even though all would have to be identified and followed up.

At 6:35 Al heard Grover on the SPIT frequency. "Package will be moving in two minutes."

A quote from Sir Arthur Conan Doyle came to mind and Al gave it voice: "The game's afoot." It was a relief to be moving; stationary surveillance had always been difficult for Al to tolerate, although it was often the most effective way to monitor an activity.

"I'm just not built for sitting, but God and John Edgar Hoover, not necessarily in that order, know I've done enough sitting and waiting in cars to earn me a place wherever good FBI agents go."

In two minutes Grover was back on the radio.

"Package moving." Rob pulled out onto the highway, heading north. SPIT Bravo was on him, and SPIT Alpha would be ready for his arrival. Rob traveled, per instructions, in the second lane at a moderate speed. As he approached the entrance ramp to the Palmetto Expressway he moved into the right lane and got on the expressway. Once on, he moved with traffic, again in the second lane. At Flagler Street he exited, looped under the expressway and drove west to the entrance to Midway Mall.

The mall parking area was crowded, and he stopped in a fire zone near the phones. People were moving around him and someone was on one of the phones. After she hung up Rob walked to the phone on his left, the west phone, and commenced a discreet search. There was no note under the phone or phone counter, just as the sector agent had reported. Rob wondered, "Will I at last get a call from Peter?" Hope began to return to him.

Alert to every passerby, he looked every man in the eye hoping for some hint of recognition. Several people smiled or passed a greeting, reacting to his direct eye contact. The first time this happened Stockton moved toward the person, sure that it was Peter, but the person continued on and Stockton's further greeting died in his throat.

After about ten minutes he heard Grover's voice in his right ear: "Look under the east phone." Stockton walked over, entered the enclosure and felt under the phone without success and then under the shelf. A note! Devastated, he muttered his disappointment in one word. "Shit." He announced his find on the bug.

Back in the car, Stockton carefully unfolded the note. In mounting shock he read into his bug: *you told police we saw your phone tapped get rid police Texaco station 104 and Dixie gas up park funeral home south leave car cross Dixie carry bag if no police you will be contacted if not she dead give bag to person says Jean do not look do not speak keep walking put note in bag now*—this note was like the others, a copy of the original.

After a second or two of silence, Stockton exploded: "You bastards, you told me he wouldn't see you! I should've done this my way, alone. I don't need you! Get away from me! Get out of my trunk! Now! Get out! Get away! Leave me alone." Stockton paused for breath, tired, drained.

Hearing Grover in his right ear, he reached up to tear out the earpiece, then paused as the calm voice said, "He's lying. He didn't see us. That same warning has been given in every kidnapping case we've ever had. If you do have police involvement, he hopes to panic you, and perhaps convince you to go alone. Forget that part of the message; it's a bluff."

Even through his anger and frustration, Grover's advice made sense. Grover continued, "We've had surveillance on those phones for about an hour and a half. He would have had to place that note before then, or we would have seen him do it."

Rob came on his bug: "Sorry I blew up like that, Grover filled me in, I understand it's just a trick. I'm okay."

The furrows in Al's forehead deepened in concern. "He really isn't okay. The strain he's been under for what—over nine hours—is beginning to show. Will he react properly under pressure? His reaction may be from the gut rather than the head, and that could be dangerous."

"We're committed now," Xavier answered. "There's no way to pull him out and substitute an agent. Our only other choice would be to abort the whole operation tonight."

"No, not yet. Let's get Grover's opinion first. Also, covering this drop should be a piece of cake for SPIT. We can grab him at the pass, or follow to the point where he might be lost and then make a grab. Or, take him home."

Al contacted Grover for his opinion on Stockton's condition, and to put the choices to Stockton.

"Al, I hear the same thing. He's coming unglued. Let me talk to him some more on his receiver. I think he can handle this one. I'll come back to you after I put the choices to him. You'll hear his answer over the bug, of course."

Switching to Rob's receiver, Grover said, "Hey Rob, you're sounding tired. Want to rest in the trunk with me for a while? Just hang in there, champ. You got sixty-plus guys out there fighting with you. You're going to win this one. You just need to answer a couple more bells, and then the referee'll declare you the winner. But you've got to be awake and alert and thinking."

"I'm okay. You're right. I guess I'm just getting tired and discouraged. I'm with it now. I won't let her down."

Grover put Al's choices to him, and Rob quickly

stammered, "No grab, please. As we agreed before, you can follow him as long as you know he can't know you're there. Please let him go."

On the SPIT channel, Al ordered, "No arrest, repeat no arrest. Surveil only. If you think you are made, or about to be made, advise."

Al then turned to Xavier, "That's as far as we go with him. The final decision on whether to arrest, if the surveillance is made, will come from here."

The SPIT team on the outer perimeter had begun to move as soon as they heard the note read, and were well on their way by the time the instructions not to arrest were broadcast. They would be the close-in surveillance on this one.

Al transmitted, "One, SPIT Bravo." Two clicks followed. "Concentrate on shopping center; let outer-perimeter SPIT Alpha cover gas station and funeral home and cross to shopping center." Two clicks acknowledged.

Grover came on the SPIT channel. "Package moving." Al thought, "The gypsies move to a new campsite." He chuckled to himself, not understanding why that thought had crossed his mind. He threw an arm over the seatback, pulling and stretching his back, sore from sitting. "Damn payoffs are sure iffy. They almost never go as planned, either by our plan or the bad guy's. When I was in Pittsburgh, we had a payoff that could have been featured on that old radio program 'Can You Top This?' "

Xavier couldn't resist. "Radio, what's that?"

Al laughed. "Man, us old-timers remember. Now, let the old man tell his story.

"A young girl, about six, had been kidnapped

in Fox Chapel, and the kidnappers had said the money should be dropped off a railroad overpass onto the tracks below. The drop was accomplished by the father, I think. Anyway, in comes a call from the kidnappers asking why the money was not dropped as instructed. Well, the guy on the phone to the kidnappers argues it was dropped. We figured that one of the gang—we knew there was more than one kidnapper—had grabbed the money and kept it. This of course complicates the expected release of the victim."

Al glanced out at the Palmetto Expressway for a moment before continuing.

"The father had insisted, and we had complied—this was before SPIT—that there be only a very loose surveillance of the drop, and absolutely no arrest until after the girl was released. Consequently we had no good leads on how the drop was cleared or who the kidnappers were.

"We went down to the railroad tracks, thinking they might have missed the money. We found nothing. A few hours later the girl was released from a car in front of an all-night diner.

"An investigation finally identified four subjects in the kidnapping, and they were all arrested. Each swore they never found the drop, but had released the girl anyway. The money was still missing, though."

By now Xavier was chuckling in anticipation of a punch line, and Al grinned as he finished up. "One of our young imaginative agents found the answer about two weeks later. A railroad track walker had passed under the bridge, and the suitcase had fallen right at his feet. Whether he thought God had dropped this $50,000 to him, I don't know, but I do know that when he saw what was in the suitcase his day was made and he was off to an early retirement." Al was wary but hopeful that planning and experience would pay off on this one.

Rob exited the Palmetto onto Route 1 and turned left into the Texaco station. One SPIT unit pulled into the station with him. He pulled up to a pump and got out of the car, remembering to lock it. The tank was almost full, so he walked over to the pre-pay cashier, gave her three dollars and began to go through the motions of putting gas in the tank.

The SPIT agent parked off to the side of the station, which doubled as a convenience store. He took his time shutting down his engine and walking into the store, where he bought a black coffee and some chocolate chip cookies. His walk back to the car was leisurely, timed with Rob filling his car.

Other SPIT cars were within half a block as Rob turned right out of the station to 77th Avenue. He went south for a block, then turned toward Dixie Highway. There on his right, on the highway, was the funeral home. He pulled in and parked.

Because Grover had to stay in the trunk, he would be of little use to Rob, who would be several hundred yards away, across the highway, in the shopping center.

Grover contacted Al on SPIT frequency. "This is the time to pretend to misunderstand instructions, or just plain tell Peter no. There's no way

I can cover Stockton from here. The car should stay close by him."

"SPIT Bravo, One. Are you in a position to afford package security when he's on foot and still maintain surveillance?"

"When SPIT Alpha joins, we'll put three cars with shotguns, and four people on foot, within fifty to one hundred feet of package at all times."

"Okay, follow the instructions. Grover, tell Stockton he can move out now."

As Rob crossed the highway and approached the busy area of Builder's Square and K mart, the two anchor stores for the shopping center, he had the bag tightly cradled in his arm, like a football. The closer he came to the store fronts, the more pedestrians he came into contact with. They flowed with him and around him.

He walked the entire length of the store fronts, and then reversed himself and began to walk back. He was again anxious to contact Peter, so he began making eye contact with everyone he approached. As before, greetings caused by the eye contact had him on a roller coaster of "This is it!" and "No, not him."

SPIT was tallying up more descriptions, but no contact. Virtually every license-plate number in the parking area was being recorded. The agents, to a man, were convinced Peter was there watching, waiting, getting up enough nerve to act. They were well aware that any action Peter interpreted as police could spook him.

Stanley and Mona were driving south on the Dixie Highway. Stanley had pretty much decided to see if he could spot Stockton at one of the drops and then figure out what to do next. He was about to turn around and head north when he spotted a "country" bar. He decided he was hungry, and certainly thirsty. Something to drink would help him decide what to do next.

They pulled into the parking lot in front of the bar, which featured a country and western band on Friday and Saturday nights. The window fronts were painted over so people could not see inside; beer advertisements were prominent over the windows. Stanley, followed by Mona, entered through the door between the two blackened windows. The inside was dim, and there was a long bar and stools off to the left, two billiard tables with overhead lights on the right, some coin machine games beyond them, and a large open room with tables in the rear. There were perhaps six high-backed booths along the right wall, and Stanley headed for those.

There were about fifteen men in the bar, no women, and Mona was mentally undressed by several of the patrons as she and Stanley walked the length of the bar to the booths. A game of pool was interrupted so the players might assess what had just intruded on their domain. Several commented loudly to each other on her entrance.

"Hey wonder if that little lady would shoot some pool? Ah got a stick and balls."

"Want me to rack your balls?"

"Ohhh my! That looks like a tight-fittin' ass."

"She sure do move it good."

"She needs an expert in shootin' . . . pool. I'd sure be happy to show her how it's done."

Stanley was deep in thought and paid no attention. Mona had experienced things more disturbing than comments, and she ignored them. Once the pair was seated and the novelty had been enjoyed, the patrons went back to pool, poker dice, and conversation.

Stanley walked over to the bar and got bottles of Bud for himself and Mona, and then walked back to the booth. After three deep chugs his bottle was empty. Stanley walked back to the bar and got another bottle, paused, then ordered a double bourbon. Concerned, Mona saw that he was going to start some serious drinking.

The double shot and beer were gone in ten minutes, and Stanley declared, "I'm hungry." He ordered hamburgers for both of them, with some french fries, and got another shot and a beer.

Mona began trying to maneuver Stanley out of the bar. "Donnie, let's drive down the Highway and see what's happenin' with Stockton. If nothin's goin' on we kin go home and I'll play your game. You can tie me over the table."

She did not like it when Stanley drank—it was those times when she was afraid of him. But her transparent attempt to get him to leave the bar only egged Stanley on to stay and drink. By seven he had consumed another hamburger and several more beers, accompanied by bourbon.

The alcohol had the effect Mona was afraid it would have: Stanley was angry. "I've put a lot into this, and that fucker has screwed me. He didn't do what he was told. He'll learn. I'll teach him who's got it. Him and his old lady. I'll get the goddamn money and shove it up both their asses. I'm goin' to fix it right now!" With that he rose to leave.

As they got to the car, Mona made a mistake.

"Donnie, the guy ain't goin' to pay. Kin we call and tell him where to find her?" Stanley answered with a fist that blackened her left eye and put her over the hood of the car. Stanley swore at her, left her lying on the hood, got in the car and started it.

Mona lifted herself up, ran to her door and got in just as the car was pulling away. She was all apologies. "Donnie, I don't mean to make ya mad, but kin we at least go back an' pick her up and put her in the trunk?"

Stanley's response closed the discussion. "You dumb slut. Ya think I can haul that broad around? What if we git stopped, huh? I put her ass in the woods 'cause there's no other place to keep her. I'm not takin' no chance on goin' back there either. Screw her. Screw him. Now shut up an' let me think."

Cowed, Mona said no more, but her knuckle went to her mouth. She thought of Jean staked out in the woods for most of the day, and now all night. "There's nothin' I can do about it. Donnie's boss and Donnie said no. Even if I wanted to do somethin', I'd never find that spot again. I'm not sure Donnie could."

After half an hour at the shopping center without contact, everyone was becoming discouraged. Al consulted with Xavier. "If Peter's here, he hasn't got the nerve to make a grab. He may be doing what we're doing, watching and trying to make a surveillance. My best feeling is that if he's still with us, he's not going to move tonight. He'll probably make a fresh contact and try again. Or maybe he just wants to see what happens when Stockton realizes there is to be no contact."

"Are you suggesting it's time to break off for tonight?" Xavier asked. "Is there some way we could send a visual or even verbal message to Peter, if he's out there?"

Al massaged his lower jaw. "There is an alternative: We could try a 'steal the payoff' routine. I discussed the possibility earlier, and SPIT is ready to do a snatch and run on the package if we give the word. If Peter is there and sees someone apparently stealing 'his' money, he may either try to get it back or stop it. It would be almost a reflex. At this point I don't see we have much to lose."

Xavier nodded in agreement. "And if he's here and sees the grab and doesn't react, he's put in the position of having to recontact to see what he can salvage of the operation."

Al paused. "Let's look at a 'what if': What if Peter is right on the edge of doing or not doing, and this grab spooks him? What if Peter sees the money go and uses this as an excuse for himself to not go through with the kidnapping? The bottom line is: Will this in any way jeopardize Jean's ultimate release?"

Xavier shook his head. "I believe that in a kidnapping, early on, the subject consciously or unconsciously has decided or at least leaned toward release or kill. At this point Peter is well into the kidnapping and probably knows what he intends for Jean. Our actions will have little effect on that decision."

Al nodded, satisfied with this reasoning. The next question was whether to consult Stockton.

If they were to try a grab, though, Al felt it had to be his decision and not Stockton's. They could never explain this to Stockton via his receiver, and there could be no give and take. Al decided, if it was done, he would take responsibility.

Al's next comment was "Okay. Let's say we do it. We've got to tell Stockton what's coming. Hell, he might fight with Jimmy. Six bystanders could come to Stockton's assistance and we could have a real mess."

Al thought for another moment. "Let's do it. The upside outweighs the downside. We put Peter in a real decision-making mode. He gets pressure. He has to make a decision. I see it as totally to our advantage."

He came on SPIT frequency: "Twenty-four–ten, One." Two clicks acknowledged. 2410 was James Lincoln's credential number. "Jimmy, you set for a grab?" Two clicks.

"Pal, tell package Peter a no-show. A friendly is going to snatch his package; he is not to fight, but should react with surprise and may chase for short distance, but should not call for help. Tell him this is done to cause reaction in Peter, if here. This decision is mine. Advise when Stockton has been informed."

Grover answered, "10-4."

Rob heard in his right ear, "Peter is obviously not ready to act, so the boss is going to set up scene to cause contact by him. An agent will run by you and snatch the package. Don't fight. Act surprised. Chase for a short distance, but don't call for help. Then walk back to your car, dejected, get in and wait until I tell you to move.

Walk now to a place where you can talk to your bug to acknowledge you understand."

Rob had started to talk as he was listening, but stopped himself and continued to listen through the whole message. If he had said what was coming up in his throat it would have come out *"No!"*

Rob moved around a corner, out of sight and earshot of the crowd. "This is crazy. We need to give him more time. He could be scared off. No, I don't like it."

"This one isn't negotiable," Grover replied. "Remember the boss told you sometimes he would call the shots; this is his call. If you don't follow instructions, you may seriously hurt our efforts to find Jean. Now get back in the flow. I'm going to tell Al to go in two minutes."

Grover waited a few seconds, then breathed more freely when there was no response from Rob. Grover knew there would be hell from Stockton if nothing came of this ploy. Grover keyed his mike, "One, Pal. Package objected but is ready."

Al responded with "Jimmy, your show. Whenever it looks right to you, go."

"10-4."

"Two units watch Jimmy, others the crowd," Al transmitted.

James Lincoln had been a track star in college, and during his four years of agent service had kept up with his hobby, marathon running. He maneuvered himself behind Rob, who was now walking south in front of K mart. He figured, "A snatch, then a straight run of about ten yards beyond Stockton, a left into the parking lot, a run to my car at the end of the aisle, and out. That should give Peter enough time to digest what has happened and do something that would point to him."

Jimmy would do a "slow" run, and speed up only if necessary. If he saw Peter interference, he would welcome it. If it looked like citizens were on him, he would speed up and his two SPIT covers could do some blocking. If he had any indication that Peter had caught up with him, he would drop the package. The recovery would go to Peter, or at worst, Stockton would get his package back. Any doubt would be resolved in favor of dropping the package.

Jimmy started his move a few feet behind Rob, pushing him slightly to one side. The expression of surprise on his face was genuine, for he had not known when or how the hit would come. As Rob took off running after Jimmy, a few people saw what had happened and called out "stop." One man began to run with Rob but stopped when he did, after chasing only a few yards down the parking aisle.

The man, who was noted by SPIT and would be followed and identified, said, "Why did you stop, what did he get?"

"Too fast," Rob replied absently. "Only some papers. Thanks for the help." Rob then walked away.

The man looked at Stockton quizzically, made a remark under his breath, and moved away. SPIT had spotted five other people who had showed a continuing interest in the scenario. Several others who saw it had just continued on their way. Charlie called in the outer SPIT perimeter to team with the inner group to follow and identify the six.

Al, seeing the sudden manpower drain, called in the sector units to cover Stockton. He assigned one more sector unit to hook up with Jimmy while he maneuvered to insure he was not being watched.

Once back in the car, Stockton shouted into his body bug, "I should have been told this was planned. Goddamn it, I would never have gone along with this. You've scared him, he'll never call. Your stupid goddamn move has killed my wife. So help me God, you son of a bitch, when I see you I'll kill you. Where the fuck do you get off playing God with my wife's life?"

Stockton's diatribe finally stopped, almost in midsentence. Knowing how exhausted he must be, Grover felt great pity and sadness for him and his family. Nonetheless, he stopped himself short as he recognized the beginning warning signs. "Come on, man, think professional, feel later. You start getting emotionally involved with the family and your objectivity is gone, and so is your usefulness."

Grover came on the SPIT frequency. "Package will move in two minutes."

Rob's transmission on the bug had been addressed to Al and Al had heard it all. "Stockton's made it clear what he thinks of me and my move. How much damage do you think I did to our relationship? Do you think he's lost trust in me?"

Xavier responded, "I don't know, Al. A lot of that was just exhaustion and bitter disappointment. Perhaps with Henry and Grover talking to him he'll come to see that the move was a calculated one and may still benefit the operation."

Al was deeply concerned. "I need to talk to him, make him understand the maneuver. He's got to trust me to make this operation work."

Grover spoke to Rob in a calm, quiet voice. "Rob, we're going home in a minute, I'll tell you when. Start the car now, okay?"

Stockton's response was to crank the engine and slip into reverse. After a short pause, Grover said, "Let's go." Grover announced his usual, "Package moving," which was repeated by Al to the sector cars.

So began the sad procession back to Stockton's house.

Henry and the children had been monitoring the headquarters frequency, and so had not heard the body bug, SPIT, or the Grover–Stockton transmissions. They were aware that Peter had apparently not appeared. Their mother's fate was as uncertain as ever.

Henry turned to them and said, "Look, your dad's going to come home tired and whipped. He's been fighting for your mother all day, and through no fault of his, he has not succeeded in freeing her. He's going to blame himself. You can help him, or hurt him more. You're obviously not happy about what happened today, but you can show hope. You can show gratitude for what he has done. You can support him with your concern for him and with a show of affection for him."

Stanley drove aimlessly for some time, thinking. Mona, holding her eye and cheek, was paying scant attention to where they were going. Suddenly she straightened in her seat as she realized where they were. They had turned right onto 184th Street, and left into Cape Cutler. They were headed for the Stockton house.

Stanley slowed and made two more turns, and Mona saw they were on the Stocktons' street. The house was just ahead on the right, then they were in front of it and past it. Mona saw there were lights on in the house, but she could not see in. Stanley did not stop, but kept on driving. He turned out of the area and got himself onto Old Cutler Road. He was silent for a while, and then said to no one in particular, "The fuckin' truck is in the driveway! What is with this shithead? He must be home. His fuckin' wife's kidnapped and he's fuckin' home."

Then he looked at Mona. "I walk away. Fuck him, fuck his wife. I walk away."

CHAPTER 10

Fading, fading; strength beyond hope and
    despair
Climbing the third stair.
   —T. S. Eliot, "Ash Wednesday"

The Datsun pulled into the garage and the door closed.

Grover stepped out of the trunk, hot and stiff. He stretched and squared himself and bent into the trunk to remove the equipment. Stockton walked by him, head down, beaten. Grover said, "I'll be in as soon as I collect all this stuff."

Stockton took no notice, and opened the door to the kitchen. As he stepped in, the rush of three young bodies startled him, and he looked up just before they came crashing into him.

Amy was enveloped in his right arm and Ben in his left. Steve was big enough to hug his father around his brother and sister.

Their voices jumbled together: "I'm glad you're home." "You must be exhausted." "We were worried about you." "I love you." "Hug me tighter." "I'll get you something to eat." "Go in the living room and rest, we'll take care of everything." "It's so good to have you home."

"What a greeting!" he said, lifted out of his despondency. "How have you guys been doing?"

"Oh, we're fine. We haven't done much except listen to the radio."

Rob's warm smile faded to grimness. "Then you know I haven't found your mother."

"Yes, but you will," Steve and Amy answered. "Tomorrow everything will work out and Mom will be home."

Grover entered the kitchen loaded down with cased shotgun, radios and briefcase. Rob turned on him. "When is God Almighty Al Lawrence going to show?"

The children were taken by surprise, not just by the language, but by the edge in their father's voice. They took a step back, as though to get out of the line of fire. Henry placed a hand each on Amy's and Ben's shoulders.

Grover walked to the kitchen table and laid his baggage on it. "Is this the place and the time? Wouldn't it be better to rest a few minutes before we get back to our problems? Take a minute and enjoy the children."

This only had the effect of redirecting Rob's wrath. "Your damn surveillance was detected by Peter. You heard his note. That crap you gave me in the car was just that—crap." Both Henry and Grover looked at each other, knowing that they had to let some of the rage inside Rob spill out.

"Your screw-up may kill my wife. If only I had told you guys to shove it. I could have done everything you did today, without endangering Jean."

Amy and Ben burst into tears. Steve, close to tears, tried to console them. Henry quickly took them to one side and said quietly, "Your father is very tired and upset. You must understand that much of what he is saying is said in frustration at the fact your mother has not yet been located. His agitation is causing him to say things he really does not mean or believe. Please, try to help and support him and he'll soon calm down and we'll go forward in finding your mother."

Amy went to her father first, then Ben and Steve. Their pain was obvious, and Rob realized his intemperate language was the cause of it. "I'm sorry, kids. I don't mean to hurt you. Calm down now and stop crying."

Grover's first glance to Henry said it all. While Stockton was with the kids Grover confided, "It looks like a complete bust. I've no idea whether he was there watching or not. It could have been just a dry run. Stockton was really pissed at Al, though, and we need to work on him to lighten him up before Al gets back tonight."

After five minutes of holding and talking to his children, Rob was once again himself.

The two agents waited for an appropriate moment, and then Henry, who had not been a direct party to the "failure" that evening, said, "Let's look at the whole day, starting with the call. Would you agree, Rob, that when Peter called you, he had already planned his moves to get money from you, and that certainly at that time he had Jean?"

Rob, on edge, defensive and ready to flare up at any moment, cautiously conceded, "Yes, he most likely had decided to leave notes for me to follow until he saw a clear chance to approach me."

"May I suggest that when he called you, the

notes were already in place? Remember, when he took Jean, he left a note in your house telling you where the first drop point would be. If you had gone immediately to the police and they had, within minutes of the call, discovered the note in your home and gone directly to the first drop point, then Peter, if he were then placing the note, might have been caught. Peter could not risk that. The same reasoning must apply to the other notes. Since each point led to the next, the police could have picked up all his notes in an hour or less. Therefore, I suggest to you that all the notes were in place by the time he called you."

Rob saw where this was leading, but had to grudgingly give in. "It looks like that's probably the way it went."

Henry continued. "The makeup of the notes themselves suggest preplanning. Consider how long it must have taken to locate all the words he wanted in the newspaper, cut them out, paste them on pieces of paper and then Xerox them all. Looking at the whole picture, this plan had to have taken at least a day in preparation. If this is the case, it would only be logical to have all the notes in place before the abduction occurred. It wouldn't surprise me to find out, after we arrest Peter, that he placed the notes the day before the abduction, or indeed several days before. He might not have been sure what day would offer the most favorable opportunity to abduct her."

Rob, despite his reluctance even now to admit that he had been misled by the note accusing him of going to the police, nevertheless nodded a measure of agreement.

Henry began to advance a new premise. "Consider this: Peter places all of these notes, including the one accusing you of going to the police, before he kidnaps Jean. All except one are at telephones. Even at the last, at the K mart shopping center, you passed phone banks in your walk. You would have answered one if it rang. You were looking for a contact. It would have been a normal reaction. What I'm suggesting is that the notes were so placed to give Peter the option to call if he saw something he wanted to communicate to you. For example, if he really had made a surveillance, he would have given you a specific warning, like, 'I saw the guy in the blue shirt. He's a cop.' "

Steve put three glasses filled with ice on the table and Amy brought over some cans of soda which the men opened and poured.

Having rather conclusively established their argument to this point, Henry introduced a leap of faith. "It is very possible—I would go so far as to say probable—that Peter never intended to make a pickup this evening. In almost every instance I can recall, the first run is dry. The extortionist may observe, study and work on getting up enough nerve to make a pickup.

"It is something like a dress rehearsal for him before he goes 'on stage' with the real performance. He is usually trying to figure out the optimum drop situation. He may watch you for this reason, or just imagine it once everything is in place."

Rob looked over at the serving counter and saw the three children perched on stools, elbows on the counter. He smiled and said, "My three monkeys." He was accepting Henry's assessment.

"His failure to make contact and his warning about police are all calculated to wear you down, to so burden and confuse you that you will not think rationally. He wants you to react to him. He is trying to weaken you by threats, by the abduction itself, and by the tiring, endless, futile following of instructions. If he can accomplish this, you will be unable to effectively oppose or interfere with his ultimate instruction, the transfer of the cash.

"You can prevent your being 'captured' by him if you understand this premise. You are aware of what this day has done to you. If you recognize the motive, and oppose it, then his strategy does not work."

Rob vigorously nodded at this. He could fight Peter. Peter could be dealt with. Rob just needed to face up to him, not let Peter scare him.

Grover now picked up the explanation. "What we have just laid out for you—Peter trying to wear you down so you don't question his orders—is one of the reasons why the boss suggested putting an agent into the role of delivering the cash and dealing with Peter."

He ended on an important note: "Don't credit Peter with being some sort of genius based on our analysis of the day. This is common-sense psychology to a criminal. He almost intuitively knows, understands and uses these ploys. They are adaptive to any crime where control of the victim is an element. Even a robber uses some of them to frighten his victim."

The all-agents conference that evening stretched on for almost two hours. No patterns, either of drops or recorded persons, were emerging. A complete computer run would be made that evening.

The notes were photographed, and would be on the first airplane to D.C. for examination in the FBI laboratory. An agent with a reputation for patience and thoroughness was assigned to closely study the wording of the notes for any distinctive characteristic that they might have, and to try to identify the very page of printed material from which the words originated.

At 5:00 a.m. several agents would dust the places where the notes were located for latent prints, and then clean the surface so no trace of the dusting would remain.

They were all dismissed, except for five agents, with the admonition to go home, get a good dinner, a good night's sleep and be ready to do it again tomorrow.

The five agents Al held back would proceed to the Stockton house in their cars and set up a perimeter around it. The perimeter would be several blocks away, but the agents would be ready to back up Henry and Grover should Peter decide on a home invasion as a way to secure the money. Those agents presently on the house would return and file their reports.

Home-invasion robberies were one of the developments that Miami suffered because of her preeminence as a cocaine distribution center. Al certainly saw it as a potential threat to Rob, who Peter could believe had $250,000 in his house.

Clothes and toilet articles had been picked up at the homes of Grover and Henry. Some bags of groceries had also been procured, all of which were loaded into Al's car. He, Milt and Xavier would meet with Rob that evening.

On the ride to the Stocktons' house Al reminded the others, "We need to let Stockton ventilate, not to the point of destruction, but to relieve tension and frustration."

There was another matter on which he was very firm. "Any advice or suggestion that you come up with is, as always, welcome. Write them down so you don't forget them, but do not, I repeat do not, voice them in front of Stockton. When I come at Stockton again it will be with a comprehensive design and a minimum of choices. I want us to make the decisions and hammer out the problems before we tell him the direction we intend to take."

Xavier voiced what Al was thinking. "There has to be a contact from Peter. Forcing or causing a contact must be the principal element in any plan. Without a contact we really have no place to go."

Al nodded agreement. "Our concern now is contact. Here are the questions that I see as needing consideration: What should we do if tomorrow goes by and we have no contact? If we decide to initiate an action tomorrow, what form should it take? Is there any way we can contact Peter through Stockton or some other agency? Assuming no contact, how long should we wait before we initiate an open, overt investigation where Peter knows, without doubt, we're in the case and looking for him? What can we do short of an open investigation? Is there a viable middle ground before we go totally overt? If we identify Peter should we step into him, arrest him or try to

surveil him? If we surveil, how long should we
give this technique before we arrest?"

Al had tentative answers already formulated.

A free exchange flowed between Al and Xavier,
as they traveled to the Stocktons'. Milt maintained a studied silence. He had not participated
in the discussion, but his mental notes would
appear in the memo he had partially drafted.

The five backup units that were on the Stockton
house had been called in by Al to insure the area
was not under surveillance, as he approached the
house. Now one unit preceded him down the
Stocktons' street and one followed. The other
three cars were at cross streets. As Al approached
the house, he alerted Henry on the radio. The
garage door opened. Because the automatic garage light had been disconnected the door opened
on a dark, barely visible, garage. Al had taken
the precaution of turning off his headlights and
tripping a switch on his console that disconnected his brake lights. He had learned early that
an inadvertent tap on the brake can turn a parked
car into a beacon noticed by subjects and marked
by them as a surveillance unit. The blacked-out,
unnoticed car slid into the dark garage and the
door closed behind them.

Mona had satisfied Stanley's cravings. He was
now untying one of her hands so she could untie
her other limbs from the small table over which
he had draped her. As usual, he had not simply
untied her after he finished, but had sat back and
let her beg him to untie her. Still thinking of Jean,
he had prolonged this after-sex ritual and had at
one point walked right out of the room. Mona

began to have some misgivings, and a tremor of
genuine fear appeared in her voice. This had
come close to stimulating Stanley to further activity, but his mind was now preoccupied with
Stockton.

Stanley was still trying to decide whether to
walk away from the thing or give it one more try.
He kept turning it over in his mind. He had made
and unmade a dozen decisions that evening. "I
can't understand why Stockton ain't followed the
orders," he told Mona as she dressed. "I got his
old lady. He must want her back. He had the
truck home the whole time. I oughtta find out
why. I called once, I can do it agin. Suppose he
says, 'I'll pay.' What do I do then?"

Stanley had planted his trail of notes so that
he could observe Stockton's progress by following him along the trail. Stanley felt he would spot
cops a mile away. He had experience with them,
and his sixth sense could always spot one. He
knew that a cop carried himself a certain way.
He could always spot them coming into a bar.
They did a quick scan, taking in everything, before they fully committed themselves. He was
certain that being at the sites and watching people around Stockton would tell him whether the
cops were there.

When he felt cool, he figured he could make a
telephone contact at one of the phones. He really
hadn't worked out the pass, but doubted he
would do a hand-to-hand. Details, especially future details, tended to escape him. He had
vaguely decided to tell Stockton to leave the bag
somewhere, and then he could have picked it up
when Stockton was gone.

Now, however, he considered the original notes dead. He had divulged the location of the Winn Dixie note, and so he had to assume the entire trail was known. He slammed his fist on the table in anger. A lot of planning and work had gone into those notes.

It had taken him two days to make up and deposit the notes. He had first carefully considered what he wanted Stockton to do. He recalled the TV program that had given him his idea. There had been a lot of contact between the kidnapper and the family. That had led to the guy getting caught. That's where Stanley had come up with the note idea. The guy had left a note at the scene of the grab, but then had started talking to the family. Stanley thought the guy should have stayed with notes and he would have been okay.

After he had reviewed his mental catalog of phones and shopping centers and possible delivery points, he drove around collecting phone numbers and making the final selection of the spots he felt notes could be concealed. He then carefully wrote out each note. He and Mona spent hours locating the words in the *Miami Herald*, often settling for letters, and finally changing what he wrote, shortening it, to accommodate what they could find to cut out. After they had pasted the words and letters on paper, he had taken the originals to the Cutler Ridge Library, and using their pay copier he made a Xerox of each sheet. He had put adhesive tape over the tips of his right thumb and index finger to handle the copies, so as not to leave fingerprints. He had dropped the copies into a shopping bag as they came out of the copier.

When it came time to deposit the notes, he had told Mona exactly what he wanted done. If anyone was going to be out front, it would not be him. He had put tape on the tips of the fingers of Mona's left hand and told her to handle the notes only with that hand. He had also given her a roll of plastic tape to affix the notes to the underside of the counters and the bench. The notes had been folded previously, again without risk of fingerprints.

Mona had been nervous and anxious to be finished. She imagined everyone she saw was watching her. Her routine was to lay the note on the counter and to take the roll of tape in her left hand, pull off a piece with her right, and affix it to the note with her left. She then would take the note and tape in her left fingertips, per Donnie's orders, and place the note under the counter, pressing the tape against the underside of the counter with her other hand.

Stanley considered replicating the note trail he had so carefully laid. It would take at least two days. Suddenly he stiffened. Stockton hadn't given the ready signal but could he have followed the notes anyway? Stanley had a sudden empty feeling. He had thought about that earlier but had not seriously considered it.

Tomorrow he would have Mona check for note one. If it was gone they would look for the second note. That would show whether Stockton had followed the trail. If he had, Stanley felt he could try again, even if he had to switch his plans; $250,000 was worth switching for. If he hadn't picked up the notes, maybe, Stanley thought, they could still be used. But that would be risky, and would depend on what Stockton had to say. "To say." Stanley thought about that last mental sentence. "Yeah, I gotta talk to Stockton again."

Jean had slept, she must have, for suddenly she was alert, wide awake, and cold. She was trembling with cold. She thought it was late, it had to be late. She had no sense of time, but she just knew it was late night, perhaps early morning, like 2:00 or 3:00 a.m. "Where am I? Where's Robert? I'm not in bed with Robert. There's no light." Her eyes were open, she willed them open, she knew they were open. She could see nothing. Then it came back over her, a dry, all-consuming terror. She was tied to the ground under trees, heavy trees that she had seen in daylight. It was a completely black void. Then it began to rain and she grew colder and colder and closed her sightless eyes. She began to slip into a slot in her mind, one that she had created, one that took her away from there.

CHAPTER
11

For courage mounteth with occasion.
—SHAKESPEARE, *King John*, II, i

When Al and the others entered the house they were greeted by a Robert Stockton they had not expected. Although he was not upbeat, he was also not the beaten, accusatory figure they had anticipated. There was none of the venting Al had expected. Al gave an approving glance to Henry and Grover: They had done their jobs well.

Henry and Grover, in Rob's presence, outlined what they had discussed with Rob.

Al then turned to the children. "Hello, I'm Al Lawrence, one of the agents working with your father to get your mother back for you. We are going to talk about some things that may happen tomorrow, and if your father says it's all right, we'd like to have you sit with us and listen, if you want to. These other two people are also FBI agents, Milt Jennings and Xavier Restrepo."

Al turned to Rob next. Grasping his right hand in his own, he put his left hand on Stockton's shoulder and looked him in the eye. "Rob, what happened tonight was not unexpected. I would have put our chance of a drop at twenty-five percent. We are at fault for not telling you this in the beginning. I guess there were just too many other things happening, and this is one of those 'givens' that we sometimes don't realize other people don't know. Nobody 'failed' today. You, especially, did not fail. Your children can be proud of their father; you did an excellent job.

"As Henry and Grover said, Peter was probably testing, trying to decide when, where and how. He wants what you've got—$250,000. That's his motive for this whole thing. Jean is of no use to him. He wants the money, and that is our strength. He'll be back. Now we have to prepare for tomorrow and we need everyone's help."

The adults all crowded around the kitchen table, the children arranged behind and around their father. On the table were some cold cuts, cheese, bread, chips and Coke. For some, this was the first food since breakfast. The FBI people each had a pad and pencil.

Al began. "Rob, we had hoped to start you on this earlier, but other things came first. We need you to begin gathering names, addresses and other identifiers such as date of birth and social security number of all your employees, ex-employees, subcontractors and suppliers. In total, everyone you have had any kind of a business relationship with for as far back as you can remember. We can have an agent meet your secretary, Kim, at your office tomorrow morning and cull your business records."

Al was building a sandwich, as were the others.

"We also need a list of all your friends and relatives and of any clubs, societies or other organizations you or Jean belong to. It is possible that, working from these lists and what we are developing in our surveillances, we will come up with a common denominator; and he will be Peter."

Al took a bite of his sandwich and checked an item on his pad. "We must emphasize again that everyone is to stay off the telephone. If someone calls, you get them off the line. We have installed call waiting, but that is not a substitute for a clear line."

Al's next question shifted gears from the phone to other communication lines. "What time is your mail delivery?"

Stockton put down the Coke he was drinking, and considered. "I think it might be about three."

Amy contributed, "If our regular mailman is on the route it's usually about two-thirty or three. If someone else is delivering, it's later, maybe four or even five."

"It's possible that Peter may communicate by mail," Al explained. "We need an authorization from you for the post office to open and examine your mail. We will be at the post office for the morning sort and before the delivery people load up to intercept any letter from Peter. We will need the same authorization for your business.

"Now before we begin discussing tomorrow, I want you, one more time, to slowly and with deliberation recount as exactly as you can what Peter said and what you said in the telephone conversation. As you are verbally recounting it, I want you to write it out on this tablet."

With that, Al tore off two pages on which he had made notes and a third page to jot down impressions from what Stockton was about to say, and passed the tablet and a pen to Stockton.

Stockton began, writing as he spoke. "My name is Peter. I have your beautiful wife Jean. I want $250,000 in twenty-dollar bills. Go to your bank now. Do not stop, call or talk to anyone. Do not call police. If you do I will know and I will kill her. She is fine now. She told me the scar on her inner right thigh [Stockton hesitated for just a second] came from a bicycle accident when she was six. Have the money by three. Go home when you have it. There is a note in your living room. Follow instructions."

Stockton hesitated, but then continued, "Somewhere in there I stopped him. I asked him where Jean was and said something like, 'What is this shit?' I think it was just before he told me how much money he wanted.

"I'm sure he was reading. I recall that when I interrupted him he said to shut up and then he seemed lost for a moment. Like it took him a second or two to find his place again.

"My impression was he didn't really know what he was saying. You know, in reading he wasn't hearing, like you guys have told me happens, and why I should repeat back."

Now Al changed subjects. "Will you consider allowing us to substitute an agent either for you, or posing as a friend, because of your emotional state? Let the agent carry on any negotiation, conversation, whatever, with Peter from here on. You have experienced the strain of responding to

Peter. Today was nothing compared to what tomorrow will probably bring."

Before Rob could respond Al quickly added, "The agent we select will have Jean's interest foremost in his thoughts. You can talk to him and satisfy yourself that he will do everything possible to get her back. You did exceptionally well today, but as I have said before, your emotional burden is too heavy to carry, and may get in the way of practical measures to get her back."

Rob's whole body became rigid. "No! I understand what you're trying to do. Perhaps from your point of view an agent could do better than I have. Maybe even from my point of view; I have to admit that a detached negotiator has the edge on me. But Jean is my wife,"—he half-turned to look at his children—"their mother, and this is my fight. I will fight. I will deal with Peter. You said he probably knows us. He's got to feel better talking to me. A stranger might scare him off."

Al moved on to the next decision. "Okay, we buy it, you've done fine so far. Listen to Henry and Grover and try to be guided by them. Just giving in to Peter will not guarantee Jean's return. Let them help you set up situations with Peter that are calculated to lead us to him and to Jean.

"Now, the next decision: Do you want to pay off in real money tomorrow, or should we do a dummy package? The package we construct will have a tracker so we can follow wherever it goes. It will be constructed to look just like real money, but it will be wrapped in such a fashion that he will be frustrated in trying to open it as soon as he receives it and will likely take it back to his base of operations where, hopefully, he has Jean."

Rob's hand held the half-eaten sandwich suspended above his plate. "I still want to use real money. I think this gives me, as you said before about my not having the money today, two shots at Peter, and more importantly, Jean. You guys are going to be on me and him if he gets the money. The real money may convince him to release Jean. If not, you guys still have the same shot at him as if we used your dummy pack."

Al nodded. "From what you've said I now take it that we can bug the package. If that is so, then I agree with your observation of having two shots at Peter. Without the bug, our surveillance will have to be less than discreet although, even with those parameters, I doubt SPIT would be made by Peter. So if you want to optimize your chances, I suggest bugging the package."

Rob pressed both hands flat on the table and gave a loud "No!"

Al poured some Coke into his glass, containing his growing irritation, and giving him a pause before continuing. "You must face the possibility that even if you pay, Peter may not release Jean. To be brutal, even if, and we must face if"—now Al was sorry the children were there—"Jean is still alive, she may only be alive to prove to you by voice or some signal that she is still alive. Once you pay she is of no use, and he may kill her. With a concealed tracker in the currency we stand an excellent chance of following him to his base, where Jean is likely to be. Without a tracker, the surveillance you have elected could lose him, the package and maybe Jean."

Rob's whole demeanor changed. His right hand was running through his hair. An air of defeat and indecision had returned. "How big is this tracker? How could it be concealed in currency?"

"About two inches by three inches, and about one quarter inch thick. It's a quarter watt, which isn't much, but with a plane and the cars we can locate it. It will transmit voice, and the battery will carry it for about two hours. We would double-bag the money and put the tracker in the bottom, between the two bags. There would be a thin wire you would have to pull to activate it. This would be the last thing you do when the drop is made."

The agents were surprised when Rob inquired, "Precisely how would you do a dummy package?"

Al, hopeful, spread his hands on the table in a gesture of explanation and detailed the procedure. "We would again double-bag the currency. It would be play money, but a good lookalike, with real bills on top of the stacks. The money would be wrapped in clear plastic so Peter could see it, and then strongly and tightly sealed with nylon filament tape. I assure you that if he does not follow the normal course and tries to open the stacks of bills and we take him, he is ours. He is our hostage for Jean. I would be lying if I told you he will tell us where Jean is, but he will receive such encouragement to do so that I would be most surprised if he declined."

Stockton moved his chair away from the table, separating himself from the discussion. He folded his arms across his chest defiantly. "I want to give him every chance to release her before you take any action. I have to go with real money. I can't chance a dummy package. Once she's released, do what you want. I'll be right there; if I have a chance," Stockton's arms left his chest, his hands became fists on the table, "I'll kill him."

"Easy," Xavier responded, "let's not put ourselves in his league."

"Okay," Al said reluctantly. "We'll go with your decision. Now another matter. We'll need you to transfer $250,000 from your bank to the Federal Reserve as soon as Barnett opens. We have your money already recorded and ready to go. The FBI carries prepared packages of ransom just for such cases. You will walk out of Barnett with a dummy package. The real package from the Federal Reserve will be at your home when you arrive, probably by ten."

Again Al switched topics. "Let's talk about contact with Peter and how you will handle it. Let us suggest two most important areas: person-to-person contact with Jean by phone or, failing that, requesting private information from her through Peter. Henry, give Rob the benefit of your insight in this area."

Henry drew his pad in front of him to check off items, insuring he covered all his points. "Let's start by talking about your business. When you look around to buy material, you deal. You have something they want—money—and they have something you want—material. I submit this kidnapping is exactly the same. You want

Jean; Peter wants money. Do with Peter exactly what you do with your suppliers: negotiate. Peter gives; you give. But before you engage in serious negotiation for material, you satisfy yourself that the supplier has that material.

"The same applies here. Insist on talking to Jean before you pay. It's logical. You want to be sure she is all right, and you actually accomplish many things by this. He is in a decision-making status, his faculties are occupied and he is not thinking proactively, he becomes more vulnerable and therefore has a lessened ability to cause us problems.

"He may have to move Jean, so escape becomes a possibility. The movement of Jean may be such that we will detect it. The movement causes another contact with you, which we can cover, and involves Jean's presence. If the trap and trace work, and our surveillance units are close enough, it could be all over."

Grover, on his second can of Coke after the dehydrating trunk ride, interjected, "We cannot overemphasize the desirability of a direct contact with Jean. It could very well put her in your arms in minutes. Try for it, negotiate. Use your business skills."

"Now let me give you a fallback position that every negotiator always has," Henry continued. "If Peter is adamant about not allowing direct conversation with Jean, suggest that you still must be assured she is all right, and therefore you would propose to pass a question through him to Jean; he can then pass the answer to you, which will prove that Jean is well. Now, if you have followed me, and I see by your nod that you have, we need that question, a question that only you and Jean know the answer to."

Rob shifted uneasily in his chair. The request had opened a wound he had been nursing all day. When not in action, while waiting at Big Daddy, while driving, he had been day-dreaming, going over his life with Jean. It had been something of a balm. It brought her close, in a bittersweet way. He had come to realize how much he loved her. With that had come the regrets at their times apart.

He accused himself for having wasted the time he could have had with her. The breakfast argument haunted him. He hadn't said "good-bye," hadn't kissed her.

Now the question, that only he and Jean knew the answer to. The night they made Steve flashed before him. This had been one of the most beautiful experiences of his life. The unexpected, unanticipated, that suddenly opens to the fulfillment of two people who care very deeply for each other. Rob could not explain how moved he was by this one union that stayed with him as the ultimate love of their lives.

Xavier saw Stockton was distracted, was not really with them, and had to be brought back. "Rob, any suggestion on a question?"

Rob's head came up, as he left his reverie, "Yes, the perfect question." Then he stopped, realizing the children were there. "No," he continued. "On second thought, that's not good." After a moment he suggested, "I can ask what old thing she wore on her wedding day. It was her grandmother's wedding ring on a chain around her neck."

"That sounds good. Remember to push for the

question if a direct conversation with her is not possible."

Al could see that everyone was approaching exhaustion, and that further work would result in diminishing returns. He thought it time to stop for the evening. "I'm sure there are additional items we need to cover tonight, but let's adjourn for now. It's important that you get some rest. Fatigue will cause mistakes."

Al then directed his attention to the children. "I have three children. They love their mother, and I very much love my wife. As you can see, I'm older than your parents. In fact, I'm a grandfather. My wife loves and enjoys her granddaughter and anticipates many more to love. We are a very happy family. I'm telling you this so you'll understand that your problem tonight is close to us and personally shared by us. We'll get your mother back, and she will be here to continue to love and care for you; and someday she will enjoy her grandchildren, just as my wife does.

"Henry and Grover will need your help, but nobody will need your love, help and strength more than your father."

The drive back to the office was largely a silent one as Al, Xavier and Milt were each deep in thoughts about tomorrow. Milt had not said more than "hello" all night. He was mentally finishing his memorandum.

Al was most concerned about Stockton and how he would handle himself.

When they arrived at the office they separated, and each headed home for some rest, but not before this teletype went out:

To: Director, FBI [7-new]   URGENT
    SAC, Atlanta, Mobile, Jacksonville,
      Tampa

Fr: SAC, Miami [7-508]

"Changed" Stocknap

Title marked changed to reflect code name "Stocknap."
Title formerly carried, "Unsub, aka Peter; JEAN
STOCKTON-Victim Kidnapping."

Re MM tel today.

Trail of ransom notes followed to various parts Dade
County. No contact from Unsub. Ransom notes consist
of Xerox type copy composed of cut out words from
newspaper. Same being flown to Lab A.M., expedite
examination requested. Fisur of drop sites developed
possible suspects. Background being developed. No
possible suspect has good potential at this time.
ROBERT STOCKTON, victim husband, elects pay off in
cash with no electronic coverage of package. Fisur of
payoff and pickup will be effected. FBI prerecorded
currency will be used and serial numbers entered NCIC.
No contact from Unsub since initial a.m. call. Events of
Tuesday depend on further contact from Unsub.
Consideration being given to options in event no further
Unsub contact to initiate new payoff. Bureau will be kept
advised. End.

After the teletype was dictated, Al scanned his
daily messages and mail. He acted on a few and
put the others in priority for tomorrow.

He finally left the office and was home shortly
after 2:00 a.m. Helen was in bed, asleep. He was
bone tired and was soon in bed but not asleep.
As he lay awake, he was seeing Helen in Jean's
place.

* * *

Jean was watching herself and her family on an island that had a beautiful beach with sand the color of snow. She was lying in the sun and was warm and comfortable, half dozing. Robert was sitting next to her and the children were snorkeling just off the shore. Ben was excitedly exclaiming that he had just seen a huge ray swim under him. Jean couldn't seem to chase away the gnats or whatever it was that was bothering her. Even though she was warm in the sun, her body was trembling.

CHAPTER 12

Stake your counter as boldly every whit,
Venture as warily, use the same skill,
Do your best, whether winning or losing it,
If you choose to play!
     —BROWNING, "The Statue and the Bust"

Breakfast was served by Mona, and consisted of instant coffee, toast and cereal with milk. A cook Mona was not. Stanley was quiet. He was still puzzling over the events of the day before. He had sent Mona out early for a copy of the *Herald*, and was examining it for news of the kidnapping while he listened to a radio news station. There was nothing in the paper or on the news about the Stocktons, or about a kidnapping. Stanley thought, "That probably means Stockton hasn't gone to the police yet. Or maybe they're just keeping it quiet."

He looked up and made a snap decision. "Pack. We're going to J-ville. This place is bad news."

Mona was afraid to mention Jean again but asked, "Ain't you goin' to check the notes before decidin' to go to Jacksonville?"

Stanley thought for a moment before answering, "Okay. We'll look for two, Winn Dixie and Midway."

* * *

By 6:00 a.m. Al was stirring. In half-sleep and first awakening, the mind seems clearer and thoughts come freely through, unimpeded. It always seemed to Al that while he slept the computer of his mind worked, and when he woke it spit out solutions to the questions and problems of yesterday.

Al sat on the edge of his bed and snapped on the lamp on the small night table. He had a pad of paper on his knee and was recording the thoughts that had come to him:

Ident Xerox machine
Jean fingerprints, hair
Psycholinguistics
F.I. Cards
Media
Fisur drop sites

By 7:00 he was in the office, at his desk. Milt had been there a few minutes before him, and others were arriving. Milt and Xavier joined him to consider the investigative direction they would take that day. Xavier was enthusiastic, Milt reluctant.

Al called Henry about 7:30 to see how the family had fared, and found that they were up and anxious for the day's events to begin. "I need to talk to Rob before he leaves for the bank. I'll try to call about 7:45."

"What about sending the kids to school?" Henry asked. "Grover and I discussed it and we both feel they'd be better here today."

Al agreed. "It'd be safer for the kids to stay in, or right around the house. A second kidnapping is very remote, but let's play it safe. Besides, the kids wouldn't feel comfortable at school today, and might even say the wrong thing to the wrong person.

"Now, another matter. Gather up Jean's personal items—hair dryer, perfume bottles, hair brush, comb and anything else from which we could get her latent fingerprints and hair samples. I want to submit them to Ident and the Lab today if possible. She's apparently never been printed, and if we get enough items, Ident may be able to do all ten fingertips and more, like palm, side of hand and fingers."

His discussion with Henry completed, Al turned to another item that needed attention. Lieutenant Young was in the office, and Al requested one of the agents to locate him and ask him to come by his office.

Jimmy was there in a few minutes and, after good mornings, Al asked, "Could you get on the phone to the District Station, or wherever, and get all F.I. cards for the past year for the Cape Cutler area?"

"Sure. They should be on file, and probably computerized. If so, I'll get them on a floppy disk and you can enter them directly into your computer. I'll have them this morning."

When a police officer talks to any suspect, he prepares a field interrogation card on that encounter. The card carries the person's name and other identifiers, the date, place, reason for the stop and other information the officer feels pertinent.

"Besides F.I. cards," Al continued, "we'd also like traffic citations issued in Cape Cutler for the same period."

"That'll be more difficult, but we'll start on it right away."

Al was looking for someone who did not belong in the area, and was also building their data base for comparisons.

As Young walked out of his office Al turned to Milt and said, "If we can identify the machine that made those copies, we have a chance of locating someone who saw them made. If nothing else, we may come up with a locale that Peter frequents and a chance on a latent print on a coin that, when we ident a suspect, will put him at the machine.

"Assign some people to contact the companies that lease or sell coin-operated copy machines. Start out by trying to determine the manufacturer of the machine that made our copies. Hopefully our photos are sharp enough for a company engineer to recognize his company's footprint.

"If we get a sharp engineer, ask whether there are enough peculiarities in the copies to identify a specific machine.

"Assuming we can identify the copy machine by company, such as Xerox, we then need to locate every coin-operated Xerox machine in the county through company records and get samples for comparison.

"This is a priority, but not to the exclusion of more pressing investigation. Use your judgment as to the number of people to assign."

Milt was making notes, mentally calculating the manpower he would need.

"Item two on our list," Al continued. "Request the Bureau to fax copies of the notes we have to Dr. Sheldon Wright at Columbia for a psycholinguistics study. I don't know if he can do anything with them, but as the man said, 'It couldn't hurt.' He may be able to give us some insight into the type of person we're dealing with.

"Xavier, item three, and in this I solicit your suggestions and of course, you too, Milt. Should we assign some people to surveil the drop sites of yesterday? The theory being that if, for some reason, Peter did not show yesterday, he could come by today to check to see if Stockton cleared the sites."

Xavier was dubious. "I think we have to assume that Peter was somewhere in the area. It would make no sense to put all that effort into creating those drops and not use them, at least to observe the activity."

Milt, expressly asked to participate, could not disengage himself. He tended to agree with Xavier. "To do a decent surveillance we'd need three to four people at each site. With the work we have now, that would be an expensive investment."

"I know where you're coming from," Xavier broke in. "It's a long shot. Let me back off on my first answer and propose a compromise. Don't cover them all. Peter would probably start with the first drop or the drop at the 7-Eleven. Midway Mall is possible, but the Winn Dixie and 7-Eleven are close together. He could even check both of them. I may have just suggested a reason for covering two. If we get the same person at two drop sites close together in time, we've got a hell of a suspect. They would be the easiest places for him to check, and human nature would almost demand that he start at the beginning."

Al nodded. "I agree that Peter will probably

start with the first drop site if he decides to do any checking, and then possibly proceed to number two. I am tempted to surveil the first two, but let's use the men to more certain and more direct advantage. Set up just on the Winn Dixie.

"Now let's move to another area that I'm sure will evoke some strong discussion. Let's assume we get no contact this morning. Do we try to precipitate a contact this afternoon? This evening? When should we move to try to cause a contact? What can we do to precipitate a contact?"

Xavier responded first. "In my opinion, if there's no contact this morning, we're in trouble."

Milt agreed. "There has to be a contact this morning. Without that we will probably have to take some action. It would appear that all we can do is go open with the case and generate as much heat as possible to convince him to release her, if she's still alive."

"I'd better talk to Stockton now," and with that, Al switched on the speaker phone and punched up the number of the office-use phone in the Stockton house. Grover answered. Al briefly told him what had been decided that morning among Milt, Xavier and himself. He asked Grover to begin to prepare Stockton for affirmative action if no contact was received by early afternoon, and then imparted the gist of what he was about to tell Stockton. Grover handed the phone to Stockton.

"Rob, Henry tells me that he thinks you had a reasonably good night. Finish up the list of names as soon as you can. We have a number of things going here, and we're ready for Peter's contact. Remember our conversation and try to follow the guidelines we've given you. When you get in contact with Peter, negotiate. You'll beat Peter hands down in negotiation."

Rob was not confident. "I understand what you're telling me, but this is a little more emotional than buying sinks. I think I'm ready, though. I just want him to contact me. I don't know what I'll do if he doesn't call."

Al had his opening. "Rob, none of us know what the next second will bring, but if there is no contact we feel very strongly that we must take affirmative action to locate Jean. In essence the longer we wait, the colder the trail. We'll discuss this later, in more detail, if we have to.

"We'll secure the money from the Federal Reserve for you just as soon as you can make the wire transfer from your bank. The money has been counted and will be sealed. You may of course, and we urge you to, recount it when it gets to your home. You'll have to receipt for it. Xavier, fill him in on what to expect."

"One of our agents will be at your bank when you arrive, and will have a dummy package for you to carry out after a suitable interval. We called your branch V.P. at home this morning. He'll have things ready for you. You'll go to the bank in the Datsun, with Grover in the trunk, just like last night. For security, three of our cars will take you there and follow you back. We'll talk to you later in the morning." And so they disconnected, and the game began.

* * *

Stanley and Mona had just gassed up and were on their way to check the notes at Winn Dixie and Midway Mall. "We can take the Turnpike to the Palmetto and be at Midway quickest," Stanley said, pleased at the possibility his scheme might still be alive.

During the drive Mona was searching for a way to motivate Stanley to check on Jean or let her go. She had not really bought into this kidnapping from the beginning, but had gone along with it, just as she went along with whatever Stanley wanted. She now found herself hoping and searching for a way to make the kidnapping work. If Stanley got the money he would return Jean or, she hoped, at least tell someone where she was. Then that nagging thought of the previous evening returned. Mona's knuckle was in her mouth. He was ready to go to Jacksonville and just leave her in the woods. If he got the money, would he bother to let anybody know where she was?

Mona was not used to thinking. It confused her. She decided to stop, and just try to make the kidnapping work. She would try to convince Donnie to go for the money. But she had thought of something last night: If things looked bad, like Donnie wasn't going to tell where she was, Mona would do it, but without anybody knowing who it was that kidnapped Jean.

When they arrived at Midway Mall, Stanley drove around trying to make any police surveillance. Twice he drove by the phones where the note had been hidden. Finally he parked a full lot away from the phones, positioning the car so he could see them.

"Mona, listen, here's what you do. Walk over toward the phones, and look as you walk; try to see if it looks like anybody's watchin' those phones. If it looks cool, walk by. Don't do nuthin'. Go in a store for a couple minutes. Come out, walk by the phones, always lookin'. Come back again. If it looks cool, give it a feel. If the note's there, leave it. If I see anythin' I'll blow the horn, and you come on back. You got that?"

"Yeah, Donnie. Don't worry, I can do it."

With that, Mona got out of the car and began the walk and inspection Stanley had ordered. When she at last went up to the phone and inconspicuously ran her hand under the shelf, she found nothing. She hurried back to the car.

"Donnie, it ain't there. It's gone. He's been here. We should've tried last night. He's goin' to pay off. You did it, sugar."

Stanley basked in the praise, even though it came from Mona. "Yeah," he said, "looks like he's goin' for it." Filled with new resolve, he went on. "I gotta set up somethin' for today. Get in, let's go."

As they drove out of the mall, Mona asked, "Donnie, should we check another one?"

Stanley thought. He originally planned to try the Winn Dixie after this. "What's the percentage, Mona? This one's gone; Winn Dixie's gotta be gone too. No, we need the time for me to figger a new delivery. With the note gone and nothin' on the news, we're still in the ball game."

As Stanley pulled onto the Palmetto Expressway, Mona took a tissue from her purse and wiped a small amount of silvery powder off her hand. She wondered where she had picked that up, then shook her head. Stanley, deep in thought, did not notice. Mona did not recognize the latent fingerprint powder. The agent who had dusted had missed removing some of it.

Al accepted a call from Channel Eight. They were getting anxious. Ralph Winslow, the assignment editor that Al had talked to on Monday, was on the line.

"What's the status of the kidnapping case we talked about yesterday? We'd like to go with something on the noon news."

"Nothing has changed since we talked yesterday. We still have no information that we can release without risking a life, and don't take that as confirmation of a kidnapping. I hope that you will continue to voluntarily hold what you have, out of concern for life. We are now discussing the possibility of a background briefing, not for use at this time, on what has happened and what we are doing. When a release can be made you'll then have a complete story."

Ralph said, "Okay, we'll hold, but can you get back to us this afternoon? Better, I'll call you about the briefing." Al agreed and disconnected.

He turned to Milt, who was in his office and heard the exchange. "What do you think? Should we do an all-media briefing to try to get everyone to agree to keep the lid on? If Eight has something, I'm sure the others will start picking it up today and somebody could blow it."

Milt hesitated. He really wanted out of this case, but Al kept at him with direct questions that had to be answered. "A briefing could anticipate and control the problem," Milt said cautiously. "If everyone knows, anybody who released a story when the others held would stand out like a real bastard. On the other hand, the temptation of a real scoop could prod a premature release. It's a real gamble." Milt smiled inwardly at his safe answer that committed him to nothing.

Al's response was unexpected, and a crooked smile betrayed his thoughts. "How about you calling all the editors and station managers for a one p.m. conference . . . here?"

In the meantime, the investigation was moving. The hundreds of leads that needed attention were being covered. Information was flowing in. Records were being checked and indexed for comparison and study. The coverage of some leads generated more leads; sometimes several leads sprang from one interview or record check. Every name the family had supplied and the business was now producing, were being checked against Miami FBI records, Headquarter's records and police records. One good piece of news came from Ident. But the bad news came first. There were no unidentified latent fingerprints on the notes. Stockton's prints were found and eliminated, as were Phil Bentley's, on the Winn Dixie note.

The good news was that there were eight partial prints, not classifiable and not sufficient to run on the computer, but enough for identification if a suspect were developed.

The partials came off both the sticky side and slick side of the cellophane tape that had held the notes to the counters. Some latents of value had also been lifted from the underside of some of the shelves. These might or might not be subject prints. The prints on the tape were, though.

The lab called later and had little of immediate value. Some fibers were found on the notes, and these were being processed. Hair, which had not been processed but appeared to be human, had been found on the notes and two pieces of the tape.

A subsequent call from the lab gave direction to one area of the investigation. They were fairly certain the notes had been copied on a machine manufactured by Xerox.

This was put out on the air, and those agents who were targeting other manufacturers were diverted. Confirmation of the Lab's preliminary opinion was sought from Xerox.

While the FBI was busy, Stockton was not. There was no contact. He was restless, became irritable, realized it, and tried to control it.

His questions were repetitious: "Why hasn't he called?" "Are you sure the phone's working? Your gadgets may have wrecked it."

When the phone did ring, Stockton dove for it.

Henry put a hand out and stopped him. "Wait! Let it ring three times before you answer. Remember, time, we need time."

The call was from a friend, for Jean, and Stockton was curt with her.

There were several such calls that morning, each treated the same.

He ranged over the house. He was short and testy with the children and immediately apologetic. The children were also upset. Each fed on the other's nerves. By noon Henry and Grover were ready to confine people to their rooms, but they understood the emotional reactions and tried to find some busy work for all of them.

Al asked Xavier and Milt to meet with him in his office. "We'll be meeting with the media soon. Before we do we have to decide if we're going to make some moves today if there's no contact. Any thoughts?"

"My feeling is," Xavier said, "that Peter has either walked away from the situation or he is undecided about what to do. We need to nudge him, and nudge him quickly. We are losing valuable time at the victim's expense."

Al said, "Okay. We nudge, no disagreement. Media blitz or something else?" Then followed a give and take.

"An ad in the 'Personals' column?"

"Nobody reads the 'Personals.' "

"A radio commercial, something like, 'Hello, this is Robert Stockton, of Stockton Roofing and Plumbing. We want to help you with your problems. We are particularly trying to help people like Peter who has not yet dealt with us.' "

"Possible."

"More to the point: 'Peter, this is Robert Stockton. The repairs you wanted can be done. Everything is ready, all you need to do is call.' "

"Better."

"We are assuming he will be listening to the radio, indeed to particular stations at certain times. What we need is a nudge that we know he'll get."

Al entered the discussion. "Should we go with the blitz today or tomorrow? And how do we handle Stockton?"

Both Xavier and Milt hesitatingly suggested

holding the blitz one more day. Al agreed. "I'll brief the media on the case and tell them we are going to buy time on radio for some short commercials aimed at Peter."

Al called Grover and told him to discuss the radio ads with Stockton. If he agreed, Grover was to arrange for Stockton to tape the commercials by phone to the stations and, of course, consult Stockton regarding payment. This was not an FBI budget item.

Within twenty minutes, Grover called Al advising that Rob had jumped at the idea and was now calling stations to arrange for the taping and payment. "I have no idea whether this commercial bit is worth shit, but the idea has saved me from having to cuff Rob in his room. Just kidding, but it was getting pretty testy around here. He's his old self now, busy and productive and easy to deal with."

Al did not get all editors and station managers, but all the media was represented. "Thank you all for coming on such short notice. I hope you will agree after our discussion that the invitation was appropriate. I am going to tell you something about a case we are working now, and then ask for your help. Channel Eight knows a little about it; they know that the case exists.

"Yesterday morning a thirty-six-year-old mother of three young children was forcibly kidnapped from her home in Dade County. Her husband received a ransom call from a male demanding $250,000. The banks were closed yesterday, which the kidnapper didn't realize since part of the instruction was to secure the cash from the bank. A note was left in the victim's home directing the husband to a certain location. The usual kidnap-extortion trail followed, without any contact from the kidnapper. The trail consisted entirely of notes. There has been no contact today. We are preparing masked commercials on radio addressed to the kidnapper, who used the name 'Peter' when calling the husband.

"The kidnapper has threatened he will kill the wife if the police are involved. We take this threat seriously, and our investigation has, so far, been very circumspect. We want to give the kidnapper every opportunity to make contact and secure the ransom. This is, of course, the most expeditious way to gain the victim's release. The kidnapper will either release her after payment, or, through the information we will develop as a result of negotiation with the kidnapper and the payoff, we will determine her whereabouts and effect her rescue.

"We know that your news sources are excellent, and that in time you all would develop pieces of the story. We felt it better to be up-front and factual. What we are requesting is that you all voluntarily sit on the story, just delay reporting it, to give us more time to establish contact with the kidnapper and gain the safe return of the victim."

Remarks were not slow in coming:

"We don't kill stories."

"My paper doesn't work for the FBI."

"The public has a right to know, and there is insufficient information for us to determine whether we are justified in holding this."

Al was afraid he might be losing the argument,

but felt this was more posturing than reality. What proved to be the final word came from a *Herald* editor. "The *Herald* will not print the story at this time. Balancing the preservation of a human life against the public knowing today or two days from now, there is no choice but one, for any responsible journalist."

That ended the discussion. The other media members all concurred with the statement the *Herald* had made, and began to leave. The reporters, who could not make such a decision, voiced a certainty that their bosses would comply. A few lingered, asking questions, trying for that additional crumb of information that signals a good reporter.

Later in the day, the agents who had concluded their day's work assembled for a short conference to update everyone on where the case was going.

Al decided to do a "I guess you know why I'm here" interview on every possible suspect that evening, and a briefing ensued.

"Xerox engineers have confirmed the Lab's impression that the notes had been copied on a Xerox machine," he began. "They added that they should be able to identify the specific machine. We're sampling machines in public places starting in the southwest.

"All of the Stockton friends, relatives, business contacts, et cetera, are in the computer and have been checked in Ident and in our files. So far, nothing of interest has surfaced. Surveillance of the Winn Dixie drop for a check by Peter was unproductive.

"F.I. cards are in the computer and citations are being reviewed manually. We've come up with seventy-five people from F.I. cards who merit some attention. Many are known to the police; some do not fit Stockton's voice description.

"All will be interviewed on a pretext, and given the 'I guess you know why I'm here' speech. Those of you who get these interviews, and the subject doesn't respond, can use the story that you believed he or she was acquainted with a fugitive. Use a fugitive photo and you might even get lucky and find him. I'll be designating at least twenty of you to do these tonight."

After some further discussion from the agents, the briefing concluded, and they proceeded with their assignments. It would be another late night.

Of the interviews that had been assigned for completion that evening, Agent Donald Jacobi was the first to get positive results. One of Jacobi's suspects was Jerald Wells. He located him at home at about nine-thirty. Wells had been F.I.'d about six months before.

Jacobi knocked on the apartment door and a male opened it. "Jerald Wells?"

"Yes."

Jacobi, displaying his credentials in his left hand, leaving his right free to respond to any threat from Wells, said, "I'm Jacobi, FBI. I guess you know why I'm here!"

Wells, shaken, responded, "Yeah, I've been expectin' you guys."

Jacobi's heart rate went up, and his right hand moved toward his hip holster. "One of the kidnappers" raced through his mind.

"I knew you'd I.D. me on the three 7-Eleven

jobs," Wells continued. "I should'a quit after the first one. The gun's under the bed."

That evening would produce two more spontaneous confessions from interviewees who would be turned over to police.

While the three arrests were the subject of considerable comment in the office, they did not further the purpose of the interviews—the solution of the kidnapping.

The leads to identify the source of the cut-up newsprint fared much better, but came far short of putting the finger on someone. The clippings used in the notes came from the February 11 issue of the *Miami Herald*.

And so, as day two of the kidnapping rapidly drew to a close, Rob's commercials were on every English-language station. Al went to see Stockton, accompanied by Milt and Xavier.

Al observed the same security precautions as he had the previous night. After the garage door closed, he came out slowly, straightening a tired back. The garage, unlike Al's, was neat, with tools hung on a peg board. He could smell not-so-fresh grass, from the mower in the corner. He stepped over the threshold and into the bright kitchen.

Jean's half-empty coffee mug was still on the table. Before he sat down, Al, out of habit, reflexively picked it up and was about to move to the sink with it.

Stockton, off to the side, shouted at him, "Don't move that mug! That mug was Jean's, yesterday. She was probably drinking out of it when they took her. Leave it on the table. She's coming back."

Al, surprised at the outburst, said, "Sorry, I

didn't know. I was just tidying up before we talked."

Stockton was still shouting as he advanced on Al, squarely facing him. "Didn't know! That's been the story for the last two days! You do things without thinking of the consequences! You make decisions without consulting me! This shit has got to stop! It may already be too late! This is all screwed up because of you! All I had to do was pay him, and Jean would be back! But you had to get this thing all complicated and confused, and he knows you're in it! That's why I haven't heard! Jean's probably dead, and it's because of your fucking interference!"

Al did not respond to Stockton's accusations, but Xavier noted the color rise in Al's face, saw his jaw muscles firm under his skin and knew that Al was exercising great self-control.

Milt took careful note of the confrontation, as it confirmed much of his criticism of the manner in which Al had handled the case.

Al abandoned the quiet, suggestive air he had previously used with Stockton. Al sensed that Stockton was losing it, and he needed someone to take control. "Rob, sit over there." This was the first test of strength. If he did, Al was on his way to winning; if not, there would be need for a solid demonstration of authority.

Stockton remained still. Al was looking him square in the eye.

Henry pulled from under the table the chair Al had designated.

The noise broke Stockton's eyes from Al to the chair. He hesitated, then moved toward it and sat.

Al sat opposite him. "Rob, if there is no contact by noon tomorrow, you and the children will appear on TV and grant interviews to the press and radio. You will ask Peter to contact you. You will tell him that you have the money, you may even display it. You will say that if he will tell you where or how to pay him, you will do so, and there will be no police involved. The FBI will, at that point, begin an open, high-profile investigation. To put it bluntly, if you want your wife back, we can't do this half-assed. We go! Now, if for some reason you and the kids won't do what I'm telling you, I will. Any questions?"

Rob was not looking at Al. He looked first to Henry and then to Grover. His expression was one of confusion. He was looking for an explanation of why he was being given orders. Then he said, again looking at Henry and Grover, "Okay, these are all your decisions. I'll do what I'm told. If this kills Jean it's your fault. I tried."

Milt's head involuntarily nodded. Stockton did not observe it but Al did. Milt saw the deep scowl that crossed Al's face. This was the first real, personal anger that Al had directed at him. Milt found himself with an uneasy feeling.

"The search for Jean at this point," Al continued, "can only benefit from an open investigation. The entire resources of the FBI can be openly committed. The whole state, indeed the nation, will involve itself. I've seen this before. There will be an outpouring of prayers, good wishes and, more importantly, concrete help. There may be dozens of people about whom we have not the faintest inkling that have information concerning Jean but don't even realize they have it. By going public, we can tap into this."

Rob, still avoiding Al's eyes, mumbled, "Tomorrow. We wait until tomorrow."

Jean was dying, the ordeal of the last twenty-four hours was taking its toll. Hypothermia, dehydration, animal bites, and despair were slowly claiming her life. Jean was on Biscayne Bay, on the family's boat. The kids and Rob were with her. They had been snorkeling off Coon Point at high tide, watching all the baby fish, and were now back on the boat and Jean was preparing lunch. The kids were excitedly describing and trying to name all the little fish they had seen. Rob was watching Jean; he would touch her, a caress, as she walked by him. It was a beautiful day. The sky was the pure, cloudless blue that only south Florida can have. She could feel the warmth of the sun and, even with her sunglasses, had to squint against its brightness. It was a nice lunch, but Jean felt there were too many flies, and she couldn't understand where all the ants had come from.

Stanley had made a decision to contact Rob through the mail. He had prepared the letter with Mona's help and then had thrown it away.

Mona was devastated. She had worked on Donnie to try to get the kidnapping moving again, and had thought that when he started clipping the newspaper and had her address the envelope, that things were going to work. Now, any hope for Jean's release was again remote.

That night Mona decided to act. She would free Jean.

C H A P T E R
13

The unexpected always happens.
    —Common saying

Al left Stockton's home and drove back to the office. Milt and Xavier went to their offices for a final check before heading home.

Al followed Milt into his office. As soon as they were alone, Milt saw Al's expression change from pleasant to "storm warning." Milt took a step back, not sure what to expect. He realized Al was about as angry as he had ever seen him.

"Your performance in this case has been intolerable. You want to do a memo to the Bureau taking issue with the direction of this case, do it. I will not tolerate another exhibition like the one you put on tonight. Your open disagreement with me, in the presence of Stockton, could jeopardize the life of the victim. Fortunately, Stockton didn't see what I saw. You will, henceforth, meticulously follow the letter and spirit of my orders. Another such exhibition and I will ask for your suspension. Do we understand each other?"

Milt was infuriated. "Your total disregard of

Stockton's wishes and skirting of Bureau rules will be responsible for the failures that are coming. We have already experienced problems that are clearly traceable to your shortcomings. The reaction you saw this evening was not intentional, but it was normal." Milt walked by Al and left the office.

Work would continue throughout the night. Al, tired and discouraged, drafted a teletype and then left for home.

To: Director, FBI   URGENT
     SAC, Tampa, Jacksonville, Mobile,
       Atlanta

Fr: SAC, Miami (7-508)

Stocknap

Remytelcon today. No contact from Unsub. Confirmed ransom notes reproduced on Xerox copier. Efforts to ident copier ongoing. Letters and words in note cut from February eleven edition Miami Herald. Media briefed, as one TV station had partial story, all holding publication. Husband of victim placed "ads" local radio mentioning Unsub's aka "Peter" and offering to do business. Over one hundred interviews conducted today of possible suspects, twelve require follow up. Three felons identified and arrested by local police as result of interviews. All acquaintances of family obtained and background being developed. Bureau will be kept advised. End.

Al was home at 11:30. Helen was up. She knew he hadn't eaten all day, or at least not properly, so she took a large steak out of the refrigerator and put it on the grill, then made a salad and prepared a baked potato in the microwave, along with some green beans. By the time Al had showered and donned pajamas, dinner was ready.

It was just after 1:00 a.m. when he fell into an exhausted sleep.

During the night the office computer made a full run on all the information that had been crammed into it during the past two days. While everyone slept it worked, sorting and matching the data. Included in that data were all the cars and people that had passed the Stockton home. Many were known to the Stockton family, the computer matched them and they were assigned for follow-up investigation.

At 4:36 a.m. it matched the name Richard Stanley, a small builder who had occasionally contracted with Rob for plumbing and roofing. On Monday evening a Chevrolet Caprice registered to Richard Stanley had driven by Stockton's house. Sue and Sam had taken several photos through the Flemings' dining room window using a telephoto night vision lens.

The photographs showed two occupants in the car, possibly male and female. With proper enhancement the photo images would be of sufficient quality for identification.

By 8:00 that morning, one of the two agents responsible for assigning leads came across the Richard Stanley lead and handed it to a clerk to fax to Phil Bentley in the Homestead R.A. Richard Stanley's address was in Florida City, south of Homestead.

Phil was in the R.A. office when the fax came in. He had a couple of other interviews to do that morning, plus a deadline civil rights case that should have been out the Friday before. He called Miami and asked for an index check and file review on Richard Stanley, and to fax the results. He could do local checks with his sources by phone. In half an hour he had talked by phone with the Florida City Police Chief and some acquaintances in the building and banking industries; he now had a pretty fair picture of Richard Stanley. With a fax from Miami of any pertinent file information, he would interview the builder that afternoon.

Al had been in the office since 7:00, reviewing not only the progress of this case but other work that could not be stopped or put aside. Many cases had been put on hold to devote the bulk of the office resources to the kidnapping, but some cases were of comparable priority and had to go forward.

Al called the Stockton house at 7:30 and talked to Grover. Stockton and the children were up, and all were in worse shape than last evening. "Stockton has come apart. It is becoming increasingly difficult to carry on a conversation with him. He has no attention span. He seems constantly preoccupied. He's just not here anymore. The kids sense this, and it adds to their feeling of insecurity. They have lost a mother, and now their father seems lost. I'm very concerned about Stockton's ability to function should we get a Peter contact. If the contact does not rejuvenate him, you may have to arbitrarily take him out of the game. The kids are not a problem. They are just quiet, withdrawn and sad—morose.

There just isn't any life left in them. They've all given up."

Mona rolled into a sitting position on the edge of the bed, stood and walked to the bathroom. The movement disturbed Stanley and brought him awake. He turned on his back and saw it was day.

He was awake, thinking, as Mona came back to the bed. He looked at her body and thought how good she had been last night when he had threatened to blacken her other eye if he didn't get something special.

"What're you doin'?"

Mona, with a puzzled expression, responded, "Goin' back to bed."

"Get dressed and go down to the store. Stockton's called the cops by now, and we're going to Jacksonville. Get some food, beer and a paper. I want us outta here before noon."

"How about breakfast?"

"Damn it, you can eat when you get back. Now get movin'."

Minutes later, Mona cranked up the old Chevy and drove down the rutted dirt road. Her thoughts were of Jean. "He really is going to leave her. This is maybe the only chance I'll have to get her out. I gotta do it now." Mona did not just go shopping.

Stanley lay in bed for a half hour after Mona left, still thinking about the $250,000, and what Stockton may have done. He finally slid out of bed and went into the kitchen where he fixed an unappetizing breakfast of cold cereal and milk. Despite his remark to Mona, he was considering whether he could salvage something out of this mess. He heated some water to make instant coffee.

While he waited for Mona and the paper and the hot water he switched on WINZ, an AM news station. He was half listening when Mona returned.

What they heard brought Mona and him to full attention. "Hello, this is Robert Stockton, of Stockton Roofing and Plumbing. I have a message for all of you out there, and especially for Peter. I have what you want. I know I can satisfy your requirements. All I ask is the chance to serve you. Peter, and all of you, should feel free to call me. There will be no strings. I want to deal."

Stanley sat transfixed. Mona was totally disconcerted by this unexpected event. Her mind was in a whirl. "What's Donnie gonna do now? I can't tell him what I done, he'd kill me."

Al, watching the morning slip away, could not escape the conclusion that Jean was dead. There had never been a kidnapping case that he was aware of in which the victim lived after so long a period of no contact. There were old cases that had taken weeks to resolve, but there was always contact and negotiation, not the loud silence of this case.

He began to prepare himself for the media blitz. He had decided to let Stockton and the kids carry it. The media and the public liked schmaltz, and this case had it. His presence would detract from what they were trying to accomplish. The police profile had to be kept as low as possible.

The media impression Al wanted to convey was

that of a bereaved family who wanted their wife and mother back. They were willing to do whatever it took to accomplish this, including the payment of ransom. The police were aware of what was happening, and were there to assist the family, but they would do nothing to interfere in any arrangement that the family might make with the kidnapper.

If this image could be conveyed, Al felt he had the best of both worlds. The American public would be aware of the kidnapping, and would cooperate to the extreme with the FBI in its inquiries to find Jean. And Peter might buy into the idea that the family was willing to pay the reward for Jean, no strings. Certainly, after such a public announcement, there could be no question of a wide open, aggressive investigation.

The result of this investigation was never in doubt in Al's mind. If Jean were alive, they'd find her, and her kidnappers. If Jean were dead, they'd find the killer. Al knew that when the FBI puts a priority on a case, it gets solved. To Al, it was just a simple fact of life he had lived with and seen, time after time.

The question now was the location for the media release. It went without saying that the FBI office was out. He considered Stockton's house. It would have the homey touch that would help make the story. The problem was control of the media, and getting them out of the area. Stockton's house was a control center; to have the media mucking about would certainly disrupt the operation.

Al was looking for a neutral locale where the only interest would be Stockton and the kids. He wanted Rob and the kids to walk on and off in five minutes. The perfect solution came to him: Rob's lawyer's office. It gave a tone of negotiation, without police involvement.

Al immediately picked up the phone and contacted the house. Henry answered, and Al tried out the idea on him. Henry saw no reason why it could not be arranged, and saw no reason why Stockton would object.

Al transferred over to Stockton and put the media plan to him, "Rob, Al. We're as disappointed as you that there's been no contact. We all hoped the commercials would do it. It's time to go open, where we can use our full strength." He then explained the rest of the plan.

Stockton was slow in responding, and when he did his voice was flat, emotionless. "Yes, all right, I'll call my lawyer."

"Good. Just tell him briefly what's happened, ask him for his help, and tell him that I'll call him and make final arrangements."

"Okay, I'll call you back after I talk to him." Stockton called within five minutes advising that his attorney, William Winder, would help and was expecting Al's call.

Bill Winder was an attorney who handled only civil cases, and had never been in a criminal courtroom. He had been Stockton's lawyer for ten years, and more importantly, his friend. Once Winder grasped the reason for the media event in his office, he unhesitatingly agreed.

Al arranged for media calls at noon, from the FBI, for a news conference at Winder's office at 2:00 p.m. Both Al and Winder made themselves unavailable, so they would not be under pressure to respond as to the purpose of the media conference.

Al did not want premature leaks on the noon news, and so the media was told only that a one-time announcement of significant newsworthiness would be made at 1:00 p.m. to whoever was able to be present. If they could come, they would be welcome. Those that could not might consider picking up footage of the release from the other stations. It was this last remark that guaranteed their attendance.

By 1:00, the conference room at the office of William Winder, Esq., was overflowing with cameras and press. At 1:15 Stockton and the children entered from the end of the room, opposite from where the press had been told to set up. Stockton began.

"I'm Robert Stockton; these are my children." He gestured toward each as he introduced them. "Steve, Amy and Ben. We have been without a wife and mother since Monday morning. Jean, my wife, was kidnapped from our home Monday morning by a person who later called me at work and told me his name was Peter. Peter asked for $250,000 for the safe return of my wife. I have that money. Here it is."

With that statement, Stockton lifted a brown paper Publix bag and dumped the money on the conference table. The cameras were eating it up. There were close-ups of Stockton and each of the tearful children. When Stockton dumped the money, there was an audible gasp in the room, and every camera zoomed in on the cash.

"If Peter will return our Jean to us, I will deliver this wherever he says.

"This is my wonderful wife, my children's mother," Rob said as he held up a photo of Jean. Copies of the photo were on the conference table for the media to take with them. Cameras focused on the picture Stockton was holding.

"The money is his, no questions asked. I have instructed the police to stay out of this. All we want is Jean. If anyone watching me tonight has any information, or can help in any way in finding Jean for me, or perhaps saw something Monday morning between eight-thirty and ten or thereafter that could shed some light on our tragedy, please call my attorney, Mr. Winder, at 237-1000."

Al had made prior arrangements with Winder and the phone company to provide three off-site extensions that connected to the FBI office. If a Stockton call came in it would go to one of those extensions, and be answered by an agent. A trap and trace was up on all such calls, since Peter could well be one of the callers.

As the presentation was ending Al was signaled by Winder's secretary that there was a call for him. Irritated at the interruption at this critical stage he shook his head.

At that moment his pager vibrated against his body. He looked. The number was the office-use line into the Stockton house. Al advanced toward the secretary and asked who was on the phone. "A Mr. Henry Adamski," she replied.

Al took the phone call in Winder's office. "Henry? Al. What's up? We're almost at the end of the press conference."

"We just got a contact. I talked to a female, saying I was Stockton. She said she was calling for Peter and that we should be ready to pay the money to Peter later today."

Al had been surprised many times before, but this one topped them all. He sat down, nonplussed. He came back to Henry after a moment during which all the implications of the timing of this call set in. "What time is the drop?"

"She said she'd get back to us with specifics."

Al hung up and headed for the conference. His mind was roiling. "How the hell am I going to stop this thing I just started? These guys got a hell of a story on tape. How can I convince them to sit on it a second time while we play grab ass with a lunatic who obviously can't get his act together?"

The paper and groceries sat untouched on the kitchen table as Stanley and Mona stared, immobilized by the radio that had just carried Stockton's voice to them. Mona was more concerned than she had ever been, for now Stanley might try for the ransom, and she had already taken some steps to help Jean that she could not erase.

Stanley finally broke the silence. "The shit wants to deal. You heard him. He wants to give me the fuckin' money. Baby, we got it. We go."

With that, he reached for the tablet and a pen and began to write out a script for Mona. As he wrote he issued instructions. "We're goin' to a pay phone a long way from here, and you call him and read this. Don't answer no questions, don't do nothin' but read this. You got it?"

Mona nodded.

The purpose of Stanley's message was to determine if the radio commercial was for real, whether Stockton really wanted to pay. If he got a yes that he believed, he would work on putting together a drop that would protect him from any possible police involvement.

A scheme was developing in Stanley's mind that he felt would be foolproof, if he could put all the pieces together. Surprise, along with the old shell game of misdirecting attention, were the cornerstones of the plan he was beginning to visualize. The message was completed, and as they drove to a public phone, he repeatedly warned Mona not to deviate from it. The phone he chose was located at Krome Avenue and 222nd Street. After he pulled into a vacant spot at a small country store, Mona got out of the car accompanied by a last warning to stick to the script and to get off the phone as soon as she delivered the message to Stockton.

Stanley had parked on the side of the store that held the phone, so he could not be observed from the front of the building. He was about fifty feet from the phone. He watched, the engine was running and he was scared.

Mona punched up Stockton's business number, and a female answered, "Stockton Company."

The call had been forwarded to the FBI office and answered by an agent.

"Mr. Stockton, please."

"Mr. Stockton's not in at the moment. May I ask who's calling?"

"No, I'm a friend, that's okay. I'll call back later." Mona quickly disconnected and walked back to the car.

The telephone company trapped the call and

traced it to the phone Mona was using. Once it was identified as a pay phone, the office alerted all operational cars that a call had come to Stockton's office from a pay phone at Krome Avenue and 222nd Street.

Xavier, advised of the developments, instructed all cars in the area to converge on the location, on the possibility this was a kidnap contact and that another call from the same phone could follow.

Mona, back at the car, told Stanley what had happened. Scowling, he reached in his pocket, took out a piece of paper and handed it to her. "Try this, it's his home."

Mona walked back to the phone and placed the call. On the first ring Grover advised, over the open line, "Incoming." Henry picked up on the fourth ring and answered. "Hello?"

The female voice on the other end said, "Mr. Stockton?"

"Yes. Who's this, please?"

"A friend of Peter's."

Henry gave Grover a thumbs-up sign. Grover had heard the statement through his earphones, and passed the message over the open line, "Female contact." This was immediately relayed to the cars on the street.

Mona read her message. "Mr. Stockton, you did not respond to my first demand. I took it that you preferred your wife dead."

"No, no," Henry interrupted. "I want her back. I'll give you the money. I followed all your instructions, but I didn't see you at the K mart center. May I talk to my wife please? I have to know she's all right."

Mona, as Stanley had before, lost her place in the script and disobeyed Stanley's instructions. "Your wife's all right, but she's in danger. She may be dyin'. You got to move fast. Why'd you not park the truck?"

It was Henry's turn to be confused. "I don't know anything about a truck. What's wrong with Jean?"

Mona continued, "He told you to leave your truck at 184th and Cutler when you were ready."

"He never told me that. I didn't know about the truck but I'm ready. Whatever happens, keep in touch with me because I've got the money and I want to pay you. Tell me about Jean. How is she? Where is she? Let me talk to her before we go any further."

Mona, realizing she was off Stanley's script, began to panic. "She's not where we are. Be ready for today. We'll call you."

With that she hung up and ran back to the car.

As Al entered the conference room a reporter from Channel Five was asking Stockton, "Did this Peter give you any instructions for paying the ransom, and if so, did you follow them and what happened?"

Rob was about to answer when Al strode to the head of the table and interrupted the answer with a restraining hand on his arm. "My apologies for this interruption. For those of you I have not had the pleasure of meeting, I'm Al Lawrence, Agent in Charge of the Miami FBI office. What I am about to say will come as a great and welcome surprise to the Stockton family, and to all of us that have been trying to contact Peter working toward the return of Mrs. Stockton.

"Most of you were aware, or at least your management was aware, yesterday, of this kidnapping, based on our briefing of the media then. At that briefing there was a unanimous decision that since a life was at stake—the kidnapper having threatened to kill Mrs. Stockton if the police were made aware of the crime—you all would, for the present, not report what you knew.

"Yesterday you had a very limited story. You only knew a kidnapping for ransom, with a death threat, was working. At the time of yesterday's briefing, the only contact from the kidnapper had been a Monday morning phone call. There had been no contact since then, and that is why we decided to go public today. It was hoped this conference would nudge him into making a contact.

"We took a calculated risk. It was possible, probable, that he would be more frightened than motivated by the publicity. Our preference would have been to allow him to believe that only he and Mr. Stockton knew of the kidnapping.

"Now you have the complete story that you didn't have yesterday, and I am about to again ask, beg, that you delay its release.

"Just moments ago, as you were addressing questions to Mr. Stockton, the kidnapper called the Stockton house."

Rob and his children registered utter amazement. Rob moved toward Al, mouthing questions which Al silenced with a movement of his hand. The media people were writing furiously; the cameras were zooming in on the expressions on the faces of the family: amazement, joy, concern. Reporters raised hands seeking recognition, and some reporters burst forth without recognition, drowning each other out.

Al stopped speaking, and then above the din asked to be allowed to continue. "*Please!* Bear with me. Let me finish and perhaps I'll answer your questions.

"You all have a good story now, a complete story, and certainly the contact by the kidnapper in the middle of the press conference is high drama. It will be high drama whether you play it today or tomorrow. I know, and you know, that you are free to go with the story now if you so choose. I hope you recognize, however, that the same reason you chose on Tuesday to delay reporting the story exists today, and even more strongly, for now we have a contact and a chance to rescue Jean. We believe this contact, if Peter is not spooked, gives us an unparalleled opportunity to do that. I regret that my opting for this conference has placed you in the position of having to share in what may well be a life or death decision. Whatever decision you arrive at, individually or collectively, I give you my word that as soon as this contact has run its course, you will be fully briefed on the events. Hopefully at our next conference we will all be rewarded with the personal appearance of Jean Stockton. The decision is yours."

There was a period of silence, no one wanting to commit. The *Herald* was again the first to commit to hold the story, conditional upon the editor's approval.

An aside could be heard. "Shit. The *Herald*

gives up nothing. They're morning and stand to be first if it breaks tonight." Channel Eight, however, followed with a similar pledge. Most of the others were not sure. Al felt certain that if the majority held the story, the fence-sitters would follow. Any station that went with the story while the others held chanced being badly hurt if Jean were harmed or if the payoff were jeopardized.

Al took Stockton's arm and turned him toward Winder's office; the children followed. "Rob, all I know is that a female called saying she was with Peter. She's going to call back with instructions, but according to her, we're on for tonight. Go home. You'll have our usual escort. I need to go to the office, get the full text of the message, and start things in motion. You can get the details from Henry when you get home. We'll talk after that. Try to stay calm and follow the script we've given you. We'll do everything in our power to have Jean home with you tonight."

CHAPTER
14

Judge not the play before the play is done.
—FRANCIS QUARLES, *Respice finem*

On the first ring of the Stockton home phone, the radio room advised of the calling location and confirmed that it was the same pay phone that had previously been used to call the Stockton business. This was followed by confirmation of a female contact.

At the time of Mona's call there was no sector deployment, as a call was not anticipated. The cars that were operational were scattered about, covering leads. The nearest car to the 222nd Street and Krome location was at 168th Street and the Highway, a good distance away, but he began to move in that direction.

In addition Phil Bentley was about to leave Homestead and head to Florida City to interview Richard Stanley. He advised he would respond. Both agents knew they would arrive about ten to fifteen minutes after the subject had departed, but there was always the chance of another call from that phone. Also, in daylight, someone might remember the caller.

The radio operator spoke again. "We have a disconnect." Xavier had picked up on the action and at his instruction, the radio operator moved additional cars into the area. Some cars had begun to move without instruction, and now advised they were en route. At fifteen cars, Xavier stopped further deployment.

While the other cars were all too far away to even think of an intercept, the action had come from a specific area, and if another call were made, it might well emanate from that same general area. A degree of saturation was therefore appropriate. Without assignment, the cars began covering the area from Homestead to about 184th Street, loosely, but they were there.

As Phil and Oscar, the agent from 168th Street, got within intercept range, five minutes away, they began trying to note license plates of vehicles going in the opposite direction. At a speed of sixty miles per hour this was impossible, and the attempt was abandoned after the first try.

This was the closest they had been to Peter, and Xavier was not surprised when the fifteen cars began to build as others found excuses to be in the area. A minor disciplinary lapse that was overlooked. They all knew that with some work, and one good break, they'd have him. Phil and Oscar Suarez arrived within minutes of each other.

They first circled the small country store and block, taking license-plate numbers and physical descriptions of those in the area. Both parked.

Oscar remained in his car observing, while Phil located the phone.

Ordinarily they would do systematic interviews of everyone in the area in an effort to locate anyone who might have seen the person using the phone. In this instance Phil decided to go slow. He returned to his car and communicated with Oscar by radio. "Let's lay back; check the cars out front. So much time's elapsed since the call it's doubtful anybody's still here from the time of the call. Any cars that don't move will be suspect, as waiting to make another call."

When they had determined that all the parked cars had moved, Phil decided to leave and resume his investigation and instructed Oscar: "Pick a good spot to eyeball the phone. If it's not used for the next call, arrange for the coin box to be removed, dust the phone for latents, and clip the handpiece to send to the lab."

The coin container would be turned over to the FBI so that all the coins could be processed for latents. Ident in D.C. could do a much better job of developing prints in a laboratory environment, using chemicals rather than powder. The Bureau would pay Southern Bell for the damage.

As they drove south and west, Mona related the phone call to Stanley, taking care to omit some of the details of her deviation from the script. "Donnie, I read the note you gave me. He said he wanted his wife back and would pay. He asked how she was. I didn't answer, 'cept to say okay. He said he had the money and did everythin' you told him to. He didn't know about parkin' the truck, he said. He kept wantin' to talk to his wife. He said a couple times he wants to pay."

Stanley's response was to the point. "Talk to his wife? Fuckin' big chance of that! But he said he's got the money?"

"Yeah, and he wants to pay."

"Okay." Stanley said, thinking out loud. "We got to figger a way to get it clean. A way we got no risk. No chance of bein' seen. When we got it set, you can call 'em back. I think I know how to do it; just like Ralph taught me with the shells and the pea. Now ya see it, now ya don't."

As soon as Al arrived at the office, he listened to a copy of the taped conversation Henry had transmitted to the office by phone. He then called Henry. "Let the family hear the full tape. There could be voice recognition, and Stockton will learn from it. The tape is a textbook exercise in dealing with a kidnapper. Just what we've been trying to teach him.

Henry was pleased. "Thanks, but she didn't let me talk to Jean, and there's no indication she will. I'm beginning to get a bad feeling about the case. I'm not sure the kids ought to hear the whole tape. I don't think Mrs. Peter was trying to scare us with the language about Jean being in danger. I believe she is in danger, and Mrs. Peter is concerned and wants to help us, help Jean, really. If we talk to her again we should try to capitalize on this. If you agree, I'll try to steer Stockton that way."

Al agreed completely with Henry's perceptive assessment, and hung up. As soon as sufficient agents could be assembled he was on his way to an all-agents conference.

Al began his briefing by playing the contact call several times. "My feeling is that the female making the contact is saying what she believes. She's not reading when she talks about Jean. In my mind, Jean is in real trouble. I don't know what the trouble is, but my gut tells me if we don't find her quick, she could be dead.

"We need to move as fast as we safely can tonight. Xavier has a grid breakdown for all of you. We are going to concentrate on the area where the notes were found and today's call came from. Respond to contact sights as quickly as possible. The radio will broadcast time of connection and disconnect, including how long ago the disconnect was. They will also tell you whether the caller is male or female. Only assigned grids move. Everyone else must maintain their grid position.

"I know I'll hear this loud and clear, but let's hear when one of you sights a caller still on the phone. At that point the whole grid that he's in should stay with him while we try to confirm one more call. At this point, no arrest. Stockton wants to try a real payoff. We'll let that progress. As of now the money pass will be clean, no tracker.

"We don't like that and will try to change his mind, but for now, that's the way it is. We may interrupt at some point, but we'll only do it at my direction. It could be a long night. Coffee thermos and empty quart jars are in order; you'll be living in your cars for a while. Anybody want a private word, I'll be around. Let's do it."

Fifteen minutes after the conference broke up,

Al had a separate meeting with SPIT. "Stay with Stockton and alternate your inner-outer assignment. If Stockton and a subject end up in a small area, things could start happening pretty fast and get a little sticky. This is the point at which he is going to be the most hinky. We know now that there is at least a male and female in this. I know you're always alert for this but I repeat, a countersurveillance must be assumed and detected. A countersurveillance detected makes a subject. Let's do it right the first time; we may not get another chance."

Everyone went to their station, and within half an hour a roll call was under way.

Al called the house again and this time got Grover. "When a contact call comes in, control Stockton. Sit on him. Don't let him run. I want to hear the call and I want to consult with both of you, and Stockton, but you two first. Start impressing upon him the concept that reasoned judgments will win, and we just can't slavishly follow Peter around. Try him again on substitution. You or Henry for him on the payoff. Hit him up again on the tracker in the payoff package. I don't want to scare him, but I think Jean is in trouble and that tracker is insurance. Quite frankly if this were my decision and not a family one, I'd grab whoever showed. I think Jean's got that big a problem and we shouldn't be pulling any punches. Come back to me after you've talked."

Dolores, Al's secretary, and the secretary for four SACs before him, had been trying to get his attention and he had put her off because of the need to move quickly. She finally just blocked his path and said, "You must read this, now!"

Al took the piece of white note paper. On it Dolores had typed: *John Straus, an attorney, called at 2:15 p.m. He said he has a client who knows the whereabouts of a kidnap victim. If we are working a kidnap, call him at 351-5700.*

Al showed the paper to Xavier. "A setup?" he queried. "Is Peter cleverly shopping for police involvement via a lawyer's inquiry?"

"I know the name," Xavier said. "I've seen it in the newspapers. He practices mostly in State Criminal Court. Can we think up a noncommittal answer and pump him?"

Al put the tape recorder on his phone and punched up the Straus number. He identified himself to the secretary who answered, and requested to speak with Mr. Straus, advising he was returning Mr. Straus's call.

Straus came on the line quickly. "Thanks for calling back. I've checked with Metro, City of Miami and Florida Department of Law Enforcement, who advised they have no kidnap working. Then I thought of you guys. I've got a person who contacted me by phone late this morning requesting me to represent him. He said he was in trouble, that he was involved in a kidnapping, and was worried that the victim might die. Might, in fact, already be dead. The caller maintains that when he took part in the kidnapping he had no idea that anyone was going to be hurt, or could be hurt.

"I believe I can locate, or help locate, the victim based on my client's information. I feel a very strong moral obligation to do so. If you have a kidnapping working, perhaps we can work out a deal for my client. A grant of immunity to the client would protect him enough that he would come forward and locate the victim."

Milt and Xavier clearly read Al's bewilderment from the change in his facial expression. "Mr. Straus, I very much appreciate your call. Your information is of interest to us, irrespective of any possible existing investigation, since you state your client has informed you that a kidnapping has occurred. Let us proceed on your information that a kidnapping has taken place."

Straus countered, "Understand that I have to both protect my client and try to save a life. My first duty must be to my client. That is not necessarily the order I would choose, but I am ethically compelled to follow this path. If you receive my client's information without a grant of immunity, he will convict himself of kidnapping, at the very least."

"I'm sure you know," Al responded, "that I can't grant immunity. I have no authority to do so. You need to discuss that aspect with the United States Attorney or Dade County States Attorney."

"Yes, I'm aware of that," Straus continued, "and I would require a grant from both of them to preclude a charge in either forum. I contacted you rather than them since I felt that operationally you would be better versed in any ongoing kidnap interest. I cannot overemphasize the urgency of this. In my judgment, time is of the essence; and I am talking hours. A day will probably be much too late."

Al was wary. "Can you give me the name of the

victim, or any other identifier that will assist us in knowing the victim? Can you give us any specifics? Can you give us a solid reason why we should grant immunity to a confessed kidnapper? You know that a grant of immunity is a very serious, deliberate act, and never done as quickly as you are suggesting. How do we know your client's not just a nut?"

"My problem is divulging client confidence. The name of the victim, which I have been given, is part of that confidence, but I do understand your dilemma. I consider that my authority to act for my client does give me some discretion to exercise judgment in this area. Therefore, I can tell you that the victim's name is Jean Stockton. She was kidnapped from her home on Monday. The manner in which she is held insures her death at any moment."

"Is your client the principal?"

"I can answer that with confidence: He is not."

"Can you describe what part your client played in the kidnapping?"

"At this time, without specific client permission, I do not believe that I can."

Al became restive, shifting in his chair and thinking, "This son of a bitch is telling me Jean is about to die, and he's more worried about some worthless kidnapper's immunity." What he actually said was, "If the U.S. Attorney were to consider immunity at this time, and I am certainly not speaking for her, my sense is that transactional immunity would not even be discussed. Any consideration of immunity would encompass use immunity."

"I would have to advise my client to insist on transactional immunity."

"I certainly don't mean to tell you your job, counselor, but use immunity would guarantee we not use what he says in any way against him. Transactional, in effect, says we can never prosecute him, even on independently developed evidence. Would your client testify for us?"

"He has said he would not."

"Is there anything else you can tell us that would assist in reaching a decision? Any other information your client gave you that you can pass on?"

"Only, and I shouldn't say this—perhaps because as an advocate I should not inject myself into the situation, but I will—only that I personally believe him. I must impress the urgency of this. Mrs. Stockton will surely be dead, if she's not dead now, within hours or minutes. My client has no way of determining her current condition."

Al thanked Straus, advising that they would get back to him and hung up.

Without a word Al quickly hit the tape eject button, punched the tabs on the cassette so it could not be erased or recorded over, replaced the cassette in the recorder, rewound it and punched the play button so Milt and Xavier could hear the whole conversation.

Al watched their faces as the tape played. They were a study in surprise and consternation. Al wondered what he must have looked like during this conversation which, he had to admit, was the damnedest turn he had ever seen a kidnapping take.

At the end of the tape Al addressed a short question. "Well?"

There was an unusual silence from Milt and Xavier. Both were deep in thought. Al pursued it. "Is Peter fishing? If we bite, showing we know about the kidnapping, does he back off?"

Xavier answered first, with the answer Al had already formulated but was testing before he adopted it. "No, this is not a fishing expedition. He's told us too much by giving us the victim's identity. If we weren't in the Stockton case before he called, we would be after."

Al agreed. "Second question: Who's the client?"

Again, Al's almost rhetorical question was answered by Xavier. "Mrs. Peter."

Al smiled. "I think so too. It could, of course, be another gang member, but the tenor of her conversation this morning fits with what we're getting from Straus. This is an interesting development that needs to be disseminated to the troops, since it sets the tone for any interview of a female subject.

"Third question: How do we deal with Straus? We don't have the luxury of endless debate on this one. I tend to agree with Straus in one respect—whatever we do, we need to do it quickly."

Milt began, "The ultimate decision is for the U.S. Attorney and the States Attorney. Immunity, as you point out, is a hell of a step. There is no way we should grant transactional. We could be giving immunity to a murderer."

"I agree," Xavier contributed, "and part of any grant, if one is given, should specify that it is contingent on the grantee not being the principal in the kidnapping."

"I hear what you two are saying," Milt said, "and I heard what Straus said, but is there really a crushing hurry? Would midnight be as good as now? I want my cake, and I want to eat it too. We work the payoff, and grab everybody, and find Jean—all without immunity. If for some reason we can't come up with Jean by a certain time, we deal immunity."

Al ended the discussion. "What I hear you both say, and I say it too, is that we are going to deal with Straus on some level. Time to call Mary."

Mary Lowe was the U.S. Attorney for the Southern District of Florida. She had been appointed two years ago to what is probably the busiest federal district in the United States.

Al placed the call to Mary, who had been briefed on the case at its inception, but had not been apprised of any of the developments of that day. He began by bringing her up to date on the investigation, and then added, "Now that you're reasonably current, let me get to the purpose of the call. The case took an interesting twist a few minutes ago, and it can best be conveyed by your listening to a short tape. What you are about to hear is a call I returned to an attorney by the name of John Straus. I'll play the tape on the speaker phone; Xavier and Milt are here, and I think we will benefit from a four-person conversation."

Mary concurred and Al began the tape.

At the end of the recorded phone conversation, Al stopped the playback. "That's it. I would imagine that whatever we decide you'll want to coordinate with Emory Steel, since it's likely the case will go to state prosecution. We've had a female contact. Based on language she used and what Straus is telling us now, it would appear that she is Straus's client. After we're finished, I'll have that earlier tape played for you, if you want. Both tapes will be available for Steel to hear also."

Mary asked the big question. "What's your evaluation? What do you suggest we do?"

"We've discussed this briefly; the call is only a few minutes old. Let me try to summarize where I think we are.

"We think you ought to discuss use immunity with Straus with the proviso that it is effective only if his client is not the principal. At this point we feel transactional immunity is too big a price. Use immunity might also be conditioned on Jean being alive.

"You certainly are entitled to ask for a more detailed proffer than what has been supplied so far. We suggest you try to pump him. He's really asking us to buy a pig in a poke."

Al looked over at Xavier, who nodded in agreement. "Bottom line: If the client is not the principal, give what you have to. We're going ahead with the payoff, but all of us are concerned with what we heard from the female subject. Jean is in trouble."

Al let this sink in before going on. "I didn't mention this to Straus, but I will when we talk again; and you may consider mentioning it also. Straus is in violation of the Rules of Professional Conduct, which I'm sure you are aware of, whereby he is under obligation to reveal information to prevent his client from committing a crime, or to prevent death or substantial bodily harm. If he doesn't comply, we can charge him before the bar and he could lose his 'ticket.'

"Also, since he is in violation of the Rules, I suggest that kidnapping, a continuing crime, opens him up to possible criminal prosecution. This could be very serious if we find a corpse, which became a corpse while he was sitting on information that might have freed her. I don't intend to beat him over the head with this, but I'll kind of throw it out there for him to chew on. It's a card we ought to play. It may even suggest an opening to him, a way to help us, since those sections provide an exemption from client confidentiality—indeed, a duty to divulge what he knows. He expressed a moral, human desire to supply the information, which I think was genuine. This may help him do that, without immunity for his client."

The warmth of the sun did not stimulate Jean's body. . . . It was Christmas, and Jean was watching her three little ones scream with the joy of Christmas and the obvious arrival of Santa Claus as they ran from her to Rob and back to her. She had trouble raising her arms to catch them, and somewhere deep in her mind she remarked on how strange the Christmas tree looked. Rob should have sprayed it before he brought it in the house. It was crawling with bugs.

CHAPTER 15

The player on the other side is hidden from us.

—T. H. HUXLEY, *A Liberal Education*

Stanley first stopped at a Radio Shack and told Mona to wait in the car. He walked into the store, looked around for a moment and then approached a clerk. "I'm interested in a scanner. My wife's not been feelin' well lately and's home a lot. She likes excitement, and I figgered a scanner that got fire and police calls would entertain her some. You got one with Metro police, maybe Homestead—and oh, yeah, how 'bout FBI?"

The clerk smiled. "No problem. Have one right here, and it's hooked up with fire rescue and City of Miami Police too. Lots of room for anything else you want to hear."

Stanley picked up the small receiver. "That work in a car, case we take a drive and park or picnic and she wants to hear?"

The clerk was very helpful. "Absolutely. It has a place for batteries, or you can plug it in at home with this wall outlet adaptor that comes with it."

"Okay, I'll take one. Might's well battery her up and give me a list of who's who on those numbers."

The clerk rang up the purchase and handed over a list of the frequencies utilized by various governmental agencies.

Stanley paid for the purchase with a hot credit card he had picked up from a waiter who worked at a local restaurant. It had been left by a customer. He carried his purchase to the car.

Stanley tore off the packaging, threw it in the back seat, and inserted the batteries in the radio. He checked the clerk's frequency list and entered the ones for Metro Police—there were ten. There were seven frequencies for the FBI, and these were also entered. He selected three Homestead frequencies and entered those.

As he listened to the police chatter he began thinking of contact points that would allow him to watch Stockton, or anyone working with him. He had to be sure there were no police. And even if he were sure of that, the pass of money had to be so good that not even police presence would catch him. The old shell game. Yes, he could do it. He just needed a little refining of his idea, and he knew he'd have it just right.

He sat for some time, thinking. Mona was next to him, watching. Her mind too, was occupied, but even if it weren't, she would never interrupt Donnie when he was in one of his "thinking" sessions.

Mona was uneasy. Had she done the right thing that morning? She had been worried that Donnie was going to just leave Jean in the woods. He had left her for so long already without food, water or clothes. The days were only in the middle seventies, and the nights got down to fifty-five. What Jean must be suffering from—cold, animals, lack of food and water—bothered Mona. Mona was also afraid Jean might die, and that she and Donnie would face a murder charge. Women had been executed for murder, and Mona wanted no part of jail, let alone execution.

Mona had had no real plan. She only knew that she wanted to have someone find Jean, and she wanted to do it in such a way that she would not get in trouble with Donnie or the law. While she was shopping the day before, she had picked up a newspaper, and in the local section noticed a story about a lawyer who was defending someone on a murder charge. The lawyer's name was Straus.

That was when the idea came to her. She could tell a lawyer what she knew. She knew he couldn't tell anybody about her, but he could get the information out that would locate Jean. She would be protected, and Jean could be found. She had looked up Straus in the phone book this morning and called.

She recalled, vividly, the conversation; it was the first time she had ever done anything like this. When his secretary had answered, "Law office," Mona had hesitated for just a second. "I need ta talk to Mr. Straus. We kidnapped someone and I'm 'fraid she's goin' ta die."

There was a very slight intake of breath on the other end and Mona heard, "Please hold a moment."

The next voice she heard was male. "This is John Straus. Before you say anything, do you want me to represent you? Do you want me to be your lawyer?"

Mona was surprised by the question but gave a weak "Yeah."

"My fee is $200 for the initial consultation. I charge $150 per hour thereafter. Is this acceptable?"

Straus got another "Yeah."

"Now, you mentioned something about a kidnapping. First, though, give me your name, address and phone number."

Mona, again caught by surprise, mixed lies and truth. "My name's Mona Little, I'm here temporary. We're at the Cavalier Motel on U.S. 1; I don't have a phone number with me. I'm callin' from a pay phone on the highway."

Mona had decided not to tell the lawyer where she and Donnie were living. The lawyer might call and Donnie might answer.

Straus continued, "I don't do business on the phone. When can you come in to see me?"

Mona got scared, and thought maybe this wasn't a good idea. She wanted to get a message across, not be drawn into these discussions. "I can't now. There's somebody with me. I have to get away from him first. When I do, then I can come in, an' pay you too." Mona thought the "pay" remark was a particularly good touch. "I don't think we can wait for that, though. The reason I'm callin' and not waitin' to be in your office is cause this woman we got may die, and I gotta get her some help."

There was a pause as Straus thought about the ramifications of this strange call. He wondered if this was a nut call that was wasting his valuable time. His intuition, developed over years of such calls, said it was for real. He also sensed that this caller was being deliberately evasive, and he would never see a fee. If he continued talking with her he would hear something he would be better off not hearing, and he would be involved in time-consuming problems with no compensation. Straus knew he had no choice, morally he had to listen. "Tell me what your problem is."

Mona unloaded. "On Monday, Donnie—he's my guy—an' me, we kidnapped this woman, Jean Stockton, from her house in a place called Cape Cutler in south Dade. It's near 184th Street and Old Cutler. Donnie called her old man and asked for $250,000. The husband didn't show Monday night with the money. Anyway, Donnie couldn't carry her round, so he took her to the 'glades and tied her to some trees. She's on her back, legs and arms tied down so she can't move, tape over her mouth. She wasn't wearin' nothin' but a nightgown, and Donnie ripped that. She's been there two days, and we ain't been back to see her. Donnie won't tell nobody where she's at, and I'm scared she'll die, if she ain't already."

"Mona," Straus said, "you did right to call. I'll help you, but you've got to come to the office. We have to know where to look for her. The Everglades is a huge area, there are no street addresses. I'll call and find out which agency is working on it and get a deal for you—immunity, which means you won't be prosecuted—but I've got to see you."

Mona knew she had to end this. "I'll try but

gettin' away from Donnie ain't easy. When will you know somethin'?"

"In an hour or less, depending on who I can reach. Can you give a good description of where you put this woman?"

Mona wasn't sure; she realized how little information she really had, but tried. "You go out 41, but don't go into the park. There's a canal on your right and you come to a Indian reservation on your left. Just a little past that there's a road to the right that goes over a dam on the canal. Pretty soon that road becomes dirt, and there's branches off it left and right. Maybe four or five miles on the dirt road there's a left road that kinda curves away, and about a mile or two down this road, you can see a hammock; and while the road doesn't look like it'll hit the hammock, it curves into it. She's in there."

Mona had done the best she could. She wasn't sure that either she or Donnie could find that hammock again, but she felt maybe she could.

Straus went back over the directions Mona had given him, and fine-tuned some of them. "Mona, I'm going to do my very best for you and for that woman. I can't do it alone. You were part of this kidnapping. You just can't walk away and dump it on me. I need you to help. You must come here as soon as possible, and I want you to call me every half hour until you do. There will be problems and questions that only you can solve."

Mona knew she would never do this, but told him, "Okay, but I can't call so often. I can only call when I get away from him. I'll do it as often as I can." Mona, satisfied that she had done pretty much all she could, thanked Straus and hung up.

Mona, watching Donnie now and gnawing on her knuckle, was both worried that the call might come to hurt Donnie and relieved that she had done something to help Jean.

Al was involved in the interminable paper work that was too much the job of an SAC. He was, at last, making a dent in the pile that had accumulated, but he readily accepted the call from Dr. Sheldon Wright, who was doing the psycholinguistics examination.

"I see you've got another one," Dr. Wright began.

"Shelly, they seem to follow me. You guys any good at removing these curses?"

"Sorry. My witchcraft doesn't extend to making life easy for Agents in Charge."

"Has your witchcraft told you anything about the guy who sent us those notes?"

"My cauldron is dry and I'm out of eye of newt. We didn't get much. His being bound by what he could scavenge out of a newspaper interferes with the reflection of his psyche in the messages. Your subject is male. He's moderately educated. High school, maybe a year of college, but I doubt it. He's been in trouble with the law before. He's probably Caucasian. I think under the right circumstances he could be violent. Age? That's tough. Probably under fifty, most likely under forty. That's about all I can tell you. I'll send the full report and back-up documentation through channels.

"As usual, when you get him, and you always do, call me and let's chat about where I was right and wrong. It's how I learn."

"Thanks, Doc. As always we appreciate the help, but work on removing my curse."

With a final laugh, they hung up.

Al called Xavier and Milt into the office and gave them a rundown on Wright's analysis.

When Al had finished, Milt reported, "I was about to call you. I think we've got a make on the Xerox machine. The samples from the machine at Cutler Ridge Library look like a match to the Xerox engineer. He feels so good about it that I've had the coin box pulled, and we're doing interviews of the library personnel."

"Damn," Al smiled. "Maybe we're getting somewhere."

Stanley sat bolt upright. He had been inspired. The whole thing had suddenly come to him out of the blue. It could be done. With a cry of triumph that shook Mona out of her reverie, he bolted from the car and returned to Radio Shack.

He found the clerk who had waited on him before standing near the door. The clerk recognized him and asked, "Something else we can help you with today?"

Stanley, excited by his revelation, didn't try to follow his prior cover story, even if the clerk cared or remembered, which he didn't. "Yeah, I'd like to see some handitalkies, the most powerful ya got."

The clerk accommodated him. "These are four watt, the most you can buy. They cover all CB channels—I assume you want CB. We have some marine radios that are a watt more in power, but they're supposed to be used only on water and they're much more expensive."

"How far will these CB radios go?"

The clerk really wasn't sure, but told Stanley, "About two miles."

A mile would have been a better guess, but Stanley took three of them, paying with the same hot credit card.

From Radio Shack, Stanley's shopping spree took him to K mart. There he bought a pair of 7×50 binoculars, because they were the biggest pair they had. The hot card did its work.

Now Stanley needed some pay-phone numbers. He didn't want to use the numbers he had previously picked, although he might use some, he'd see. Right now he was studying the best spots. He spent over an hour driving to shopping centers, checking phones, their locations and numbers. He wrote down the locations and made notes as to whether they were observable, and whether they would do well or only marginally well.

Stanley was really working on this project; he was—rare for Stanley—expending real thought and effort.

One thing Stanley knew for sure: He was not going to front himself, except for one contact— the money. He would put Mona out front. If the cops were there, it would be Mona's voice on tape, not his. If the cops were watching, they would see Mona on telephones, not Stanley. He had to be sure that Mona followed orders. He had less than complete confidence in her intelligence or her ability to follow his instructions.

The CB radios gave him the ability to direct the scam without him actually showing, and to be sure everything was in place before he moved.

If he could rely on Mona, he should be able to keep abreast of what was going down.

Stanley wondered if he should steal or borrow a car. They could use another car under his new plan. He decided, though, no. For now he would go with the car they had. They could use cabs if they had to; a hot car might prove a real liability if it was reported and spotted.

They reached the house and Stanley parked. They both went inside. Stanley unwrapped the CB radios and tuned them to channel twenty-four where he couldn't hear any transmissions. He gave one to Mona and sent her outside. Stanley, using the other two, talked to Mona to make sure they worked.

Satisfied with their performance, he summoned Mona back inside, and talked to her for half an hour until he was sure that Mona knew what he wanted her to do.

Mona left, alone, in the car. On her way to Perrine, a small community in south Dade County, she stopped to call Straus. The lawyer came on the phone as soon as Mona said who was calling. She needed to know whether she and Stanley were in trouble as a result of her call. "What's happenin'? I only got a minute, and you told me to call."

Straus was visibly upset. "You've got to come here, now! This is getting more serious. I've talked to the FBI and the prosecutors. They know about Jean Stockton; I had to give them a name. You've got to get out now, or both of us could have problems. Get out now and I think I can fix it so you're clean. Right now they don't want to give you absolute immunity—that is, promise never to prosecute you; they only want to promise not to use what we give them against you."

When she didn't reply, Straus realized she was confused. "I really can't help you in this without your being here where we can talk as I talk to them. You just can't continue working in a kidnapping and trying to deal with the police at the same time. Come out. Come to my office."

Mona was silent for a second. "Thanks, I know you're doin' right, I'll try to get there. It ain't easy. He's here. I'll call agin." With that, she hung up.

Though troubled, Mona had an overriding loyalty to Stanley. While she might try to save Jean's life on the one hand, she could not walk out on Stanley. Mona could not see the contradiction in this. The fact that he had told the FBI about Jean worried her also, but she saw no other way to deal with it. Stanley had told her his scheme was "police proof"; that even if the police were in the case they would never be caught—and she believed him. The bottom line was she had to go through with his scheme. And she couldn't tell him about Straus.

She got back in the car and, following Stanley's orders, drove to a place in Perrine called The Porch. The name was not official but the most descriptive and widely known. It was a large, old building with an old-fashioned, southern-style, roofed-and-columned porch across the front. It was a hangout frequented by idlers, thieves and dopers. If you wanted to buy or sell stolen merchandise, this was the place. It was also a hiring hall for any criminal enterprise. One could stop by here and announce a projected burglary or robbery or larceny and recruit accomplices with ease.

Mona parked a few yards away from The Porch, got out and walked over to some twenty men, seated and standing about, conversing in small groups. As she walked toward them, an unusual figure in their male world, the conversation died and she became the sole object of attention.

She stopped and looked at them; there was silence among them. Mona broke it. "I'm lookin' for a man with a small skiff or canoe with a outboard to do some night work."

The reply was much whooping and hollering and laughter about the kind of night work they could do for Mona. She just stood and looked. This ribaldry didn't come close to fazing her. The men soon sensed this was business, and they calmed down.

A voice challenged, "You payin', momma?"

"I'll talk with the man that's got what I want."

A heavy man of about Mona's height separated himself from the others and moved toward the stairs. He came down and walked over to Mona. "I'm Adam, the men call me Ad. My bro' got a boat lak what you want. I use it."

Mona had her man. "Let's talk." As she began leading him away, the other men called out sexual comments, accompanied by obscene gestures that followed Adam and Mona to Mona's car.

Adam, at Mona's hand motion, got in the car asking, "What you want this here boat fo', an' how much you pay?"

Mona put him off. "Got to talk to the man 'bout that. Hey, I only fetch and carry." Then, taking a long, hard look at Adam, said, "Maybe I can do a few other things."

Adam started getting hard, and wasn't even sure why.

After Mona crossed to the east side of the highway she stopped at a small grocery that had a phone. It too was populated by men waiting for the opportunity for a quick score.

Mona looked at Adam. "We got to call the man. Can you handle these dudes, or do I have trouble?"

Adam smiled. "Why momma, when you with me, you okay."

With this less than assuring answer, Mona parked the car, and she and Adam got out to the curious stares of the idlers and their laughing, lurid remarks. Adam ate it up, exchanging good-humored banter with everyone. Finally he stopped it. "Okay, now hush it up; we got business and need ta use the phone wifout a buncha brayin'."

Mona dropped in a quarter and punched up the phone in the house. Stanley came on. "I got someone who says he's got the boat you want. His name's Adam."

Mona handed the phone to Adam, who greeted Stanley and heard in return only, "Describe your boat."

"It be 'bout fourteen feet an' got a real flat bottom, sure is skiff, square ends, got a three outboard. Ma bro' use it fo' fishin' canals. When you want it, and what fo'?"

"I need it tonight for about two hours. A man is goin' to give me a package, an' I don't want his friends finding me later. You dig?"

Adam understood that kind of a deal. "Yeah, I got it."

Stanley continued, "Nothin' heavy, I just need insurance. It'll be worth $200, for the two hours. The girl'll give you $20 now an' $180 in cut halves of twenty-dollar bills. You get the other half when you show. If you do good and this works, you'll get somethin' extra."

Adam, suspicious, asked, "This here a dope deal? I git heavy bread fo' dope deals."

"No, this ain't no dope deal. You'll see it ain't. I'm owed some bread, but I need to collect careful. You won't be hurtin'."

"Okay, man, I'll do 'er."

"Fine. Take the girl to see the boat, put it in the water and run it to where she tells you so you know exactly where to be tonight."

"Okay, man, you got it."

Adam and Mona got in the car, and Adam directed her to his brother's house. When they arrived he told her to stay in the car and he'd get the boat. After a few minutes Adam and another man exited the house and went around back.

After about five minutes Adam walked up to the car and advised Mona the boat and trailer were hooked up to his brother's truck. He would lead Mona to a ramp to launch the boat, if Mona would now tell him where she wanted to go.

Mona described the area she wanted to get to, and Adam told her to follow him to a launch site. When they arrived there, it was only a matter of minutes before the boat was in the water. Mona spent about half an hour with Adam showing him what Stanley wanted him to do. After they finished and put the boat back on the trailer, Mona gave Adam one of the radios and showed him which channel to use. Then Mona gave Adam an unexpected dividend, as ordered by Stanley, which guaranteed his presence that night.

While alone at the house, Stanley had spent his time scripting out the calls. He would have Mona copy them in her handwriting. If she were picked up, he wanted nothing of his on her. Then he would dispose of his copies. He was trying to think of anything she had, or if there was anything in the house, or on him, that would in any way tie him in to the kidnapping. He had to be careful now. Things were going to get tough soon.

For $250,000 he decided he would kill Mona or Stockton or both. He dug out an old Colt Detective Special. He had traded for it some time ago, and had kept it hidden in a drawer with some old junk. Mona didn't know he had it. It was now in his waistband.

Then he turned to his police scanner. He was upset with it. He was getting Metro and Homestead fine. He thought he had figured out what frequencies would most likely be used to watch for his kind of activity. But he couldn't know that the scanner was on main repeater channels, and for this kind of an operation Metro would use point-to-point communication, not a repeater. If they had county-wide surveillance they might then take a repeater channel. The close-in work would be point-to-point. It was the FBI he was upset with. Some of the channels he had been given came in fine, but on others, all he got was a burst of static. He finally called Radio Shack complaining that there was something wrong with his scanner. The clerk who answered said that some FBI channels were scrambled and could not be understood. So Stanley decided to settle for what he had. He had covered most of the police frequencies and felt he'd hear if something was going down.

He was waiting when Mona drove up. He got in the car and told her to drive to a barbecue. "I want something to eat." Stanley read the messages he had written out and numbered. When they arrived at the barbecue, he ordered and, as Mona ate, she copied the messages and numbered them to conform to Stanley's originals. Stanley told her the copies were necessary so he could have a set also.

The day had come out of the east, clear and warm and beautiful. Wednesday, February 20 was a perfect day in "paradise."

The sun penetrated the thick canopy of trees in the hammock with thin slices of light that moved as the day aged.

A casual visitor to the hammock, such as the small black snake now inspecting Jean, would not have detected any life in the small, dirty body lying spread eagle on the forest floor. The breathing was so light that the chest wall did not move. Her body temperature was now in the middle eighties; her eyes were closed. Jean had not been conscious of her surroundings for about the last six hours. For the twelve hours before that, only a sharp pain or external trauma brought her back to her terror. She had been able to escape to her

family during most of her ordeal, but now there
was nothing, just a void.

Her exposed body was stung and scratched and
bitten as the animals and insects of the forest
probed and feasted.

CHAPTER 16

Time shall unfold what plighted cunning hides.
—SHAKESPEARE, *King Lear*, I, i

M ona, this is it," Stanley said. "This is our big chance, the score we been waitin' for. You and me together, baby, we can do it. Just do what I tell you, listen to me and do it right. I planned it out. I'm goin' to be lookin', and I'll take the big chance at the money. You just gotta make some calls while I watch for cops. Ain't nothin to be scared of, long as you do exactly what you're told. You got the notes I wrote. Read! Just read! Don't talk with him. Don't answer questions. Read an' get off the phone. If he interrupts or asks questions, read that special line I gave you. Just stop and read that sentence, then go on and don't stop again.

"Keep the radio in your purse. If I see anything, I'll call you. You do the same for me. We'll use channel twenty-four, where there ain't no noise just like I told you."

* * *

Al sought out Lieutenant Jimmy Young and played the Straus tape for him, advising him of the call to Mary, and that Mary would be calling State Attorney Emory Steel. Jimmy updated his commander and called Steel.

Mary called Al and related that within the space of an hour she had three interesting talks with Straus. On the second occasion she had used some tough language with him. She had picked up on Al's lead regarding "duty to divulge," and had pointed out that she would not hesitate to indict him, along with his client, if the facts warranted. She felt that Straus was concerned about Jean and, in part, continued in the case because he felt morally obligated. Mary wanted information, and so she had reluctantly put this added pressure on Straus.

Straus was concerned about his criminal liability. He recognized that what Mary had said in the heat of discussion was not without merit. He nevertheless felt compelled to continue to demand transactional immunity. However, he wasn't sure how long he would hold out. He had agreed to contact his client and attempt to reach a compromise that the state would accept. The last negotiating position of the state was (1) absolute assurance that the client was not the principal—if the government proves by clear and convincing evidence that the client was the principal, immunity will not apply; (2) use immunity with no testimony; or (3) no immunity, testimony and a three-year cap on the sentence.

Mary relayed the gist of the third call to Al. "The client was to have contacted Straus every hour, but there have only been two contacts.

Straus has never met his client face-to-face. Everything so far has been done by phone. Straus says his client is under someone's control and doesn't know how to reach him. So, we've just been waiting for a client contact so Straus can put our offer to him. Straus is becoming more and more concerned about Jean, and about his own position. Straus's closing question to me was, 'Why me?' I think if Straus does not hear from the client within the next hour or so, he's going to act. I don't know what he'll do, but the result may be that we have his information." Al thanked Mary and they both agreed to keep in close touch.

Agents in cars spread out all over Dade County waited impatiently as the minutes dragged by. Rob sat, got up and paced, sat, got up and paced. His mind was churning, going over again and again what he had been instructed to do and say. He weighed his responsibility to Jean and again declined an offer of substitution. Henry and Grover checked and rechecked their equipment. The Datsun was inspected. Over all, there was an expectant silence; no one would miss the ring of the telephone.

By five o'clock everyones' tempers were wearing thin. "Take it out! Get the damn thing out of the package!" Rob said adamantly. "I want a clean package. I'm not taking a chance he'll find it."

Henry and Grover had fitted the tracker into the double bag, and had been about to show Stockton how to activate it. He refused to even look at it.

Henry called Al, and Al got on the phone with a man who was not in a mood to listen.

Al heard deep fear in Stockton's voice, fear that came out as anger. "If Peter tears it open to look at the money, or feels the hard spot in the bottom of the bag, he could find the radio. I know why you want it, but it's too risky. I told you, I want a clean payoff!"

Al tried to reason with him. "I can't guarantee he won't find it. I can't guarantee my car will start when I go to join the surveillance. You're accepting several risks on faith when you go forward with this payoff. The question is, are they acceptable risks? Is the potential return worth the risk?

"Let me offer a compromise. If Peter lets you talk to Jean, there is a greater likelihood that he will release her on payoff. The money is double bagged, and the tracker is between the bags in the bottom with some cardboard stiffener to mask it. If you talk to Jean, tear off the outer bag and drop the tracker. If he won't let you talk to Jean give him the bag with the tracker."

Stockton was confused by all this talk. He wanted what he wanted, but he stopped and composed himself. After a long pause he partially agreed, more to halt the discussion than anything else. "Let me consider that. It's possible I could buy that, but I lean toward trying to do it without any chance of his finding out you guys are on this."

Phil Bentley was not on station as yet. He was trying to clear up some remaining F.I. leads, and the Richard Stanley lead. He was in Florida City, a little south of his sector. He wasn't in his car. He carried his hand-held radio, which would announce any contact, at which time he would go mobile.

Telephone company security people were at their computers. The trap and trace on Stockton's home phone would register the calling number on the phone company computer as soon as his number was dialed, and before it even rang. The originating number and address would be in the hands of the surveilling units almost before the first "hello" was even spoken. With this timely advice, the surveillance stood a much better chance of being on the originating phone before the kidnapper disconnected.

It was a race between caller and surveillance. The FBI needed every edge it could get if they were to win the race.

At precisely 5:30 Stockton's phone rang. Since it was expected that the initial call would come to Stockton's home, Henry was on an open line to the office.

At the first ring Henry, wearing earphones connected to the recorder, hardwired into the phone line, said one word to both the surveillance radio and office: "Incoming."

The phone company security officer almost simultaneously told the office, "Pay phone, 12335 Kendall Drive, Phillips 66."

The office radio broadcast, "Incoming, pay phone, Phillips 66, 12335 Kendall."

On the fourth ring Stockton picked up and said, "Hello?"

Seventy cars had slipped into gear and five were moving toward the Phillips station.

"Mr. Stockton?"

"Yes."

"This is Peter's friend."

Henry spoke two words to the office and simultaneously on the radio: "Contact, female."

Phil had introduced himself to Richard Stanley, who had checked out as being a reputable Florida City–Homestead contractor. He had lived in the area for about twenty years, and had been building small- to medium-scale homes for about the last fifteen.

Phil started out explaining that he was chasing some leads for that damn Miami office, and confessed that he didn't really know what it was all about. "They never tell us guys in the country what the hell they're doin'. They expect us to be mind readers. Anyway, someone wants me to check on an old blue Chevy with a license plate that comes back to you, AIZ-954. The car was probably seen someplace; hell, the number could even be screwed up. You know this car?"

Richard Stanley thought for a minute, and then Phil saw a flicker of recognition cross his face. "Yeah, I think so. That must be the old car I had in the barn up in the Redlands. A ten-year-old blue Chevy. I own an old farm out there, and I'm leavin' my cousin Donnie stay there. He's kind of in-between jobs. Donnie found the old car and fixed it; he did get a license plate for it about six months ago. The title's to me, so he would've registered it in my name, probably. Come to remember, I did get the registration mailed here.

Donnie's just kind of keepin' an eye on the farm for me. Hope he's not in trouble again."

Phil perked up at that last remark. "What kind of trouble has he been in?"

Richard Stanley was somewhat embarrassed. "Nothin' real serious. Some small thefts mostly. I heard he did one or two county-jail sentences in other states. He's been a problem, since he's a boy. Hasn't caused me any problem, though, since he's been back from up north—that's 'bout six months now. Really hadn't seen or heard much for a coupla years. 'Fact, ain't seen him but two or three times since he's back."

"Just for the record, can you tell me what he looks like?"

"Sure, he's 'bout twenty-five, don't remember his birthdate; he's twenty years younger'n me. About six-two, weighs two hundred, maybe two-ten, well-built, good-lookin' guy, sometimes wears glasses, brown hair parted in the middle—strange way if you ask me."

"Wouldn't happen to have a photo, would you? Maybe the easiest way to get Miami off our backs is to show this as the wrong car."

"No, sure don't. This is soundin' serious."

"Just routine police-type stuff. Always got to ask the questions from the list, or the boss gets pissed. What's the address in the Redlands where he's staying?"

"Man, you'll never find it without a guide, but it's 35071 Southwest 289th Street."

"Is your cousin working?"

"Don't really know. Figure he got to be doin' somethin' to live. I give him a few bucks, but not enough to live for six months."

"You know any of his friends?"

"Nope."

Phil decided to go further. "You're pretty well known down here, got lots of friends, business acquaintances. Your cousin ever meet them, or work for you where he'd meet them?"

"Not this trip. But a couple years back, I recall, he came down for the winter, kinda like now, and I gave him some construction work. So, he woulda been out on jobs then and met some business people."

Phil thanked him for his time, told him not to be concerned, that he was sure it was very likely a Miami mistake.

As Phil left he concluded that Richard's cousin Donald warranted attention, and received the "contact" message on his hand-held as he was walking toward his car. The call was in another sector. Phil was moving into traffic when the radio announced, "Disconnect five thirty-three p.m., one minute ago."

Stanley and Mona were driving down Kendall Drive looking for a pay phone and found one Stanley liked just west of 123rd Avenue. "Mona, you got the right note? It's the one with the number 'one' on top. Don't get 'em mixed up. In fact, leave 'em all on the seat 'cept the one you're goin' to read. Take the special one for interruptions along too. Remember, stick to what's there, don't let him get you into talkin'."

Mona exited the car. She knew all these needless instructions from Stanley were just signs of his nervousness. Stanley had parked up against the back wall of the Phillips 66 station. Of the three open sides to the station, one side faced the street, and the other two faced rows of pumps. The station was self-service and also had a convenience store. There were two banks of pay phones consisting of two phones each, a bank on each side of the building, facing the pumps.

Mona walked around the corner of the building to the phones on the east side of the building. The phones were not being used, and Mona lifted the receiver of one and dropped in a quarter; she punched up Stockton's number. As soon as Stockton acknowledged his identity, she began to read.

"Take the money, in the brown Publix bag, and use the Datsun. Come alone. Anyone with you, or we see police, and Jean is dead."

At this point Stockton broke in: "I want to talk to Jean. I told you last time I wanted to talk to her before we arranged for delivery of the money."

Mona looked at the other piece of paper she had in her hand and read, "Don't interrupt or you will miss these important instructions. There is no room for questions or requests. You do it our way or we stop now and Jean dies."

Mona again commenced reading. "Be at the middle public phone in front of the Burdine's store, Dadeland Mall, at five-fifty-five. You will be contacted."

Stockton jumped in just as she was about to hang up, and caught her unawares. "Let me make sure I've got it right, I'm writing it down. That's Dadeland Mall, Burdine's store, middle phone in front of the store, use the Datsun, $250,000 in brown Publix bag. Got it right?"

Mona responded with a natural reflex, "Yes."

Stockton knew he had her talking, off script. "Okay. Now if something happens, I get a flat tire or whatever and I don't show, call me again right away, okay? I want to pay."

There was no response to this from Mona, but she stayed on the line listening.

"Now, how about passing a message to Jean if I can't talk to her? I'd like an answer back to be sure she's all right."

Mona, not sure what to do, answered, "No, there's no time. You've got to do what he wants right now."

"What can I do to speed this up? Could you and I meet somewhere to talk about Jean?"

Mona was getting more uneasy. "No, no way," came the immediate reply.

Stockton began to push. "Who's the man I talked to first? Is he the problem?"

Mona was panicked. "No! No, I can't talk. Do as he says." There was a click. Mona had hung up.

Henry, listening in on the call, heard the drop instructions through his headset. He was on the radio simultaneously with the call. "New drop, center phone in front of Burdine's, Dadeland Mall at five-fifty-five."

There were several sector cars at the Dadeland Mall. As soon as Mona hung up, Henry was dialing Al, and Grover was punching out the erase tabs on the cassette and rewinding it. As Al came on, they were prepared to replay the tape for him, Xavier and Milt.

After the tape had been run through, Al remarked to Henry, "I like it less and less. Rob did a great job. Do you or Grover have any thoughts?"

Henry put the question to Grover, who responded negatively.

"Let me talk to Rob for a second." Stockton came on. "That was excellent. Henry couldn't have done better. Keep that up and we'll have them. What about the tracker?"

"Leave it in the package; I'd better go."

"Okay, we're with you."

Mona disconnected and walked back around the corner to where Stanley was parked and got in beside him. She had barely closed the door when he was backing out of the parking slot and pulling out onto Kendall Drive to head east toward Dadeland Mall.

His first words as he put the car in forward gear were "What the fuck took you so long? I told you not to talk with him."

"I didn't; he asked a question one time, and I read your special note and then went on. When I finished, he just said, 'Let me make sure I got it,' and he repeated what I told him. Then he said, if somethin' happens, like a flat tire, to call him again', he wants to pay."

Stanley wasn't sure how to handle this. He had wanted Mona off fast, but he admitted to himself that Stockton had to understand the directions, not like the stupid truck problem they had Monday. He compromised by swearing at her, and telling her to get off the phone next time as quick as she could.

The sector cars covering the area in which the Phillips 66 was located had about two minutes, from advice to disconnect, to locate the phone and caller, assuming the caller would leave immediately after hanging up. One car was there within four minutes of the announcement of the location. That car, driven by Jack Petersen, actually passed Stanley. He was heading west on Kendall as Stanley was heading east. He saw Stanley's car along with a dozen others, but could not get license-plate numbers over his shoulder. There would have been an advantage to two-man cars in this kind of situation, but Al had opted for the heavier saturation that one-man cars afforded. His manpower pool was not bottomless.

Petersen entered the Phillips 66 station area on the east side, announced his location on the radio, and spotted two phones; neither was in use. He circled around behind the station to the west side and saw two more phones; one was in use. He parked, got out and strolled over. Reaching into his pocket for a quarter, he stepped into the empty phone cubicle. He could not make out the muted conversation next to him, so he deposited his coin and punched up 271-9311, the number that had been used to call Stockton. If he got a busy signal his neighbor would be the subject of continued interest. He got a ring. He hung up, retrieved his quarter, and walked around the building to the other phone bank. His neighbor caller's description was nonetheless noted.

The phones on the east side of the building were still not in use. Jack checked the area but could not focus on any loiterers or anyone giving any indication of interest in him or the phones. He walked up to them as another sector car pulled in; the driver saw Jack and they established eye communication.

The second car pulled up next to the west side of the building and parked. The agent, Debbie Sanchez, left the car and walked into the convenience store. Jack knew she was just going to listen and observe. Perhaps a customer was lingering too long. People who came to these stores were usually in a hurry.

Jack had identified the phone that Mona had used, and was considering posting an OUT OF ORDER sign, but then decided to wait for another contact, to make sure the subject had gone elsewhere. As he was considering what to do next, a young lady emerged from the store carrying a bag and placing change in her purse. She walked over to a red Pontiac that was parked at a gas pump opposite the phone that was used to make the Stockton call.

As she approached her car, Jack walked over to her, displaying his credentials and introducing himself. "Hi, I'm Jack Petersen, FBI. Got a small problem we're working on. Could you spare me a moment for a quick question?"

The woman stopped, and Jack accepted this as agreement. "While you were filling up at the pump did you notice a woman making a call at that phone over there?"

"Yeah, I did. I wasn't really looking, but I did notice her. She kind of ran away from the phone and went behind the station, got into an old car with a guy, and they took off in a hurry."

Jack thought, "Bingo. Now go slow, but keep her." He continued, "I really hate to inconvenience you, but it's pretty important for me to get what you can recall about them. Tell me what the girl looked like."

The woman was interested, and launched into a description. "I did take notice of her. There was nothing else to look at while I was pumping the gas. She looked about thirty-five, tall, maybe five-ten and thin, skinny, maybe a hundred and thirty pounds. She had blond hair, not natural. There was nothing striking about her, but she was attractive. No hat. She had on a red blouse, real low cut, but not very much up there to show, blue jeans, sneakers, I think, and a big brown shoulder bag. She had hoop earrings and a gold chain necklace, plain. She wore no lipstick. Her hands looked funny, but I can't place why. Oh! she had a real shiner, left eye."

Jack, busily taking notes, remarked, "Anytime you want a job with us I'll recommend your powers of observation."

She laughed, pleased. "You guys think us girls look at you? Hell no, we look at each other, to size up the competition." She laughed again, and Jack got her name, address and phone number.

"Was the woman white?"

"Oh yeah, white woman."

"Did you notice the car, can you describe it?"

"Not too well. It was blue, GM, big, like a old Buick or Chevy or Olds."

"How about the man? Can you remember him?"

"No, except that he was white. That's about all I noticed." Jack thanked her and told her he might bother her again.

He was rewarded with a bright smile and "It won't be no bother."

Jack went back to his car and immediately broadcast the description of the car and occupants as possible suspects. Then he moved his car far back in the lot and opened his hood. He took his hand-held radio, laid it out of sight in the motor well, and began making spurious repairs. Debbie exited the store after five minutes, everyone else having preceded her and left the area. She saw Jack's cover and drove her car over to his and stood with him.

She had, when she arrived, advised her sector units that the Phillips was covered. This freed up the cars for any other calls in their sector.

The rest of the sector kept moving in their area but drifted east toward Dadeland. Part of SPIT was off to Dadeland before Stockton had hung up the phone, and would be in place a good ten minutes before Rob would arrive.

One of the sector agents entered the enclosure of the middle phone in front of Burdine's, lifted the receiver and dialed 200-222-2222. A computer voice responding to the dialed number supplied the number of the phone he was dialing from and he advised the office to insure that the trap and trace was up on the correct bank. This was done well before Peter could have arrived from the Phillips station. The phone company was up on all three phones. SPIT was soon close in around the contact phone trying to spot a surveillance of the phone by Peter. The outer SPIT perimeter was with Rob, moving toward the drop site.

When Rob arrived, he would be "handed off" to the inner SPIT perimeter; his escort would then begin taking license-plate numbers of cars that attracted their attention, and would also try to make a countersurveillance. A survey of the area by SPIT did not detect any pay phones from which the contact phone could be observed and Al decided to put the Cessna up. It would lock onto the Datsun. Even though Stockton gave a running account of where he was over the body bug, Al liked the redundancy of the Cessna following the tracker and the tiny infrared strobe on the Datsun. Also, if the package were dropped with the other tracker, the Cessna would be the best receiver of its quarter watt of power. The plane could also follow a car that an agent might spot and mark. The airplane was never seen or heard and, unlike a car surveillance, could stay with a subject, one-on-one, and never be made. An ice-pick hole in a rear red light was a beacon to an airplane.

It took Stanley ten minutes to reach Dadeland. He was in place on the fourth floor of the parking garage, overlooking the Burdine's store, a good two hundred yards away, and separated by a huge parking area. His binoculars were out and ready.

The scanner had produced nothing. The police frequencies were busy with chatter about activities referred to by numbers that Stanley did not understand, but there was nothing even remotely suggesting any interest in his activities. He couldn't get much from the FBI channels, just bursts of static.

Phil had picked up on the "big, older model, blue, GM" that Jack had broadcast. He needed to give the information he had to the command post, but it was too lengthy and involved to put out on the air. He hesitated; if he left his car during this crucial period, he could be late in answering a contact in his sector. He decided to make a call instead, but selected a phone where he could park his car right at the phone.

Taking his hand-held radio with him, he punched up the office number and was soon on with one of the command-center agents. He provided the results of the Richard Stanley interview, emphasizing that the only link was the color of the car and the fact it was old and a GM product which, as Phil said, "leaves a lot of room for a lot of cars."

The agent who took the call conferred with Milt, and he decided to release a carefully worded radio transmission. He didn't want any of the agents to get the impression there were known subjects. The woman and the car at the Phillips station was most definitely only a suspect. The information from Phil created a possible suspect only if the Phillips information identifying a suspect was valid.

Sally, the radio operator, broadcast, "All units prepare to copy." She paused for a moment. "Suspect vehicle from 66 may be, repeat, may be 1982 blue Chevrolet Caprice, four door; Florida license AIZ-954, occupied by Donald Stanley, WM, twenty-five, six-two, weight two-ten, brown hair, center parted, muscular build."

Rob arrived at Burdine's at about 5:55. Stanley, using his binoculars, had detected nothing for the past fifteen minutes other than the usual flow of people and cars that were a part of the Dadeland shopping center. Several people had used one or more of the phones during that period. Finally he saw the red Datsun pull into the parking area and circle, passing the phones. He watched as Rob found a parking place several lanes away from the phone.

Rob walked toward the phone bank, carrying the brown paper-bag package cradled in his arm. He walked over to the center phone and stopped, staring at it. After a few minutes he began to pace back and forth, in front of the phone bank.

As Al and Xavier approached Dadeland, Al said, "We came mighty close at the 66. We only needed another minute. I think I know how to get that minute and maybe more." He picked up the mike and called Milt, asking him to switch to another channel so their discussion would not interfere with the surveillance channel.

"Milt, have the telephone company, using the computer, busy out the contact number but continue to trap it for incoming. When Peter or Mrs. Peter calls the contact number, he's going to get a busy signal. SPIT told us there are no phones that can observe the contact phone. Peter will have to assume someone is using the contact phone to make a call, or that he dialed the wrong number. Peter will probably pause for a moment to figure this out, and then will place the call again. We will have the originating number before he can place the call a second time. When Peter hangs up after the busy signal, the telephone company can unbusy the number. I'm tempted to keep it busy for two Peter tries, but I'm afraid of spooking him."

Milt hesitated, thought about suggesting that Stockton be told this, but held back. It would be included in the memo. His response was noncommittal, "10-4. I'll relay your request to the phone company."

Stanley watched Rob. More precisely, he watched the brown paper bag, for about a minute. After a last survey of the area around Stockton, he walked over to the blue Chevy and tossed the binoculars on the front seat next to Mona, got in, started the engine and pulled out of the parking garage.

They drove to the Falls, a shopping center on 136th Street and the Highway, about ten minutes from Dadeland. Stanley turned right on 136th Street and then left into a large parking area. He drove through it and stopped on the street in front of two public phones just to the west of the front entrance to the Oyster Bar. As Mona got out he snapped, "Now this time read the goddamn message and get off the phone."

Then he continued on to a parking garage just west of the parking lot.

As soon as Mona reached the left phone she punched up the number of the phone at the Burdine's store. It was now 6:12 p.m. Al's arrangement worked. Mona got a busy signal and listened to it for a moment, surprised. She hung up, undecided what to do next. Stanley hadn't told her what to do if this happened. For a moment she thought of going to the garage to ask Stanley what she should do, then she just redeposited the quarter and tried again.

The phone company computer had traced the busy call to the pay phone in front of the Oyster Bar, in the Falls at 8805 S.W. 137th Street. Sally advised the surveilling units of the location. This was on the edge of two sectors, and the supervisor allowed the first five responding cars, regardless of sector, to move toward the phone.

Rob was growing nervous. He had been there for almost fifteen minutes, and he was worried he had not gotten there fast enough, that Peter had gotten scared and left.

Grover's reassuring voice was in his ear, "Easy, he's delaying the call on purpose, just to try to spook you."

Stockton relaxed a little, but only a little. He just wanted to get this over with. The phone rang. Stockton said to his bug, "Phone ringing."

The phone company computer had shown the second incoming call and supplied the same number and location. Sally transmitted, "Contact, same phone."

Grover heard the call as Stockton answered the phone and broadcast, "Contact female."

Rob picked up and said, "Hello."

"Mr. Stockton?"

"Yes."

Then came a surprise. "Stay where you are. We'll call again."

Mona hung up before Rob could respond. He had utilized his bug mike to transmit the telephone call as it was taking place. He had slipped the mike between the phone earpiece and his ear so he could hear and transmit simultaneously. SPIT, Al and the surrounding units picked it up.

Sally broadcast, "Female contact, disconnect six-fourteen, one minute ago."

Al turned to Xavier. "What do you make of that? Why a contact for nothing? They didn't have to make that call. All they accomplished was to confirm Stockton's presence in Dadeland. We know that at least one of them is at the Falls."

Xavier was considering the occurrence. "The purpose of the whole treasure-hunt scenario is to make a police surveillance. I think this must be viewed as a concentrated effort."

Al agreed. "All units, from One. Consider this contact a close countersurveillance check." At the moment they were parked on the outer fringes of the parking area near Burdine's. Al sensed the action was moving south and that the Falls would be crucial. Peter had to be there. He was experimenting. He probably didn't really know what he was looking for, nor precisely why he did what he did.

Al decided to move toward the Falls. He had no direct-line function, but always reserved himself as a rover. Xavier pulled out of Dadeland and headed south.

Stanley, using his binoculars from the second floor of the parking garage, noted no activity around the phones. He was becoming comfortable. He only needed one more call, and he felt he could do it. He continued scanning the area. He knew cops, and he saw nothing. No cops. Nobody running toward the phones. In fact, nobody had even used the phones since Mona left them.

Mona walked up to him in the garage as he was scanning. "See anythin', Donnie?"

"No, looks clean. I think we can do the next one. Go ahead, make the call, but keep your radio on low so I can talk to you if I have to."

* * *

The five agents responding to the Falls had now all arrived. The supervisor had put three on foot and kept two moving in cars. The first arrivals had missed Mona by less than a minute. Marcus Brown was driving by the phone as the office was broadcasting, "Female contact, disconnect six-fourteen, one minute ago." Had Mona delivered payoff instructions, they would have had her.

Brown and the other agents on foot concealed their hand-held radios in shopping bags or under jackets. They moved into the area looking for the blond woman and the male, Stanley. One of the cars was parked to observe the Oyster Bar phones, should Mrs. Peter use them again. SPIT remained stationary around Rob.

Rob, puzzled by the last call, was uneasy but hopeful. At least now they were in contact, and things were moving. The phone rang. Rob said, "Phone ringing," and the ritual of advice to the phone company and radio advice to the surv-eilling units went out. On the third ring Stockton picked up. "Hello?"

"Mr. Stockton?"

"Yes."

"Patience."

Stockton blurted out; "Please, how long is this going on? I've got the money. I've done what you asked. I want my wife."

Mona strayed from her instructions. "I'll help your wife. Stay where you are. This's goin' to take some time, but we'll be back to you."

By the time Mona was saying "Mr. Stockton?" Sally was broadcasting, "Gene's Jeans, in the Falls, no specific street address. Pay phone, 239-1132."

This was inside the Falls area, which was a large, open space with roofed-over broad walkways encircling pools and waterfalls. On one side of the walkways were shops, the other, water. The walkways meandered about. The foot agents, who were spread throughout the Falls area, consulted locator charts, and began to converge on Gene's Jeans.

Mona left by one of the many side exits rather than walking the inside perimeter of the center and again the surveilling agents missed her. Too late, the sector supervisors added five more agents to the Falls coverage on the possibility of another call from that area.

Mona's exit point was just west of the Oyster Bar, directly in front of the garage where Stanley waited. Within three minutes of her hanging up she was in the car with Stanley. They left the Falls and drove south forty-four blocks to 180th Street, to a restaurant he liked bearing the incongruous name Momma Charlie's.

Momma Charlie was a huge woman who presided over a select clientele. If she didn't like the way you ate, your attitude, or anything else, she invited you to leave. This was the one place where Stanley behaved himself, because Momma had the best chicken barbecue in Dade County, and maybe all Florida. Her barbecued ribs were a close second, and Stanley ordered those while Mona had the chicken.

They did not hurry the meal. Several times Stanley had to slow Mona down. She was hurrying, anxious to finish the night's unpleasant work. They finished eating just before 8:00, paid their check, said a cheery good night to Momma and used the pay phone outside her restaurant to call a cab.

Mona took the cab to the K mart at the shopping center at 190th Street and the Highway. She asked the cab to wait while she made a quick call from the pay phone there.

Stanley raised Adam on the CB radio. Adam said he was in place.

CHAPTER 17

Oh God! that one might read the book of
fate.
　　　—SHAKESPEARE, *Henry IV, Part II*, III, i

It had been an hour and a half since the
last contact. Al, along with everyone
else, was puzzled at this long delay. Besides playing psychological games with Stockton, did Peter
have something he was about to pull that took
an inordinate amount of time to set up? Where
would Peter surface next? If it was a psychological ploy on his part, it was working. Rob, despite
the reassuring occasional voice in his ear, was
nearly a basket case. He was convinced that
something had been screwed up. He was even
worried that Peter might have been in an auto
accident and there would never be another call.

FBI agents were accustomed to waiting. Much
of their Bureau lives are spent waiting for a subject to move, waiting for an event to occur, waiting for someone to say yes or no to a plan of
action. It is a major part of law enforcement; part
of that unglamorous, dull, plodding, day-to-day

routine that TV programs never show but is essential to solving cases.

At 8:07, the phone rang. It startled Rob so badly that it was the second ring before he announced it on his bug.

Sally broadcast, "Incoming." Everyone became instantly alert, discouragement vanished in the flash of action.

At the beginning of the fourth ring Stockton picked up. "Hello?"

"Mr. Stockton?"

"Yes."

Mona began to read, "Drive to Tony Roma's at 188th and the Highway, east side of the street. Park in the restaurant lot. There is a pay phone in front of the restaurant. Take the package with you to that phone, wait for instructions."

Rob was using his bug to transmit Mona's voice as she was speaking, and outer perimeter SPIT was already en route to the new location.

Stockton did not forget his training. "Okay, that's Tony Roma's at 188th and the Highway, east side. Phone in front, bring money and wait for call. Right?"

Mona departed from the script and answered, "Yeah."

Stockton immediately picked up. "What about Jean? You said you'd help her. How? Let me talk to her."

"No. But I'll help." Mona hung up.

The telephone company was advising the office of the phone location on the first ring; Sally was transmitting, "Incoming, K mart, 190 and the Highway, 240-1187."

The sector units were converging; the nearest

one was in the K mart shopping center. He drove from Tony Roma's restaurant at one end of the center to K mart at the southern end. He could see the phone bank as he approached. There was a young black woman on one of the phones, and a cab was pulling away from in front of the K mart.

Harry Richardson copied the cab number and license-plate number, and keyed his mike, "One line still in use. She on?"

Sally was about to transmit when Harry did, and she responded with her intended transmission. "Disconnect eight-oh-nine, one minute ago."

Harry was about to begin a search of the parking lot for occupied cars but stopped. He left his car in the fire lane and walked up near the young woman, entering the phone stall next to her. He was certain Mrs. Peter had left. He decided to approach the woman on the phone, and try to mask the approach as though he were making a phone call. The question was, should he wait for her to finish her call and contact her away from the phone, or do it now? He realized the risk, but he was so close behind Mrs. Peter that he felt it worth the risk.

"Miss, FBI. Got to interrupt your call. This is an emergency."

She looked up, puzzled, and saw his badge.

"Did you see a woman making a call from"— he glanced at the number of the phone he was standing in front of—"this phone, just a moment ago?"

"Yes sir, there was a lady makin' a call from there."

"Please hang up, but keep the phone in your hand like I am; we'll talk to each other, but it'll look like we're still on the phones. I'll pay for your call. I need to talk to you right away."

The woman, still puzzled, said to the phone, "Police here. They need to talk to me. No problem. I'll call you back."

As soon as she depressed the cradle, Harry asked, "Did you see where she went after she left the phone?"

"No, I sure didn't. I wasn't facin' out. I was facin' like now, talkin' to my son and lookin' toward the phone."

Harry's next question was to establish the sequence of the two phone users. "Were you on the phone when she came up, or did you come up to the phone while she was on?"

"I come up to use the phone while she's talkin'."

"What did you see as you walked toward the phone?"

"Didn't see nothin'; saw this blond lady talkin'. There was a cab parked opposite her."

"How long after she hung up before I started talking to you?"

The young woman looked confused. "I don't understand. What's this about?"

"Please, try to tell me how long a time there was between her walking away from the phone and my talking to you."

"Maybe half minute, a minute. You should've seen her. It was that quick."

"Can you tell me what she looked like?"

"A little, didn't pay her much mind. Blond, tall,

skinny, wearin' jeans; had on a blue denim jacket, couldn't see a shirt."

"How tall, and how much did she weigh?"

"Maybe between five-nine and six feet, she was kind of hunched over the phone. She was skinny, the jeans was tight."

"How old was she?"

"Don't know, best I kin do is under forty."

"Would you know her if you saw her again?"

"No, really didn't look at her face. I do remember she had a good amount of eye makeup. Her left eye was bruised. That's all."

"Thank you very much, you've helped me a lot; let me pay for the phone call I interrupted." Harry passed her a quarter, which she accepted. "Could I have your name and address just in case I have another question? I assure you there's no problem."

At first she hesitated, but then cooperated.

"Thank you, miss. Once again, you've been most helpful."

Harry went back to his car, drove a short distance away from the phone area into the parking area and keyed his mike. "Station, eleven–seventy-seven."

"Eleven–seventy-seven, go."

"At K mart, witness gives description of female caller matching that at 66 call except now wearing denim jacket. Believe female Unsub left area in Yellow cab number 9-8-8-9, license NOV 2-4-5."

"10-4, eleven–seventy-seven. All units copy. Unsub caller at K mart same description as at

66, now wearing denim jacket. May be traveling Yellow cab number 9-8-8-9, tag NOV 2-4-5."

Milt had one of the monitoring agents on the phone to the Yellow Cab company to identify the driver and determine his shift. He also asked Yellow to contact the cab by radio and inquire if he had a fare. If the answer was yes, Yellow would tell him to contact the dispatcher as soon as he discharged his fare.

Yellow soon determined that the cab had a fare, and obtained his location as en route to Franjo and Old Cutler. The information was passed to Sally and she broadcast, "All units, suspect cab en route Franjo and Old Cutler. Sector George, respond that area, locate cab, surveil, and determine if occupant female Unsub."

Ralph Aldrich, the sector supervisor, responded "10-4."

Arriving at the Publix supermarket at Franjo and Old Cutler, Mona told the cab to wait, and got out to use the public phone to the west of the Publix entrance. She took out her CB radio and raised Stanley. "I'm makin' the call now."

Stanley gave a nervous "Okay."

She punched up the number at Tony Roma's.

Hearing the phone ring Rob announced it on his bug. On the third ring, he picked up.

"Hello?"

"Mr. Stockton?"

"Yes."

"Listen and don't speak. Do this right now or Jean is dead! Walk northwest through the parking lot to the far corner right at the Highway. At

the corner of the parking lot, step into the trees.
You'll be met."

Ralph Aldrich was watching Mona place the
call to Stockton. He welcomed Sally's "Incoming, Publix, 20425 Old Cutler, 240-8979." And
later, "Female contact."

It was needless confirmation of the "skinny
blond" he saw, and the Yellow cab waiting for
her. Sally came back on with the disconnect time,
and Aldrich had his mike in his hand. "Station,
forty-three—oh-seven."

"Forty-three—oh-seven, go."

"Have Unsub female on phone, sector George
units switch channel five for fisur."

Sally responded while Al and Xavier let out a
large cheer.

Sally followed up. "Sector George units, respond as directed, use channel five for surveillance, acknowledge."

They acknowledged.

All the units around Stockton had received the
simultaneous transmission of Mona's instructions. A SPIT vehicle was in the parking lot on
the east side of the restaurant. Another SPIT vehicle was at Wings 'n Things, a restaurant south
of Tony Roma's but in the same shopping center
and just across the access road, and was actually
viewing the telephone at only about fifty yards
away. Two SPIT agents were in the lobby of Tony
Roma's, just inside the door, a dozen feet from
the phone. Another SPIT unit was driving into
the parking lot. Others were in a perimeter
around the parking lot. The one unit in the lot,

and the second looking for, and finally finding, a parking place in the lot, were out on foot.

Grover spoke in Rob's ear, "Don't go into the trees. Stay at least five feet away from the trees; make him come to you. Pull the tracker switch."

The SPIT agents in the restaurant lobby exited and were slowly coming around the corner of the building as Rob, unnerved, activated the tracker; then, frightened, he pulled off the outer bag and tracker and threw it into a trash can. He walked toward the corner of the lot.

The four SPIT agents saw him disappear into the trees at the corner of the parking lot; they moved closer, but not so close as to attract attention, wanting to give the impression of diners going for cars or moving toward the restaurant for dinner.

The Cessna and the two tracking cars heard the tracker activate and the noise of crumpling paper. They did not know that they heard the tracker being discarded. They were homed in on the parking lot garbage can.

Rob, when he stepped into and soon out of the thin layer of trees, saw a canal in front of him. There was a figure—low and huddled against the canal bank. The figure raised an arm and Rob stopped.

He heard the figure whisper, "Toss it to me. Turn, take three steps into the lot, close your eyes, don't look back, count to two hundred. Do it right, Jean will call, five minutes."

Rob tossed the package and saw the figure catch it and scamper toward a large culvert that apparently ran under the highway. He turned, took his three steps which brought him out of the trees and into the lot. He began to count.

Rob's bug did not pick up the whisper, or at least the transmission was so low that no one heard it. Rob did not repeat it, so the surveillance was unaware that a pass had been made, although they were sure that such was, or soon would be, the case.

Mildred Hailey, one of the SPIT agents on foot, reported in. "Canal on the north perimeter of the parking lot. Package walked into the trees on the canal bank. Could be a drop to a boat. Package now exiting trees, standing at edge of lot. No bag visible. Drop probable."

Grover asked Stockton via his receiver, "Did you make a drop?"

Stockton replied, "Yes."

Grover announced, "Drop made."

Within a second of that transmission they heard an outboard cranked once, then twice, as it caught and roared to life. The boat headed west, under the culvert, across the Highway, while everyone was on the east side of the highway.

Hailey, in the lot, went through the trees to the canal bank about seventy-five feet east of where Stockton stood and saw only the remnants of a boat wake. "Unsub in boat headed west, under and clear of Highway."

The Cessna reported, "Got a visual, but tracker not moving; still in lot."

Al broke in, "Eye, stay with boat, SPIT, Pal, contact Stockton."

Grover spoke in Rob's ear. "Now, tell me what happened!"

As SPIT reached him, he began to answer Grover. "There was a guy laying on the canal bank as I came through the trees. He said to toss him the package, turn around, count and Jean would call in five minutes. I saw him head for the culvert under the road, and then heard the outboard."

"Did you activate the tracker?"

"Yes," Stockton ashamedly admitted, "but I threw it in the garbage."

Grover contained himself and broadcast, "Disregard tracker. Still on scene, not with package."

Al came on: "Stockton to go home. Grover, exit trunk, ride home and debrief on the way. Advise anything pertinent. Sectors and SPIT, parallel the bank. Move in where you can. Eye, don't lose him; you're all we've got."

"He's going through an industrial area, warehouses and the like," the Cessna reported. "He could stop anywhere. There are a hundred ways away from the canal. Suggest bring in all units, come down from the west. This is Black Creek canal; it goes under Quail Roost at 109th Avenue. I don't know if he can do it. Chances are he'll exit between 104th Avenue and 105th Avenue at 186th Street. Quail Roost is the only way in there."

Al spoke. "One agent at canal, protect scene, process later." Then, "Pal, anything from Stockton?"

"Peter said Jean would call home, five minutes. He only saw Peter. Stockton believes it was him. He thinks he recognized the voice. He saw no boat; it must have been in the culvert. Best description he can give, since Peter was lying on the bank and later moving toward the culvert.

Peter is WM, twenty to forty, tall, maybe six feet, heavy build.''

By 7:00 p.m. Straus had run out of options as he saw them. He totaled up the score: He had had no further contact from a client whom he had never seen and had never talked to before today, a client who had not stayed in contact as she had promised, a client who apparently had not heeded his advice to abandon the kidnapping. As a human being he had responsibilities to an innocent victim of the kidnapping. He certainly recognized his precarious position in having knowledge of an ongoing criminal enterprise, especially one with human life at stake. At 7:45 he finally called Mary.

"Mary, on behalf of my client, if I have one, please prepare to record this, and I hope we can have an agreement.''

Mary switched on a tape recorder attached to her phone.

"Go ahead, Mr. Straus.''

"I truly believe Mrs. Stockton is in extremity, based on what I have been told. I have never met my client, and have had only two telephone conversations. This was contrary to my instructions and contrary to her agreement to call me every hour. I have had no contact for more than seven hours. I instructed my client to abandon the kidnapping enterprise in which she found herself involved. I do not know whether she followed those instructions. She requested that I attempt to obtain immunity for her in return for certain information. I have been unable to effect what I consider a satisfactory arrangement. The information she gave me cannot be held any longer, and so I exercise my best judgment on her behalf.

"I accept the United States Attorney and States Attorney's offer of a recommendation of a three-year maximum sentence if my client is not the principal, and if she has not participated in any homicide. My client agrees to testify in this case."

Mary replied, "We accept." Then she added, "Rather than pass this information through me, call Milt Jennings at the FBI and give it to him directly."

Straus agreed and called Milt. After receiving Straus's call, Milt broke into the radio traffic. "One, Station."

"Station, go."

"Al, switch channel four. Your ears only." This was a signal to Grover and Henry of a transmission not to be overheard by the family.

Al pressed the switch. "One on four."

"Al, Straus caved. Since he lost his client contact, he took the three-year cap. His client is a Mona Little. No description. She and a boyfriend, Donnie, no description, abducted Jean. Jean has been staked out on the ground in the Everglades, without protection, since Monday morning. We've got a sketchy description of where she is. Finding her in daylight's going to be tough. Night, impossible."

"Milt, what kind of a location description do you have?"

"The best we can get from Straus is off Route 41, before the park. There's an Indian reservation on the left. Just after you pass that, there's a road over a dam on the canal on your right. We're talking about heading west now, remember, so the road would go north. That road is paved, and then becomes dirt. Here's where it gets tough. Somewhere off that dirt road, maybe four or five miles, there's a dirt road to the left, west, that wanders into a hammock; and that's where she is. There are, apparently, numerous dirt roads left and right off the main dirt road."

"Milt, call the Miccosoukee Indian Police. See if they can scare up some airboats and some people that know that area. Put at least one agent on each airboat for radio communication, and start searching the hammocks to the west of that road."

At this point Jimmy interrupted Milt, who at his request passed him the mike. "Al, we've got four Metro helicopters at Tamiami Airport that are equipped with thermal imagers. We use them mostly to find subjects hiding in woods or fields, finding lost kids, stuff like that. Depending on where she is on the hammock, how much cover she's under, the imagers may pick up her body heat and you'll actually be able to see her on the screen."

Al immediately embraced the suggestion. "Can you get on your radio and get the necessary authorization to use as many of them as is practical to search the area? We'll give each bird one of our radios so they can communicate with the airboats."

"You got it." He passed the mike to Milt.

Al continued, "Milt, get an agent with four hand-held radios with earpieces to meet them. We need to be sure the airboats and the helicopters are on the same channel. If you want, put four agents out there. If the load limits permit, they can go up with the helicopters to give us better communication.''

An old blue Chevy pulled straight out of the parking spot that it had backed into, up against the canal. It was in the lot just to the east of Tony Roma's lot.

CHAPTER
18

Behold a pale horse:
    and his name that sat on him was Death,
and Hell followed with him.
    —Revelation 6:8

Mona left the phone in front of Publix, walked over to the cab and, reaching through the driver's window, paid him and let him go. She walked east in front of Publix and then south along the row of now-closed stores to a small restaurant, the Orange Cafe, where she went in and ordered coffee.

After a few minutes she got up from her coffee, went to a pay phone in the rear of the restaurant and punched up a number.

Aldrich, with Sherry Montalvo, one of the other surveilling agents, had entered the restaurant within minutes of Mona and had also ordered coffee. There were about ten other patrons there; most were having dessert, or just finishing dinners. The restaurant was not large.

A long counter was on one side, where two patrons sat drinking coffee and chatting with a waitress. The main part of the restaurant had, perhaps, fifteen tables. The cooking was apparently done in a room behind a serving area that faced the counter. To the rear of the restaurant were the rest rooms and two pay phones.

When Mona moved to the phone, Sherry moved to the ladies room, next to the phone. The phone that Mona called rang and was picked up on the third ring. "Hello, Straus speaking."

"This is Mona."

"Mona! Where the hell have you been? I've got to see you, now! I had to tell the FBI what you told me, because I had no contact from you. I made a deal for you, the best I could, in my judgment, and we need to talk about that. We have some serious problems."

"I'm glad you told them where she was. I'll call you again, but I can't come and see you right now, Donnie is going to call me where I am, and then we're going to meet. After I get back with Donnie I'll call."

Straus began to protest, but before he could utter a syllable Mona hung up.

The use of the boat and the information from Milt was all Al needed to make his decision. He keyed his mike first on the surveillance channel and then on five, the channel being used by Aldrich. "All units, this is One. Arrest. Repeat, arrest. Advise when accomplished. Immediately interview to locate victim and advise. Available information indicates she is staked out in the Everglades off Route 41. Need exact location."

The Cessna was tracking the boat without problem. It showed up beautifully, silhouetted against the water and creating a phosphorescent wake. The boat did manage to fit through the culvert at 186th and keep on going. The units had received Al's transmission to arrest, and now were trying to figure a way to stop the boat.

The Cessna suggested two attempts, one set up at the culvert at 184th Street west of the turnpike, and the second at 168th Street. The boat could stop and discharge its passenger anywhere along the bank.

Larry Barret and Sylvia Neely were already set up on 184th Street looking south onto the canal below, and knew precisely what to do. The Bureau had a rule about warning shots: Agents don't fire warning shots. Larry and Sylvia agreed with the rule. What they intended was not a warning shot but an attention getter. They figured they had to let Peter know they were there and that they wanted to talk to him.

As the boat rounded the curve, changing direction from west to north, Adam looked into the blinding high beams of a car that was parked across 184th Street and was facing the canal. He could also make out a rotating blue police light on the roof of the car. Larry put the shotgun to his shoulder and aimed about thirty feet in front of the boat. He let go with three 12-gauge magnum rounds, just as fast as he could pump the gun, into the water in front of the boat. Larry figured If you're going to get his attention, get it good.

The sound of those three rounds in the canal was ear splitting. The buckshot hitting the water in front of the boat graphically illustrated to Adam that the people he now noticed on the roadway he was approaching intended for him to stop—now!

If the skiff had brakes it could not have stopped any faster. Adam made a hard right, almost capsizing the boat, ran it up on the bank and killed the motor.

Larry stayed in position, announcing, "FBI. Out of the boat, hands high. Freeze."

Adam looked into the barrel of the biggest shotgun he had ever seen and stepped out of the boat onto the bank and raised his hands as high as they'd go.

Sylvia was in front of him in an instant, and Larry raised the shotgun and walked down to the canal bank. Sylvia ordered Adam to his knees, ankles crossed. She came around behind him, put one foot on his ankles, and cuffed one hand, brought it down behind his back and then, when he lowered the other at her order, cuffed it. A frisk didn't locate any weapon, and Adam was brought to his feet.

Larry announced on the hand-held radio, "Boat subject in custody."

Other agents arrived and began searching the boat, while Sylvia and Larry interviewed Adam. A search warrant was not necessary for the boat, as probable cause existed to believe that the boat held evidence of the commission of a felony. And there is a warrant exception for mobile craft, such as cars and boats.

Larry advised Adam of his Miranda rights, and when he finished, asked, "Do you understand these rights? Are you willing to talk to us?"

Adam nodded his head up and down and swallowed. "Yeah."

One of the agents searching the boat turned and said, "No money here."

"What's your name?" Larry asked.

"Adam. Adam Jackson."

"Adam, what'd you do with the money?"

"Man, that what you want? It's in ma right pocket. Take it, ya can have it."

Sylvia reached in his pocket and extracted some twenty-dollar bills that had been cut in half, along with five whole twenty-dollar bills.

Larry saw what Sylvia had and said, "Adam, you're short about $249,000. Where's the rest?"

"Ah don't have that kinda money. Don't know 'bout that."

"How'd you come by this money?"

"Man, he give it ta me, back under that culvert un'er the highway."

Larry began to have a bad feeling. "The man who gave it to you, where is he?"

"He stay un'er the culvert."

Larry got on the radio. "All units, boat subject advises Unsub remained in culvert when he took off in boat."

Al's response was "Shit!" They were now at 184th and the highway. Xavier made a U-turn and they headed back to Tony Roma's.

Al broadcast, "Unit at drop culvert, hold; this is One, be there in two and back you up." Al knew Peter wouldn't be there.

Stanley had caught the package tossed by Stockton and moved into the culvert. He threw Adam five whole twenties and said, "Go!"

Stanley was out of the culvert before the outboard was cranked and about thirty feet from the canal, hidden by trees that ringed the western perimeter of the parking lot, separating it from the Highway. Lying flat he saw someone walk through the trees to the north, those that bordered the canal, about twenty-five yards east of where Stockton stood. The person who went to the canal bank apparently looked west up the canal and then returned to the lot.

Stanley stayed where he was for about five minutes, watching the agents contacting Stockton. At first he was terrified. "The son of a bitch did tell the cops. They're gonna find me."

As the voices and people left, his courage returned and he began congratulating himself on his masterful planning. He saw that only one cop stayed behind. He rose to his hands and knees, and crept down to the canal and along the water's edge to where his car was, in the second lot down from Tony Roma's lot.

Larry continued his questioning of Adam. "Who was the man you left at the culvert?"

"Don't know. I be told be there un'er the highway. He call me on the radio an' come down the bank an' meet me."

"Do you know Jean Stockton?"

"No suh."

"Where were you when she was kidnapped?"

"Don't know nothin' 'bout no kidnappin'."

"If she dies, you go for murder; you're part of the gang. Now where is she?"

"Man, I swear, I don't know nothin' 'bout no murder or no kidnappin'. Ah be at the Po'ch today, jus' jivin', and this here gal comes 'long an' asks fo' anyone got a skiff. I do, ma bro' do, so Ah say so. She put me on a phone with this dude, an' he offer $200 fo' two hours; say he owed money and got ta pick it up careful. She gimme twenny an' some cut up twennies, say I get the halves after I do.

"Ah gets the boat an' she an' me go down this here canal an' she show me to be un'er the culvert at 7:30 an' she gimme a radio. The dude'll call to see if'n Ah'm there. Well, man, he do call an' Ah be there. He come down an' see me, give me my other twenny halves an' then he go lay on the bank.

"Pretty soon this other dude come 'long an' toss 'm a sack. The first dude, he catch it, an' move un'er the culvert. He look at sumpin' in a sack an' gimme five whole twennies an' he tell me ta go an' he go roun' the corner by the culvert. Man, I go."

"What did the man who met you look like?"

"It be dark, man. He got som'thin' on his face, couldn' see no nose or eyes. He big, bigger'n me, had a hat. Wore doctor gloves, 'member that."

"What about the woman?"

"Whooee! Oh man, Ah sure 'member her. Af'er Ah gets her back ta 'er car she grab ol' Adam an' lay back inna fron' seat. Man, Ah do this here job fo' nothin if'n she come back. Ain' never had no ride lak dat."

"What did she look like?"

"Ah kin tell that good! Ah sure seen alla her! She tall's me, skinny lak, blon' hair but it ain' real, man. Ah knows! Som'body whack her inna eye. She got gol' loop ear'ins, red shirt, nuttin' un'erneeth. Jean pants, nuttin' un'erneeth."

What little description they had of Peter was put on the air.

*   *   *

Sherry had just rejoined Ralph at their table and was about to tell what she had been able to overhear Mona saying, when another surveillance agent entered and walked over to them. "The boss says take her."

Sherry and Ralph rose and walked toward Mona. Mona was looking into her coffee cup, deep in thought, and didn't see them approach.

Sherry said, "FBI, Mona, you're under arrest. Keep your hands where they are and don't move. Now, I'm going to take a wrist, and he's going to take the other. When we do that, you get up and we walk out, no fuss, okay?"

Mona nodded. Sherry, on Mona's right, and Ralph, on the left, each grasped an elbow and hand at the wrist in come-along holds, lifting Mona out of her chair and walking her outside, where they placed her hands against a Bureau car. Sherry moved Mona's feet back by command and by nudging Mona's feet with her own foot. Ralph held Mona's purse. When Mona was angled to the car, Sherry spread Mona's legs, locked one with her own foot for a trip, and frisked her.

Afterward, Sherry hooked one handcuff on Mona's right wrist and then moved her up slightly so her head was resting on the car. She brought the handcuffed wrist to her back, and ordered the other hand there. Mona was supported against the car by her head. After she was cuffed, Sherry and Ralph lifted her away from the car.

Sherry felt nothing on Mona's person during the frisk. The purse yielded a hand-held CB radio, an Illinois driver's license, and some other identification in the name Mona Little, some tissues and six condoms. Her wallet held forty-five dollars and change. There was no local address or phone numbers. A search of Mona's jeans pockets yielded nothing. Her jacket pocket had several pieces of paper, the texts of some of the messages that had been delivered that night, along with the telephone numbers they were called to.

Sherry advised Mona of her Miranda rights, and began interviewing her. "Where's Jean Stockton?"

"I told Mr. Straus: He told me he told you, but I'll help find her. I'm not sure I can find it in day, and at night would be real tough." Mona repeated the directions to the site where they had left Jean and in answer to questions, described in detail the condition Jean was in when they left her. The additional detail was relayed to the command post, and Mona was transported to the office, with blue light and siren, for further interview so she could review aerial photographs of the area Jean was in.

As they rode Sherry asked Mona, "Where's Donnie?" Sherry noted Mona's head come up sharply.

"Don't know no Donnie."

"Mona, we know about Donnie; he's left you. You're going to face a kidnapping charge. Mona, you're looking at life. If Jean's dead, you could get a death sentence. Help yourself now. Donnie's gone with the money. He doesn't care about you."

Mona began to cry softly. She knew what Sherry said was true. Mona didn't fault Stanley; it was what she expected. After all, she was of little value to herself or anyone else. Somewhere,

deep inside her, were untapped feelings of pleasure, satisfaction, fulfillment.

Sherry continued, "Who were you talking to
on the phone, at the restaurant?"

"My lawyer, Mr. Straus, the one I told where
she was." Mona went back to her thoughts. "I
wonder if Donnie was comin' for me? I'll probably never know. You got me before he could
call."

The pay phone at the Orange Cafe was ringing.
Arnold Hyde, the owner, happened to be near it,
so he answered. "Orange Cafe."

"Hello? I'm tryin' to reach a tall blond girl
who's havin' coffee there. Can I talk to her?"

"I'm sorry, she's not here now. If it's the one
in the jeans and denim jacket, she left a few minutes ago with two men and another girl." The
line went dead.

Stanley was concerned. Not about Mona—he
had already decided to kill her. He was upset that
the police got to her first. He was headed home,
but decided that was not a good idea with Mona
arrested. He was glad he had stopped and called.
He had intended for Mona to take a cab to a
nearby motel and spend the night there. If she
was still "cool" in the morning, he was going to
pick her up some place, drive her out into the
'Glades, and leave her.

He figured he needed out of this area, did a U
turn on the Highway and began heading north,
looking for the first turnpike entrance.

Phil came on the radio. "One from twenty–oh-
seven."

"Twenty–oh-seven, go."

"Suggest B.O.L.O. on Donald Stanley. We place him, with female, drive-by of Stockton house, in a old blue Chevy Caprice; 66 makes an old blue GM car, big, with male driver. Adam's and Stockton's descriptions are close to Stanley. I monitored Milt's transmission on the victim, Mona says Peter is Donnie—as in Donald Stanley?"

Al considered a "Be On the Look Out" message with some additions. He felt Armed and Dangerous necessary in the B.O.L.O. due to the violence of the crime and to protect any officer who came upon him.

Al chose a "Terry stop" as authority to detain Stanley. This requires a reasonable or founded suspicion of criminal activity by the person to be stopped. It permits a temporary detention of a person for the purpose of allaying the officer's suspicion of criminal activity.

"Thanks, Phil, I agree. Milt, put out a B.O.L.O."

"10-4. You want that arrest, surveil and advise, or stop and question?"

"Make it stop and question in a kidnapping, and advise us when sighted. Carry him A and D. We have enough for a Terry stop, but I feel we're just a hair shy of probable cause for an arrest. We need to include our Terry elements in the B.O.L.O."

By this time Al had arrived back at the culvert. Together with Xavier and Jacob Preston, who had been left on the scene, they explored the culvert and the canal bank for a reasonable distance on both sides of the highway. They found what they expected to find—nothing.

Al apologized to Jacob for having to ask him to stay there. Jacob understood that a thorough crime scene search, including soil samples, would be required as soon as agents could be spared.

Al and Xavier were just buckling in and preparing to head for the office when they heard "All units, am following blue Chevrolet Caprice, AIZ-954, one occupant, north on the Highway approaching 217th Street. Request backup."

Al pressed the mike button. "One, 10-4."

Al's car turned west on the access road toward the Highway, on a perfect intercept course ahead of Stanley. Al had recognized Phil's voice.

"Target east on 216th Street, turnpike interchange, may head north."

Al turned to Xavier. "Phil may be right; head for Quail Roost and that interchange. We'll know before we're committed. Let's move, Xavier."

As Xavier headed north on the Highway, Al put the blue light on the dash and hit the siren. As they turned left onto Quail Roost they heard "Target taking turnpike north."

"Phil, we're on Quail Roost. Will enter there." As they approached within four blocks of the turnpike, Al killed the blue light and siren. He asked, "10-20?"

Phil came back, "Just cleared Quail Roost exit."

Another voice came on: "Thirty-nine—thirty-three entering 1-5-2 north."

And another: "Ken, this is Bobbie, I'm right behind you."

Al ordered, "Let's do a box after we clear 1-5-2. Ken, you and Bobbie fill both lanes when he comes up behind you. Phil, stay on his ass. If he's in the right lane I'll pull next to him and give him the light and siren. When I do that, Ken and Bobbie be prepared to shift right in case he tries for the swale."

Al got three "10-4"s.

Within a minute Al transmitted again. "Okay, Phil, we got you; we see him. Directly in front of you, right?"

Two transmitter clicks answered.

"Ken, Bobbie, I see tail lights ahead. Touch your brakes. Okay, we got you. Hold for a minute till we get closer. When I pull out on his left I'll flash my brights. When you see that, double lane him, and we'll do the stop."

When Xavier judged that they were positioned, he pulled out past Phil and flashed his brights. Ken pulled into the left lane, and as they came abreast of the Chevrolet, Al hit the blue light and gave the siren a quick blast. Then he switched the electronic siren to loudspeaker. Al's window was down, he was watching Stanley, his Combat Magnum in his hand. The shotgun had been moved to the front seat and was now barrel-down between him and Xavier.

With his left hand Al keyed the mike, now on loudspeaker. "FBI, Stanley. Stop right here." Stanley slowed. Ken and Bobbie slowed. Al said, "Ken, Bobbie, shift! Stanley, follow them onto the shoulder."

As Ken and Bobbie moved right, Stanley stood on the accelerator and shot through the small opening between Al's car and the rear end of Ken's car.

Again Al shouted, "Shift!" Xavier was right behind Stanley, and the other three cars in close behind Al. The old Chevy had a big V-8 engine and moved out, but Xavier was on his tail about fifty yards behind.

Stanley knew he couldn't outrun the cars. He was desperate. He had just passed Killian Parkway when he reacted more by impulse than judgment. Now past seventy and approaching eighty miles per hour, he suddenly hit the brakes and pulled left across the broad median to head south and exit into the city at Killian and try to lose them in traffic.

Fortunately for him, he was wearing his seat belt. Within one hundred feet of the turnpike, the wheels bit into soft earth and the car stopped as though it had hit a wall and almost flipped over. Stanley threw the transmission into a wheel spinning reverse.

Xavier had kept pace with Stanley, but the sudden braking and swing to the left across the median took him by surprise. He stood on the brakes, and even then overshot Stanley's turn. Xavier came around and pulled onto the median, heading for Stanley at about twenty miles per hour. The other cars were in varying degrees of disarray behind them. When they were within thirty feet of Stanley, Xavier stopped and Al leaped out of the car, moving toward Stanley. Xavier, with the long-barrel shotgun, had to maneuver out of his seat belt, as well as maneuver the gun out of the car. He was about ten feet behind Al.

Stanley released his seat belt when he couldn't move the car, grabbed the money bag, opened the door and rolled out. He was up and running when Al shouted, "Freeze!"

Stanley had the money in his left hand and the .38 somehow had gotten in his right. Infuriated that they were about to take his big score, he swung around and fired once, paused for a split second and then fired again at Al and Xavier.

Al, running toward Stanley, stopped when he saw the gun pointed at him and had the Magnum up in a two-handed grip at the first shot. Simultaneously with Stanley's second shot, he fired off six rapid-fire shots. Xavier would later say he thought Al had a machine gun.

Two rounds hit Stanley square in the chest, one penetrated his right side and one went into his right arm, through it, and into his side, as he turned going down. The last two rounds missed, passing behind him. From behind Al Xavier fired twice with the shotgun. The pellets impacted low in Stanley's body. Stanley's third shot was a reflex as he died.

In one continuous motion, Al opened his cylinder, dumped his empty cases, flipped open his cartridge pouch, secured his speed loader and in four seconds was reloaded and training his gun on the downed Stanley.

They stood for a moment, looking down at Stanley, knowing he was dead. The other cars pulled in.

Al turned to those who just came up and quietly said, "Call the office, tell them Stanley's down." Xavier touched Stanley's carotid artery and shook his head negatively. "And dead. Ask for Metro's shooting team and an ambulance."

Bobbie relayed the information on her radio.

Phil spotted the brown Publix bag next to Stanley's left hand. "Guess we better leave everything alone for the shooting team."

Al turned to Xavier, shifting his gun to his left hand and extending his right hand. "It would be my pleasure to ride with you anytime, thank you." Xavier shook his hand.

There was a bond that night. They had both looked death square in the face and side by side had defeated him. They had together killed their common assailant. There can be no closer bond between two men than to have shared that.

This was the second time in twenty-three years that Al had fired his gun at someone.

"Xavier, I'm going to exercise an SAC's prerogative. We're going to leave the scene. I know it violates Metro shooting team's rules, but since I don't work for Metro I can break them." He turned to Phil and said, "Give the team my apologies. I'm available for a statement as soon as we find Jean. Tell them since we're still working we kept the guns, but they can have them when we make the statement."

Nodding to all three he said, "Bobbie, Phil, Ken—good job. Stay here and give your statements to the team."

Abruptly he turned to leave. "Xavier, let's go. That's not the way I wanted this to end. He might have helped us find Jean, but we don't always get what we want. I don't understand his shooting. He just couldn't have been thinking. There's no way he could have escaped." Shaking his head as he slid into the car, he said, "Let's see how Milt's doing. Station, One."

"One, go."

"Xavier and I are coming in. Have the troops been reassigned?"

"10-4. We're processing crime scenes."

"How we doin' on the search?"

"Metro gave us two helicopters. It would be too dangerous to use more in that limited search area. Miccosoukee Police have four airboats with people who know that area well. The thermal imagers may not be too effective. If she's under a heavy canopy of trees, the heat that the imager measures may not escape."

As Al sighed in disappointment, Milt went on: "Mona just got here; she doesn't know about Stanley yet. She's looking at aerial photos now. The helicopters should be airborne in ten, and the airboats should start searching within a half hour."

"Milt, I'm going to the site rather than the office."

"10-4."

"Xavier, let's get there as fast as we can.

"Milt, alert the air rescue helicopter, we may need him in a hurry at the site. And contact trauma at Jackson and explain what we're likely to bring in so they can be ready."

"10-4."

CHAPTER 19

I stand on the terrible threshold, and I see
The end and the beginning in each other's
arms.
   —STANLEY KUNITZ, *Open the Gates*

Xavier stayed on the turnpike and, traveling between ninety and one hundred, had them at Route 41 in five minutes. The trip west on 41 involved traffic, and Xavier had to slow down.

As they made their way to the Miccosoukee reservation, Al said, "I know I don't have to say this, because I'm sure you know it, but I really do appreciate everything you've done these last couple of days. Without your counsel, investigative skills," Al gave a kidding smile, "not to mention driving skills, this would have been impossible."

Xavier smiled. "Just keep the paychecks comin'."

When they arrived they could see the helicopters doing search patterns off to the north. Frank Roberson, the lead agent on the scene, met Al's car as it pulled in. "The airboats should all be here shortly. There are two already here, on the other side of the canal. The chief wants all four together so he can lay out search grids so nothing gets overlooked.

"He's good. Says if we don't sit on these airboat jockeys they'll be all over the 'Glades hopping from one place to another, crisscrossing each other, and not getting the job done."

"Sounds like you've got it together, Frank. Chief inside?"

"Yeah, he is. Want to go in?"

"Yeah, I need to call Stockton."

Al went in the police building and met and thanked Howard Gilbert, the chief, for his help on such short notice.

"Howard, I don't know how much Frank has been able to tell you about this, but let me go at it even though I may repeat some of what he's said. The woman we're looking for has been staked to the ground since Monday on one of those hammocks out there.

"You know better than me what the animals and bugs might do to her. She's had no food or water, so she's going to be dehydrated. For all practical purposes, she's nude. The daytime temperatures have been about seventy-five to seventy-eight, and the nights have been right around fifty-five. Hypothermia may have already killed her. When she's found, tell the guys not to try to see if she's alive. Assume she is, wrap her as warm as they can, and call in air rescue. They'll be here shortly, standing by. We welcome any suggestions you might have, Howard, since this is your turf."

"No, Al, I think we got it covered. I know the

area and the people, and if you agree, I'll handle the search."

"It couldn't be in better hands, Howard. Mind if I use your phone? I'd like to call the victim's husband. Haven't brought him up to date since the payoff."

"No, go ahead, I'll leave."

"No need to, Howard. Stay, and maybe what I tell him will fill in some holes in this mess we dumped on you."

Al punched up Stockton's number and Grover answered. "How's the family doing, Grover?"

"Rob's beside himself. He's into guilt again. I told him Jean's tied up in the woods. Now he knows Peter was lying about her calling here, and he's saying he should have let the tracker go with the money and let us grab everybody. I've had the radio off. I don't want him to hear anything raw."

In a subdued voice Al said, "Stanley came up shooting, and we had to kill him. Let me tell him. Mona's in the office trying to locate the site on aerials. Two helicopters with thermal imagers are working the hammocks. Airboats are going out in a few minutes. I'm confident we'll find her. I'm not confident she'll be alive. You and Henry stay with them through the night; we'll get you out tomorrow. You both have been magnificent. Let me talk to Rob, unless you have something else?"

"No, I'll get him."

"Al?"

"Hello, Rob. Just checking in. We've got two helicopters up with thermal imagers. They read heat and translate it into an image on a television screen. If the imagers can see Jean, they'll read her heat as different from the surrounding area and throw a picture of her on the screen. We've also got four airboats that will physically search every hammock out there. Air rescue will be standing by, on the scene, to take her to Jackson as soon as we find her. The female you talked to is in our office trying to pinpoint the hammock from aerial photos.

"Peter, whose real name was Donald Stanley, resisted arrest and shot at us. We had to kill him. The minute I hear we've found Jean, I'll call you."

"Al, should I go to the hospital?"

"You can if you want, though I doubt if you'll get to see Jean right away. The doctors there usually do a complete exam before they let the family in. I'd say it'll be a couple hours after she arrives before anybody gets to see her. The kids might benefit from your being with them until word comes in."

"Okay. How about my coming there?"

"Not much to see or do here. The helicopters and airboats will be working; I'm just sitting in an office."

"Okay. I'll wait. Thanks, Al."

Al hung up and called Milt. "Milt, a loose end. Did the media sit on our story?"

"They sure did, Al. I wouldn't have bet on it."

"I told them I'd call as soon as I could when the kidnapping broke. There may be another day when we need their help, so let's play square and have someone call in the bare bones. You write it out. No comment beyond what you write out at this time. Questions will be answered in the morning. You can say we shot Stanley when he pegged three shots at us. Xavier and I shot him, but leave that out. Let the shooting team handle that. You can say we're searching for the victim, and include Mona's arrest."

"Okay, Al. How're you doing, by the way? Any problems with the shooting?"

"Thanks, Milt, I'm fine. The shooting doesn't bother me. I'm not immune to feelings, don't misunderstand, but I've been around shootings, had one once before. I don't have a problem with it, it's just the way I am."

The other two airboats had arrived, and Al went with Howard for the briefing.

Frank raised the helicopters on his radio and inquired as to their assessment of the effectiveness of the thermal imagers. The reply was what Al had expected. Both operators were convinced that the heavy canopy of trees in the hammocks made the imagers almost useless.

Al suggested altering the task of the helicopters, using their powerful ground illumination capability to light up the hammocks and aid the airboats.

Howard agreed, and Frank relayed the decision. Both helicopters switched on searchlights that could cover a football field with daylight.

The four airboats were off. Two went to a central starting point about four miles down the dirt road and close in to the road. One worked north, the other south. The other two also started about four miles down and worked north and south but farther out into the Everglades. One helicopter covered the south group, and the other the north group; each responded with light whenever an airboat was at a hammock.

Air rescue had arrived and was down, waiting. While it also had illumination capability, all agreed that in the interests of air safety, two helicopters were enough; and they seemed to be serving the airboats satisfactorily.

Al had contacted the office and got the latest from Mona's examination of aerial photos. She had selected four hammocks as "better possibilities," and these had been described to Howard, who was able to identify the ones she chose on his charts. They were in the center of the start zone, where two of the airboats were working.

The airboats had searched five hammocks, pulling up to each, and then going in on foot. Some hammocks were large, three or more acres, others small, only an acre. Then the unexpected happened. They found her.

Al couldn't believe it. Nothing this hard ever came this easily. He had been prepared for an all-night hunt.

The airboat that found her wrapped her in a survival blanket. Air rescue flew out, loaded her on board, and they were off to Jackson.

Frank marked the hammock for a crime scene search the next day.

The airboat crews came back in, and Mike Holleran, the FBI agent on the airboat, together with Dick Two-Bears, the airboat operator, reported in to Howard and Al. Mike, a ruddy-faced Irishman always full of good humor, was pale and he was somber. He sat at the table and asked for a cup of coffee. Two-Bears was also quiet.

Al sensed Mike's problem. "How was it?"

"Al, I don't want to ever see anything like that again. The helicopter lit it up, even though the trees were thick. We had our large lights, so we saw it. Al, she was spread out. Her legs wide apart. Her arms at full length pulled to each side; all tied to trees. She couldn't move.

"She had duct tape over her mouth. Part of a nightgown and house coat were on her back and around her sides. She was laying in her own excrement. Flies and ants were all over her. She had been bitten by bugs and God knows what all over her body. I didn't see one area of her that had not been bitten into raw meat or swelled up. She's just all . . . kind of puffy.

"I couldn't find a pulse or feel respiration. She was cold. Like ice. Like dead. Al, she's dead. God, how she must have suffered."

Two-Bears, his eyes cast down: "Your man said it. I've been in the 'Glades forty-five years. I've pulled people out before, but never seen nothin' close to that. Man who did that deserves to die like that. You show him to me, and I'll do it."

Al was devastated. He had expected it, but hoped it would not be this bad. He thanked all who had worked so hard in the search, excused himself, turned to Frank. "Stay and pick up any loose ends. I want to know everyone that helped tonight. They deserve a personal thank-you. I need to leave."

He extended his hand to Howard. "I can't express my appreciation for your help. Howard, I've got to go to the hospital. Let's talk further tomorrow."

Howard shook Al's hand with silent understanding.

Al asked Xavier, "How quick can you get us to Jackson? We've got a family to consider."

Xavier went right down the Trail, with blue light, no siren. They were there in twenty minutes. Xavier and Al went into the trauma center and were directed to Jean's doctor. Al finally located him.

"She is alive, but just barely. Another hour out there and she probably would have been irreversibly lost. She may be lost now. When I got her, we couldn't measure her body temperature, and she was extremely dehydrated. The animal and insects bites covered her. I've never seen a case like this before.

"Our first concern was to raise her body temperature; we're trying to do that now. We're also giving her an IV to get fluid in her, and antibiotics for the bites and stings are in the IV. She has had some atrial fibrillation. She was apparently brutally assaulted. We haven't been able, as yet, to determine the extent of external and possible internal injuries from this."

Al shivered under the impact of the doctor's words. Xavier shook a downcast head.

The doctor nodded grimly. "She's in very serious condition. If she survives the next few hours while we get her temperature up, she has a chance. How much permanent damage the cold did to her organs, I can't assess yet. We're concerned about circulatory problems in her extremities, not only from cold, but from the constriction of the ropes. Amputation is a possibility. I'm being brutally frank. I've never seen a worse case. We haven't even considered brain damage yet, both organic and psychological. Right now we're just trying to save the body. The prognosis is not good."

Al thanked the doctor and moved slowly to a phone. Using the main house number, he called Stockton. Henry answered.

"Henry, we still hardwired in?"

"Yeah, we are; haven't pulled it down yet."

"Henry, I can't say this twice. Give the phone to Rob and you use the headphones."

Stockton came on the phone with a subdued "Al?"

"Hello, Rob. Not good news, friend. We found her, and she's alive. The doctors say she's in real bad shape. Hypothermia, dehydration and just general exposure. She was outside for at least three days. They just don't know at this point which way she'll go. She is alive and there is hope. You're free to come to the hospital. I'm sorry, but I didn't ask about you seeing her. I would think that you probably won't be able to for the next several hours. They're really working on her, especially to get her temperature up."

Al stopped for a moment, waiting for a response, but there was none. "Rob, I couldn't be more sorry at this news. I wish there were more I could do."

Stockton said a quiet "Thank you" and hung up the phone.

Al and Xavier went back to the office, and Al drafted and sent the following teletype:

```
To:  Director, FBI (7-23571)          IMMEDIATE
     SAC, Tampa, Jacksonville, Atlanta,
        Mobile

Fr: SAC, Miami (7-508)

Stocknap (Changed)
```

Title marked changed to reflect identity of Unsub, Peter, as DONALD STANLEY, FBI number 347521-F, deceased, and to add MONA LITTLE, FBI number 887331-D, and ADAM JACKSON, FBI number 947185-C as subjects.

Remytel 2-18. Contact call received approximately 1:20 p.m. 2-19. Call followed by several others. ROBERT STOCKTON, husband of victim, made final drop of currency approximately 8:15 p.m. 2-20. STANLEY, at canal bank picked up same and diverted attention by having accomplice JACKSON flee in opposite direction in boat. JACKSON apprehended. JACKSON claims no knowledge of kidnap and hired by STANLEY for diversion under pretext. Surveillance identified LITTLE who was arrested after last ransom call. She had previously contacted local attorney, furnishing information on location of victim, seeking immunity. U.S. Attorney and States Attorney, with concurrence this office, agreed to 3 year cap and testimony before LITTLE identified and apprehended. Since LITTLE continued in criminal enterprise after agreement some question as to whether prosecutor is bound to honor same.

STANLEY identified as Unsub Peter through investigation. STANLEY detected fleeing north. During efforts to stop his car on Florida turnpike he turned onto median and became mired. He came out of car firing handgun and was shot and killed by SAC and SA Xavier Restrepo. Office, with concurrence U.S. Attorney, will accept investigation by Metro shooting team. FBI shooting team should be dispatched. Ransom money recovered.

Victim located in Everglades by search team from Miccosoukee Police in airboats with agents and Metro helicopters. Victim had been staked, spread eagle, to the ground, essentially nude, from the time of abduction without food or water. Victim had been sexually assaulted. Suffering serious injury from assault and extreme hypothermia, dehydration and extensive bites over entire body. Doctors advise prognosis for recovery poor. If victim lives may suffer organ and extremity damage from assault and cold. Psychological problems not explored.

No federal jurisdiction developed. Case being turned over Metro Dade Police today. Recommendations to follow. End.

E P I L O G U E

Xavier Restrepo was transferred to FBI Headquarters and today is an inspector, on his way to becoming an SAC.

Henry and Grover arc both happy as field agents and have expressed a desire to continue in that path.

Phil Bentley retired soon after the case.

All four received awards from the director for their work in the case.

Milt submitted his memo on the handling of the case. FBI Headquarters sent four inspectors to Miami to review the investigation. Al's judgment was confirmed. Milt received a written censure and probation for his failure to fully support the investigation. Shortly thereafter he was transferred to another office as ASAC and resigned. He is now vice president and general manager of Incomparable Computers at three times his former Bureau salary.

Mona pleaded in state court to a reduced

charge of false imprisonment and was sentenced to three years confinement and five years probation. She was free in a year but on probation. She followed the only trade she knew, prostitution, and has now contracted AIDS.

Al Lawrence continued with the FBI for another eighteen months and then, to Helen's relief, retired. He works as a consultant in law enforcement and management areas, and as a volunteer in a victims' rights group. He is devoting more time to Helen and the multiplying grandchildren.

Robert was under the care of a psychiatrist for a year. He has been able to overcome his sense of guilt and has reconciled himself to their circumstances.

He and the children lost Jean.

The Jean that eventually returned from the hospital was not the same. Physically she was impaired. After months of therapy she regained substantial use of her hands and feet. The real damage was emotional. She remains under the care of a psychiatrist, and will require medication and therapy for a prolonged period.

The family is loving and devoted, which has made Jean's recovery possible. She reciprocates to the extent she can. There is, however, a wall that was not there before. Jean carries a mental parasite, one that preoccupies her and drains her energy: a recurring nightmare.

Her sleep is induced by medication, for she is afraid to sleep. When she is awake and her mind unoccupied, the parasite sometimes surfaces and she falls into the horror of her ordeal. Slowly the parasite's hold on her is receding, but she is not yet the wife and mother they knew. She is not yet Jean.

All pray that time, which heals all wounds, will soon complete its cure.